THE MARVELS OF YOUTH

Also by Tim Bowling

Fiction
The Bone Sharps
Downriver Drift
The Heavy Bear
The Paperboy's Winter
The Tinsmith

Literary Nonfiction
The Call of the Red-Winged Blackbird: Essays on the Common and Extraordinary
In the Suicide's Library: A Book Lover's Journey
The Lost Coast: Salmon, Memory and the Death of Wild Culture

Poetry
The Annotated Bee & Me
The Book Collector
Circa Nineteen Hundred and Grief
Darkness and Silence
The Dark Set: New Tenderman Poems
The Duende of Tetherball
Dying Scarlet
Fathom
Low Water Slack
The Memory Orchard
Selected Poems
Tenderman
The Thin Smoke of the Heart
The Witness Ghost

THE MARVELS OF YOUTH

TIM BOWLING

A Buckrider Book

© Tim Bowling, 2023

No part of this publication may be reproduced, stored in a retrieval system or transmitted, in any form or by any means, without the prior written consent of the publisher or a license from the Canadian Copyright Licensing Agency (Access Copyright). For an Access Copyright license, visit www.accesscopyright.ca or call toll free to 1-800-893-5777.

Published by Buckrider Books
an imprint of Wolsak and Wynn Publishers
280 James Street North
Hamilton, ON L8R2L3
www.wolsakandwynn.ca

Editor for Buckrider Books: Paul Vermeersch | Copy editor: Jennifer Hale
Cover design: Peter Cocking
Cover image: Don Sparrow
Interior design: Jennifer Rawlinson
Author photograph: Jacqueline Baker
Typeset in Adobe Caslon Pro and Franklin Gothic
Printed by Rapido Books, Montreal, Canada

10 9 8 7 6 5 4 3 2 1

 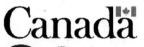

The publisher gratefully acknowledges the support of the Canada Council for the Arts and the Ontario Arts Council. We also acknowledge the financial support of the Government of Canada through the Canada Book Fund and the Government of Ontario through the Ontario Book Publishing Tax Credit and Ontario Creates.

Library and Archives Canada Cataloguing in Publication

Title: The marvels of youth / Tim Bowling.
Names: Bowling, Tim, 1964- author.
Identifiers: Canadiana 20230496490 | ISBN 9781989496749 (softcover)
Subjects: LCGFT: Novels.
Classification: LCC PS8553.O9044 M37 2023 | DDC C813/.54—dc23

For my parents
and their grandchildren

You are what you eat. You are also the comics you peruse as a child.
    Carlos Fuentes, "How I Started to Write"

What is the use of being a boy if you are going to grow up to be a man.
    Gertrude Stein, "What Are Master-pieces and Why Are There So Few of Them"

I

Lari Edison, doyen of the Haunted Bookshop, is dead, and my eyes return at once to their tenth year of seeing. Kierkegaard wrote, "The characters we will have are largely formed by the age of ten," and if I could step through the crowded arras of the years and let my eyes scan the shelves of worn paperbacks that constituted half of Mr. Edison's small enterprise, I wouldn't be surprised to find there some tattered copy of the old Dane's wisdom.

But sales of Kierkegaard pay no one's bills; they didn't even pay Kierkegaard's. So we must face the cold, blunt fact: Lari Edison, whose storefront window on a skinny, potholed street starting at the post office and ending at the river sported a dishevelled and sun-faded edition of Christopher Morley's *The Haunted Bookshop*; whose son, Stuart, my age but afflicted with a harelip that made him lisp so that for years I thought of that peculiar malady as a "hair lisp," sometimes worked behind the tall counter; whose daughter, Norah, round as a fluffed sparrow and freckle-faced pretty, perhaps fourteen, also sometimes appeared, and so calmly it was as if she didn't know that with such a name she belonged in the pages of James Joyce's biography and not in a tiny fishing town redolent of oolichan oil and pool-hall tobacco smoke and fresh rain landing softly on puddles of old rain; whose wife, as thin as her husband was stout, took the weekday morning and early afternoon shifts while he made his primary living as a window cleaner hanging from the office towers of a Vancouver that still used the sawdust from century-old red cedars to cover up the vomit of the drunks leaving the Gastown hotels, and who didn't seem to know or even to care that issues 96, 97 and 98 of *The Amazing Spider-Man* were unusual because they lacked the official approval of the comic authority's barcode (due to their depiction of the Green Goblin's son's acid trips) or that she might have played Laura in *The Glass Menagerie* if the part called only for frailty and soft-spokenness and the ability to move like a scent carried by invisible bees; Lari Edison – the spelling of whose first name was never questioned, let alone explained, whose blue eyes were kind but who never brooked a disrespect to any authority except schoolteachers, policemen, politicians, truant officers, dogcatchers, ministers/priests/pastors/reverends, librarians, employers, Revenue Canada, literary critics, art critics, theatre critics, music critics and God, and who always gave discounts to the elderly ladies when they bought more than six copies of Agatha Christie at one time – is dead. And I am left with the mystery of the single "i" of his first name, which might be solved, and of the years, which have no resolution, only continuance.

Though four decades have passed since that bittersweet spot of time between the release of *Jaws* and the release of the first Star Wars movie, the rain still falls on that familiar street the colour of rhinoceros hide when dry and panther skin when wet. It falls so hard that the minute hand on the town clock, which has never kept the right time, almost drops and I almost see the last turns of my bike wheels again as I pedal hard for the sanctuary of story. Children didn't wear backpacks in the 1970s – we had lunch kits and Thermoses like our fathers because we went off alone to jobs just as our fathers did, without choice, without undue brooding over our lack of choice. So how did I carry home my assignment to distinguish between Upper and Lower Canada? In what way did I keep dry the field-trip permission form to visit the Dairyland factory in the city? I must have folded such paper into my lunch kit and dangled the kit off my handlebars, my fingers as red as the autumn maple leaves hanging over the granite cenotaph for the World War dead, those leaves I just passed under as I rode through Memorial Park, except I can't really show them to you unless the rain falls harder and the minute hand descends another minute on the left side of Time's battered face.

But instead, the rain stops. Now the tea bag of my little hometown begins to seep. It will seep for days, spreading a curious olfactory flavour through the air, much as time spreads the same brown flavour through the pages of the books Lari Edison prices in pencil as I shiver like a wet stray in the transom between the world and worlds. Outside, against the plate-glass window, my Mustang bicycle leans with Irish insouciance, the rust forming in its steel like the foxing that waits inside the chemicals of the paper in Christopher Morley's forgotten novel. In my eagerness, I have left my lunchbox hooked to the handlebar; I have left the question of Canada to Canada's weather.

Mr. Edison's eyes are the soft, powdery blue of the chalk for the pool cues next door. I am allowed into that establishment only briefly, to retrieve my brother who is twenty-seven and full of swagger and small-town bonhomie (though he'd hate the use of a French word to describe him, given how much he dislikes the Montreal Canadiens). The pool hall is called Hurry's Place, on account of the elderly Greek owner whose name – Harry – and whose pace – frenzied – naturally combined to form Hurry, but during much of the week the pool hall is no livelier than the bookshop. Indeed, it is like a gentleman's den from the Victorian era into which you could conduct your fresh copy of *The Strand Magazine* and recline, with some fisherman's Lab or springer spaniel at your feet, and breathe in the strangely exciting smells of stale Hickory Sticks, cigarette smoke and Mrs. Hurry's bubblegummy perfume. Mrs. Hurry is a little younger than my brother, and, since this is the 1970s, she's actually referred to as "Hurry's wife." As far as I can tell, from eavesdropping when Mrs. Maxwell is having a cup of Red Rose with my mother, Hurry's wife is a little chippy who has her claws into the silly old fool for all he's worth (to which my mother, as was her wont, politely demurred, citing "the girl's unfortunate upbringing"). Mrs. Maxwell's gossip, however, doesn't change how I look at Mrs. Hurry; on the contrary, it has the surprising effect of altering my perception of her husband, who ever afterward scuttles through the streets, his claws stuffed into his pockets to hide his crustacean heritage. For who could attract a little chippy with claws except a wily old crab?

Mrs. Hurry is violet-eyed and raven-haired, her bosom small and high. She wears tight jeans the colour of the inside of a mussel shell, plenty of rouge and eyeshadow, and charm bracelets on both wrists, as if she's recently freed herself from bondage to a jeweller who specializes in miniature astrological signs, killer whales and peace signs. Also, she has a large gap between her front teeth, which is somehow both attractive and unsettling. It'll be over a decade before I come upon the medieval notion, as applied to Chaucer's Wife of Bath, that such a gap in a woman's smile is a telltale sign of promiscuity, but even as a boy I'm mesmerized by the way she sometimes covers the gap with her tongue. The truth is, I'm a little in love with Mrs. Hurry; she's like Veronica in the *Archie* comics, or would be if Riverdale had a wrong side of the tracks and Veronica had grown up there.

"Hey, Sean," Mr. Edison says between bites of a giant Wonder Bread sandwich that consists of half a head of lettuce and half a jar of mustard, "you're in luck. The new issues just came in."

I look at my red-raw and rain-sueded hands. There's no way I can handle a mint condition comic book now! My hair is dripping and my windbreaker's like a Jackson Pollock canvas in process. I look up. Mr. Edison waits with his customary patience. A drop of mustard lands on his already-stained T-shirt, which is a dingy white otherwise and doesn't quite reach over his belly to the top of his faded jeans. A clutch of chest hair, tough and thick as crabgrass, pokes out of his collar. His smile is tired but sincere. He's one of those rare adults who genuinely likes, rather than suffers or pretends to like, children.

Before I can look at my hands again, an old woman shuffles out of the paperback stacks and approaches the huge cash register, which is solid steel and covered on its back and sides with stickers about American politics peeled out of *Mad* magazine. It has all the sacred aura of a real writer's typewriter. Whenever Mr. Edison pounds away on it, his expression grows serious; he might be Franklin W. Dixon or Mickey Spillane or even the totemic Christopher Morley himself. The old woman, recognizable as one of the dozens of pensioners to whom I deliver the afternoon *Vancouver Sun*, is tiny, sharp-nosed and bespectacled, prone to holding her head of frizzy white hair to one side like a robin listening for worms. Mr. Edison often says, and always with the unspoken admonition that we are not to repeat this to anyone, that he believes the characters in Agatha Christie's books shop in his store in order to learn what they're supposed to do next. Mrs. English, who is Scottish, must be Mrs. Marple, who is English. This makes her only mildly interesting, however. Like the other elderly people on my route, she's worthy of my full attention only at the end of each month, when she carefully considers whether to give me a wee tip and perhaps a shortbread cookie the weight of a horseshoe.

I look away from her and gaze at the wall behind and above Mr. Edison. It's covered with Mylar-jacketed copies of comic books I could never afford to buy, many of whose covers, in fact, show superheroes travelling the cosmos. From a wood-cased radio in a corner comes the faint sound of David Bowie singing about fame.

The ordinary world is gone now. It's fallen away and I will have to concentrate very hard to remind myself to re-enter it. After all, I have newspapers to deliver, six days a week, thirty papers a day, my route covering several miles – the thirty dollars I earn each month is usually the only money I have to spend on comics. Already I am learning life's hard and fundamental lesson: you must engage with the world so that you can escape the world. It is the lesson I see in the eyes of the drunken men who spill out of the Arms and the Legion and, on weekends, the pool hall – and I also see it in the eyes of Mr. Edison whenever he doffs his window-cleaner's cloth cap and picks up a freshly sharpened HB2 pencil and begins to doodle on the clean foolscap he tapes all over his counter, inviting any of his patrons to join in. My feeble stick figures and only slightly more confident block letters have already adorned several countertops' worth of paper. Sometimes, if I'm in the shop when a fresh piece of foolscap is required, Mr. Edison lets me keep the doodled-on sheet – one of them is taped to my bedroom wall where nightly its weird characters invade my dreams. Perhaps if I take some of the correspondence drawing courses advertised at the backs of the comics, the ones recommended by Norman Rockwell, I could become a real artist. But I dream of something else: I have already written a *Hardy Boys* mystery in which Frank, Joe and Chet travel into outer space and encounter a group of thugs with laser vision. But better than that, I have started to create my own comic book. Well, not just my own; my best friend, Jay, who's two years older and a wizard at cartooning, is really the main creative force. We've already named the strip *Cosmos* and created a superhero named Blackstar. At school, we regularly skip out of our multigrade class, hide in the paper supply room on a top shelf behind stacks of carbon and mimeograph paper and plot our first issue. If I could live in the paper supply room and the bookshop, with brief periods away to visit my family and perhaps get in a spirited game of road hockey, I'd be as happy as a black Lab romping through the marsh to retrieve a mallard.

"But there are three mysteries in this one," Mrs. English says. "So if you add these other books, that makes six."

Mr. Edison sighs. He looks longingly at the sandwich he's placed on the counter. "Six stories, yes. But not six books. An omnibus edition is still one book."

Mrs. English tilts her head even more to the side. She clutches her purse to her breast as if to staunch a wound.

"Listen," Mr. Edison says calmly, "it will cost you four dollars for these books and you'll get to read six stories. Otherwise, if you put the omnibus back, you'll need to buy three others to get the discount, which would be five dollars for six stories. So you're saving a dollar."

"Ye-e-e-es." Mrs. English reaches deep into her bloodstream and draws up all the Glaswegian suspicion she can find. "But I've already read one of the stories in the omnibus." The last syllable of this last word she pronounces "boose," as if it rhymes with "puce." "And that would make it four dollars for only five stories."

Mr. Edison looks at me and winks. "Here's a thought. Spend the four dollars and give the extra dollar to Sean here. He's writing his own comic book and you can be one of the first subscribers."

Mrs. English gazes at me over the glasses at the end of her nose. "I already subscribe to his newspaper. And if he's a good lad and actually brings me a copy before suppertime, he might just get that dollar as a Christmas tip." She clears her throat. "I'll just put this omni-boose back on the shelf, then. That'll be three dollars."

"Never mind. I'll put it back. Just leave it on the counter." Mr. Edison takes her proffered bills and makes a quick jab and counterpunch on the register.

As kind and patient as he is, as much as he tolerates the antic behaviour of his shop's younger patrons, Mr. Edison isn't without a temper. When he gets angry – for example, when a non-initiate into the joy of comic book collecting roughly handles a choice item, or when Jay and I sometimes forget that he's running a business and not a schoolyard at recess – his cheeks redden, his saloon barkeep moustache trembles and his forearms become particularly burly as he crosses them over his chest. Fortunately, these occasions are rare.

Once Mrs. English has gone, I realize that I'm dry enough to look at the new comics. As usual, Mr. Edison anticipates my request and, carefully moving his sandwich out of harm's way, begins to pull out the crisp, mint issues of *The Amazing Spider-Man*, *The Fantastic Four*, *The Avengers*, *The Incredible Hulk*, *Conan the Barbarian* and *Thor*. Now even the world away from the world disappears. I've shrunk into little squares and dialogue balloons as quickly as Dr. Bruce Banner explodes into the Hulk. New comics cost twenty-five cents each and I have a limp two-dollar bill in my pocket, which I earned by selling one of my brother's used goalie sticks. A collector must always be resourceful, and over the past year, since the Haunted Bookshop opened, I've learned to read the various material hungers of my peers. Many exceptional transactions have occurred because some bug-eyed classmate couldn't live without a complete set of the 1972

7

THE MARVELS OF YOUTH

Team Canada hockey cards. And I once sold a bright green banana seat off a rusted old Mustang I found stuck in the mud of the riverbank. It pays to keep your eyes open. Although, as life often proves, it sometimes pays to keep them closed as well. The trick lies in knowing the difference.

The phone's jangling ring brings me back to earth. Mr. Edison picks up the receiver, then reaches it across to me, unwinding the cord. Sotto voce: "Your mom."

Sheepishly, I take the receiver and mumble into it. My mother reminds me that I need to complete my route quickly today because my father is "going out for the dark set" and he wants me to come along. How could I have forgotten? Normally, I love going out on the boat with my dad, but ever since seeing *Jaws* in the summer, I've been apprehensive about being on the water – even drifting in a swimming pool, my torso and legs have felt intensely vulnerable to attack. Of course, the Fraser River, let alone a swimming pool, contains no great white sharks, but in the years of unlicensed imagination, anything is possible, all worlds and all seas intersect. How could I know for certain what deadly creatures my father might yank unknowingly to the surface in his gill net? After all, the white sturgeon, grotesquely prehistoric and potentially as large as a small whale, frequented the murky depths of the Fraser River estuary and sometimes rose thrashing to the stern of our boat (though I'd never seen one more than four or five feet long, which was long enough). As for a swimming pool, I'd read enough comics and newspaper articles to know that humans are capable of placing deadly creatures into unexpected places. If a python could live in the sewer system and surface in a toilet bowl, why couldn't a killer shark somehow find itself in a rectangle of backyard chlorine? Sure, it was unlikely, but at age ten, my febrile enthusiasm for possibility had yet to be polluted by the logic and statistics of the world.

I tell my mom I'll go as fast as I can, speaking more softly into the phone because I'm embarrassed to be tying up the line. But Mr. Edison, happily grazing on his leafy sandwich, pays no attention to me until I hand him the receiver and ask him to keep my purchases safe behind the counter while I finish my route; I don't want to risk damaging the comics when I'm folding newspapers. The soft blue of his eyes, the yellow splash of mustard on his shirt; there's something Mediterranean about his presence that girds me for the dark and the rain and the lonely revolutions of the splashing wheels. "Excelsior!" I ought to shout, but "Bye" is all my secular Anglo-Protestant background will allow as I slide like a muskrat into the day's black current.

The rain hasn't started again, but it feels imminent, the sky a trembling wheelbarrow about to be tipped. A streetlamp sizzles on at the river end of the street but it isn't dark enough yet for the yellow light to make a difference. Far along the sidewalk in the other direction, Mrs. English stands, hunched over, gazing into a shop window, probably of the clothing store. Several elderly people find the female mannequins offensive, and it's true that the hard nipples are quite visible through the fabric, but there's nothing risqué about even a fully naked mannequin compared with Mrs. Hurry, and she often appears for hours at a time in the pool hall window, seated behind the cash register. But I suppose a wax dummy *could* be moved, whereas Mrs. Hurry wouldn't move a single long eyelash unless she felt like it. As my brother says, "That girl's her own boss. Not even Hurry can make her do a damned thing she doesn't want to do."

Across the street from Mrs. English, Jiggs, a grizzled black Lab of the neighbourhood, is making his slow way home. He pauses to chew on some lime-green grass growing up through the cracks in the sidewalk, and then, as he gathers his strength and goes on, I can almost hear his bones clack. He's like a sunken couch, worn velour-smooth with the years, that shivers out loose change and dust whenever it's shifted.

I draw a deep breath of the rain-sweet air. A dozen barn swallows swoop beneath the telephone wires in front of the vacant lot across from me. I'm tempted to pick up some rocks and practise my aim, but there isn't time. And besides, just then the bell of the gas-pump hose outside Brownlows' garage dings and there's every chance that some fussy adult will take me to task for even thinking about throwing rocks in the vicinity of windows and windshields.

I still don't move right away, however. This is the most important street in my life and though I am not, as I am now, a six-foot vessel filled with memory and the dust of older memory, I seem somehow to recognize and appreciate the beautiful simplicity of this straight travelling line, the perfect mathematics that allows me to move from one part of my world to another with familiarity and ease. Delta Street is not long, not well paved, not even busy most of the time. The small shops along each of its sides sit like the shunted boxcars of trains for which there is no destination. To the east, there's the bookshop, pool hall, barbershop, Royal Canadian Legion, the museum, an insurance agency; to the west, a clothing store, bank, butcher shop, convenience store, a notary public, dry cleaners and a shoe store. There are also a dozen vacant lots and empty stores, including the sunken grassy space where my grandfather, who died a decade before I was born, had his plumbing shop and residence. It's the mid-1970s and North America's economy has slumped. Even the harbour at the north end of the street is quieter than usual – no creak of a winch hoisting nets, no gunning of outboard engines, no shouts of fishermen.

But Delta Street, even in the autumn rain, shines with promise as brilliantly as any long impression in the grass shone for a group of medieval pilgrims setting out for the Holy Land. It shines still, though I'm not there to see the streetlamp's filaments reflect in the puddles and all of the old businesses are surely gone. But it shines, I know it does, and probably for children and old ladies and anyone else prey to these brief and inexplicable epiphanies of time that the world cannot suffer because the world must make its living. And I am part of the world and must make mine too.

Forty years ago, I did the same.

For the next two hours after leaving the Haunted Bookshop that day, I biked through the wet streets, a canvas sack of newspapers slung over my shoulder, as darkness crowded around the streetlamps like Homer's wine-dark sea and dingy flocks of seagulls flew silently inland, spiralling away as if I had tossed them out of my sack. The town, already quiet, grew quieter. The first few stars appeared faintly in the north, over the mountains beyond Vancouver. Raindrops fringed the telephone lines and the telephone poles remained flushed from the previous storm. The weeping willows and horse chestnuts and monkey puzzle trees along Arthur Drive – one of our town's original streets, lined with Victorian and Edwardian houses set far back on huge lots – trembled with the black and silver remnants of the rain. Finally I parked my bike in the cluttered side yard of our modest bungalow and hurried on foot to the twenty-foot-high gravel dike at the end of our street. By then, the bulb of the corner streetlamp had pinged on, but the air still wasn't dark enough for the light to show. Since it took my father only ten minutes to reach his preferred drift on the river, I knew we'd have time to make our set.

    I heard my father a full minute before I saw him. When I reached the government wharf and paused at the top of the cleated wooden gangway angled steeply down to the dozen small floats chained and roped together on mossy and creosoted logs that served as moorage for the fishing fleet, a familiar whistling drifted across the damp air and caressed my attention. This time, I recognized the music, because we had just watched *Fiddler on the Roof* on TV a week earlier. *Sunrise, sunset, sunrise, sunset, slowly through the years...* It had surprised me as a boy, but makes perfect sense to me now, that my father's eyes moistened during the wedding scene. How heavy and pain-filled even the most joyous events can be when we sense that there's no holding them! My mother and father must have looked tenderly at each other, must have recalled their own wartime wedding in Toronto thirty years earlier, must have touched silently on the painful loss of my brother, stillborn three years before my birth, and then, like Tevye and all the suffering fate-tossed Jews of the musical, returned to the ordinary flow of the days, buying, selling, working and wondering, their lives carried along on tide-drawn boats rather than horse-drawn carts, and the cry of "Rags! Bones! Bottles!" that my mother had heard as a child in the west end of Toronto during the Great Depression somehow serving as the undersong of every labouring family's unregarded drama.

    The whistle came to me, and I followed it to the source, as physically unlike the burly, thick-bearded, kohl-eyed Tevye as a robin is unlike a raven. My father was a small man, five foot seven in his stocking feet, and without an ounce of fat on his lean body, though he was then over fifty years old and a pack-a-day smoker whose only exercise came via manual labour. When he wasn't wrestling tides and fish, he drove a tractor on the potato fields on the outskirts of town; when he wasn't working, he puttered in the backyard, looking after his bountiful vegetable garden or drinking endless cups of tea in front of winter's driftwood fires. A lover of solitude, he had earned the nickname of "Ghost" for his annual absence at most community events, though most people unknowingly called him by another nickname, thinking it was his real name. Heck or Hecky (a garbled version of Harold that had clung to him in childhood) sometimes became Hector. But these names mattered less than my father's reluctance to correct anyone. For forty years, the farmer who employed him and the packer to whom he delivered his catches on the river called him Hector, while nearly everyone else called him Hecky. No one ever called him Harold. I'm not sure that he would even have looked up if anyone had used that name.

 He stood in the stern of his twenty-four-foot flat-bottomed gillnetter, in the small space between the wooden drum on which the net was rolled and the wooden rollers over which the net would be wound into the river. Wearing a black skullcap and a blood-stained black floater jacket, a lit cigarette held loosely between his lips, he had stopped whistling and was tying a coal-oil lantern beside the bright red scotchman at the end of his net. In the faint forsythia glow of the wharf lights, he looked both as apprehensive and cheerful as an elf in Santa's workshop. I understood the apprehension better than the cheer, for we were going out on the river to fish, and the river and the fishing were both dangerous. My understanding of a middle-aged man's contentment wouldn't develop for over forty years, and even then would prove a complex and confusing business, which is another way of suggesting that such contentment might just be a myth.

 But in the autumn of 1975, I was more concerned with great white sharks and the oily darkness into which our boat would soon be disappearing. Not even my father's calm voice and assured presence could distract me from the image of those gaping jaws widening as they rose toward the hull of our boat. I could imagine the planks snapping as easily as balsa wood;

worse, I could feel the awful numb solidity of my own legs and torso. It certainly didn't help that, as my father and I began the process of leaving harbour, the first few strands of a typical October fog slid in off the Gulf of Georgia, in their whiteness and gliding stealth a kind of phantom version of the evil I most feared.

We undid the thick, wet ropes that bound us by stern and bow to the wharf on one side and to another gillnetter on the other. Sometimes as many as four other boats would have to be slid out of their position, held in the current and then re-moored, before we could free ourselves. It was a delicate, graceful ritual, requiring a deft movement from one bow or stern to another, a hurried untying and retying of ropes – a slower, heavier version of the maypole dance that the girls performed each spring in the park, but done often in darkness without admirers (like so much of the life of that vanished salmon fishing world). This time, however, I had only to step, at the exact right second, from our stern to the wharf with the neighbouring boat's stern rope in my hand as my father pulled our boat forward. The concentration on the timing settled my nerves briefly, but once we had secured the other boat and my father had swung our bow downriver and we'd idled past moss-coated net sheds, rusted launching ways like dinosaur fossils in the muddy bank and a few float homes sagging like birthday cakes left out in the rain, I felt so vulnerable that I moved from the stern to the main deck just behind the cabin.

After a few seconds, my father emerged from the gasoline-dense interior in order to guide our passage the mile to the fishing grounds from the outside steering wheel.

"Well, Monk," he said, using the nickname he'd given me, presumably because I was so often to be found alone, reading, and because my head was close-cropped when I was a little boy, "your brother didn't come in for supper, so we have some catching up to do." He put the cigarette between his lips as he considered the steering wheel. "Ah, somebody else has been working hard too." I watched as my father carefully lifted a strand of spiderweb off one of the wheel spokes and tried to connect it to the cabin without destroying the web or harming the spider; he looked like a

13

small child playing pin-the-tail-on-the-donkey but finding only the air. At last, satisfied that he'd done the best he could for his co-worker in the catching arts, he removed the cigarette from his mouth, exhaled at length and smiled at me. "We might just beat the dark at that."

We did, but not by much. The cottonwood trees on the shores of the two silt islands between which our two-hundred-fathom-wide section of the river flowed faded like colour from the wallpaper of abandoned Georgian houses, and I could see only a few fathoms of our cork line as the drum rolled and the nylon net – forty meshes deep, a hundred and fifty fathoms long and stretched down to the murky bottom by a thin line of lead weights – passed like flax through my father's bare hands.

"Upriver," he called firmly but calmly from the stern. I turned the outside steering wheel to the north, where the ski lights on Grouse Mountain beyond Vancouver were just coming clear with the first low stars. Ten seconds later my father called, "Downriver," and now I turned the wheel to the darker south. This call-and-turn, designed to lay the net out in soft loops so that the meshes would hang loosely enough in the current to keep the salmon from striking and backing out, happened once more before we'd crossed from the bank of one island to the other. "Upriver," my father called to me. "Downriver." And my hands moved. "Sunrise," he whistled out of the lost years. "Sunset."

Once the whole net had rolled off the drum, I could see only the light of our coal-oil lantern blinking rheumily as it bobbed in the current. But the darkness did nothing to hide the shark's jaws still rising toward my numb legs and torso, the same awful rising as depicted in the movie poster.

"Shut her off, Monk," my father said.

I ducked into the greasy, gasoline-drugged cabin and turned the key in the ignition. The uncovered engine, which took up much of the interior space, shuddered like a sleeping animal, and then fell silent. Now what had been a low thrumming quiet turned pure and much deeper, like flowing water become ice. Alone with the black engine – a freshly dug and wet grave in the cabin's darkness – I felt my panic grow and so almost flung myself on deck. My father was gone.

I stared and stared against the night, but it took several seconds before I could see his black outline in the greater blackness. The pick-up light – a 100-watt bulb encased in a metal arm clamped to a spot beside the rollers and extending over them – hadn't been switched on, so only the slight shifting of his body as he lifted the burning red end of his cigarette to his mouth at last made his presence apparent. As always during a night set, my father trained his attention on the coal-oil lantern: if it stopped moving (or got hung up, as the fishermen would say), that meant the net was snagged, and either the meshes and light lead line would break and the lantern and net would drift freely again, or else the snag was a bad one and we would have to leave this end of our net attached to another lantern, take the boat across to the point of the snag and try to pull the net off – a stressful process even in summer daylight. But in October, in the dark and thickening fog, my father's anxiety must have been considerable, though he showed it only by the amount of cigarettes he rapidly smoked. All these decades later, I don't know that I've ever stared at anything as intently as I stared at the lantern on the end of my father's net, except perhaps my father's face on his deathbed.

But that foggy night, we stood a dozen feet apart, listening to the current slapping the hull, breathing in the rich musk of mud, brine and leaf mulch, silently asking the river for free passage over its mysterious depth. Somewhere below us, where the channel turned west and, picking up speed, eventually spilled into the sea a few miles away, my older brother Dan must have been pulling in his own net by hand, straining against its weight and its catch of leaden dog salmon and white springs, of branches and wildly rooted stumps, readying himself to return to the top of the drift and make another set. Down there, too, would be old Rod Beveridge and Big Hoot and Little Hoot, the drunkard Mackenzie, perhaps my aunt and uncle and – most eccentrically of all, dangerously and deliciously so – Edgar Winterbourne, quick as a spider in a squall, dark as a ruined cannery piling, whose singular speech was matched only by his tumultuous, probing silences.

One of these fishermen's boats would eventually emerge out of the darkness, first as a puttering or thrumming engine sound, then as a faint mast light, and sometimes as a voice of greeting or warning. The presence of these other boats was complicated, for even as they alleviated the terror and risks of the night fishing, they also lessened our profits by competing for what was too often a meagre catch.

I stayed on deck, tensing for the great white shark's explosion through the rippling, oily surface around our boat. But the stillness remained, and our lantern, winking in three second intervals, never stopped moving. Nor did the fog and the cold, which began to pierce my jacket and jeans and gumboots so that I shifted my weight from one foot to the other, no doubt attracting the attention of every creature gliding remorselessly over the river bottom. Within seconds, I could no longer see our lantern or my father's outline as the fog fully set in. From a long distance off, north of the Steveston lighthouse, rolled the two-noted call of the foghorn, the second note even deeper than the funereal first.

"Better start her up," my father said at last. He might have been standing right beside me or on the bank of the far island.

With great care, I felt my way through the skinny entrance of the cabin and, fumbling as inexpertly as my father had expertly moved the spider, found the key and started the engine. Then I flicked the switch for the pick-up light.

Back on deck, I heard the words that I'd been dreading: my father's call to join him in the now dimly lit stern. It was my job to stand to one side of the rollers, gaff hook in hand, and gaze into the river as the net came in, on the lookout for fish or sticks or whatever else might be pulled to the surface.

I swallowed hard and tried to ignore the feeling of deathly whiteness that the fog created. My father stepped on the drum pedal with his left boot and the drum lurched into motion, turning like some horrible spinning wheel in a fairy tale. The light bulb's glow barely penetrated the dark and fog. Mesmerized, I watched the corks slide toward me like the black, dripping scales of a serpent, like apples pulled from a barrel of blood. But the corks, ominous as they were, provided at least some minimal comfort – for when I stared to the side of them, at the dripping fog and dark, I felt myself plunging forward and down even as I held perfectly still. Now my body had lost all substance. I couldn't feel the wood of the gaff in my bare palm. Over my head, the foghorn boomed, and the sound echoed and died in my rib cage. On and on, the net rolled in, fathoms of meshes empty except for mud and bulrush stalks like the clammy fingers of corpses. Just when I thought I couldn't stand the tension any longer, my father took his foot off the pedal, the drum's squeaky revolutions ceased, and I heard the current again, sucking like a beast at the hull. With his bare left hand, my father took up the cork line, feeling his way along it for several inches and then pausing.

"Give me the gaff," he said in a clipped tone.

Now I couldn't bear to look down, except that not looking down was even worse. Inexorably, my father pulled a half-fathom toward him. The black corks had vanished, which meant that something had pulled them under, something heavy. My father leaned far over the rollers, cork line now in his left hand, gaff in his right. The seconds passed so slowly that they began to move backward, as the river itself sometimes did.

Though my breathing sent steady clouds across my eyes, I wasn't aware of it. "Please," I urged to the night and river in general, "please be a stump or a salmon, not –"

The river exploded. My father wildly swung the gaff, overhand, as if throwing a baseball. I closed and opened my eyes in furious succession as the net and the fog and my father's body merged into one amorphous shape of white and black, which appeared and disappeared in what seemed a strafing of strobe lights. For a few terrible seconds, I saw and heard the fish – a rising, quivering mass of pointed scutes that, once struck by the gaff, roiled and thrashed like the river itself until my father, with an uncharacteristic curse and a heave of breath, lifted his empty gaff as high as a lightning rod against the light bulb's jaundiced glow and then appeared to slump back against the drum behind him, though in truth he hadn't moved more than a foot.

A strange silence settled over us for a few seconds before the familiar world gushed in, a flood of clarified shapes and sounds – the roundness of the rollers, the bunched net at my father's waist, the idling of the engine and slavering of the current and, finally, my father's calm and low voice again.

"That was a real monster. One of the giants." He turned his face skyward as he spoke, as if to reorient himself between the river and the invisible stars. "I'm lucky the gaff didn't catch. Might have broken my arm."

By now, I realized that he was referring to a white sturgeon and not a great white shark. But what difference could any knowledge make to me at such a moment? I had been convinced of our imminent deaths, of our limbs being ripped from our bodies, of our blood erupting like lava into the fog. As a result, I couldn't find any words equal to the occasion. So I just stood, arms limp at my sides, until my father stepped on the drum pedal and began picking up the net once more. But when he returned the gaff to me, I remained a foot back from the rollers, unable to face the river surface. My father, no doubt consumed by his own reflections, didn't seem to notice my position. He resumed his work as if nothing out of the ordinary had happened.

The drum turned. The dripping meshes rolled in. My father untangled a few dog salmon – eight-to-twenty-pound sharp-toothed fish with dark purple streaks along their pewter scales – and some chunks of driftwood. Every few minutes the foghorn sounded, a low note, then a lower one. Finally, an engine sounded above our own, just below us, approaching along the near bank. Then the black shape of another gillnetter – I couldn't tell whose at first – loomed up almost right at our gunwale, not even its running lights or mast light visible in the fog.

"Better reel 'er in, Hecky, better get a move on."

The rapid-fire nasally voice couldn't have been more distinctive.

"She's runnin like bat shit in the slough. Better pick faster, Hecky, goddamn ya."

The laugh that followed fell somewhere between a witch's cackle and a dog's growl.

My father said, "Did you see Dan down there?"

Another laugh, longer and more gleeful. "Danny's pickin' pickin'

pickin'. Below the dynamite ship. Mebbe through the bridge into the gulf by now. What's he doing on that chunk of bark, Hecky, eh? Jesus Christ."

Then my father mentioned the sturgeon.

"That old bugger," the voice cried out with childish pleasure. "Ripped a big hole in my net last week. Big old bastard. Older than you, Hecky, goddamn ya."

By now I could pick out two figures through the fog. Their dark shapes seemed to stand in the air – one tall, the other below knee height. It was Edgar Winterbourne and his dog, a hairless yellow sort-of terrier mutt named Bullet, which Edgar always called Bully. No comic book duo – not Captain America and Bucky, not Batman and Robin, not Warlock and Pip – were as inseparable.

"Gonna catch him this fall, Hecky. Drag him in like a big old red cedar, eh? Guts full of tin cans and shoes and shit."

Then the figures slid away as if they'd never been there at all, the weird voice dissolving into the current and finally drowned out completely by yet another long booming of the foghorn.

Our net drifted on, the river running faster to the west as the fog still crept in to the east. Soon, we entered the narrower slough between two other silt islands and my father's pace – normally measured to the point of meditative – intensified. If the net wasn't picked up within the next few minutes, we'd risk wrapping it against the cluttered mainland shore of wharves and deadheads and – most notoriously – the carcass of a rusted forty-foot ship that had once been used to transport dynamite for logging companies.

But I could tell that my father was distracted by something else. He kept peering downriver, away from our lantern. I suspected that he was concerned about my brother. Dan was an experienced fisherman and had been running his own boat for several years, but the boat he had been renting all summer and into the fall was named the *Driftwood* for good reason. Flat, without either a cabin, a drum or an inboard engine, it was little more than a fifteen-foot-long sheet of plywood propelled by a Mercury outboard. Even in fair weather, the *Driftwood* was a challenge, as the net had to be pulled in by hand; in foul weather, especially in the fall, with more rain and fog and darkness, the boat was a constant source of worry to my parents. My brother, on the other hand, was devil-may-care, a product of the free-spirited '60s who wore his scarlet hair long and his ginger beard bushy, drove a gold El Camino and worked long and hard so that he could play the same way. Because he still lived at home and still fished, I saw a great deal of him during my childhood.

This night, however, he was nowhere to be seen. And so, once my father had pulled in our dimly glowing lantern, he hurried to the cabin, put the boat in gear and turned the bow to the south. But we didn't speed up much. The current was already moving fast, and the fog made visibility almost impossible. Our small searchlight made little impact, so my father stuck his head out of the cabin window, listening as much as looking for guidance.

Strange pings and cracks and what sounded like sighs emerged from the fog. Even more than previously, I felt exposed, convinced that we had left the river entirely and were now drifting over the ocean where, of course, much larger and more dangerous creatures than giant sturgeon lived – killer whales, for example.

Slowly we descended with the current, the sharp tang of brine increasing with every fathom. Where were the other boats? I couldn't see any mast lights or in fact any lights at all. Perhaps everyone had returned to harbour on account of the fog. Dog fishing in October wasn't lucrative; most of the year's fishing income was made during the summer sockeye runs. My father, because he kept to the same part of the river and didn't chase up and down the coast with the "highliners" (a fishing term for the most ambitious, or greedy, fishermen), barely made a subsistence living, so he needed whatever income he could earn from the fall and even the rare winter openings.

Soon we must have left familiar waters, for my father pulled his head in and shut off the engine. Now even the little pinging, cracking and sighing sounds had stopped. I pressed myself against the large exhaust pipe on the outside deck, not for the heat but for the solidity. It seemed as if the deck had been slid out from underneath me.

The interminable floating into blankness continued. My father came on deck and, warning me first, shouted my brother's name. It broke heavily against the stillness and then echoed dully into a deeper silence. Finally, the arching black length of the wooden suspension bridge – that mostly provided farm vehicle passage from the river mouth's largest silt island to the mainland – loomed into view, almost right over our heads. Quickly, my father slipped into the cabin and reversed the engine. It would be impossible to navigate passing under the bridge in such conditions.

The act of moving backward felt painful, as when you accidentally swallow an ice cube. Yet we were returning to the familiar, to home and routine, even the routine of the extraordinary. I didn't know it at ten years old, or even for decades later, but that reversal in the fog would come to represent my purpose and my meaning, as I sought the heat of old firings and my father's voice died on the waters running away all around me.

We backed up against the river's whole force, pressing down from Hell's Gate in the Fraser Valley and from the Rocky Mountain source hundreds of miles beyond. Then we turned and inched our way against the terrific black flow, hoping to find our own blood in the still chaos, as the salmon themselves do, willing their genes on to the death that spawns life. When my father called for my brother again, turning the engine off to do so, our boat was flung downriver several fathoms before the name died on the dripping air.

Eventually, after what seemed like hours but was more like twenty minutes, we reached the top of the drift again. There was still no sign of my brother.

"He's probably gone in," my father said as he moved toward the stern to make another set. I knew that he was speaking to himself more than to me, so I didn't respond. I also knew that he didn't believe what he said.

But in those years, when few fishermen on the Fraser bothered with radio communications, much had to be done on faith and instinct. My father, knowing what he was up against with the fog and the tide, must have chosen to accept his fate, and the fate of his eldest child. He took out yet another cigarette and struck one of his wooden Eddy matches to light it. I could almost hear the paper burning down as my father inhaled.

"Upriver," he called out.

Even now, through all that fog, I can see my boy's shivering hands on the wheel.

An hour later, with the tide finally slowing down but with the fog just as thick, we were idling up the drift to make another set when a strange glow appeared low on the northern horizon. At first, staring at it was like staring through the lens of a microscope to focus on an amoeba on a slide – a blur inside a blur. But once my father cut the engine and only our momentum carried us toward the light, I heard the joking, work-raspy voices of other fishermen and knew that the cannery packer had arrived.

It was a much larger boat – a dozen feet longer than our gillnetter and twice the width – and lit up from mast to deck like a Ferris wheel in an abandoned carnival. Old car tires hung all around its gunwales to provide protection from the boats that tied up alongside it, and its well-lit deck, pressure-hosed clean after each delivery, was many times the size of ours. Most interesting of all, a coffin-shaped aluminum box sat on a weighing scale over the main hatch, with a hook as thick as a man's wrist dangling to one side.

As we entered the shimmering glow, I saw the packer and his deckhand flinging salmon from the deck into the aluminum coffin as easily as if they were flinging nothing at all. Meanwhile, a fisherman kept bending out of sight and reappearing to toss with his hands another dog salmon from his side locker onto the packer's deck, now viscous with slime and blood. The slap of each fish as it landed, and the light crunch of the fish picks (less curved than gaff hooks) as they pierced the salmon's heads and gills, created a discordant soundtrack to the teasing comments coming from the stern of a gillnetter tied to the other side of the packer.

"You still got something hidin' down there? A regular highliner. High boat again. Too bad that never happens in July."

The fisherman tossing the salmon straightened up, rubbing his hands across the chest of his slick black oilskins. "What the hell are you doing way down here anyway? Get homesick for the old lady's cooking, or did the grizzlies chase you out of their rivers again?"

"The only old ladies I ever see around here are you old buggers. Hanging out your doilies. Can't believe you catch anything with those hankies. Lead line breaks if you sneeze on it."

Slap. Chunk. Slap. Chunk.

We idled near the packer's stern, waiting for one of the two boats to finish delivering so that we could pull alongside in its place.

The fisherman on the far side of the packer – a fortyish man I recognized but didn't know, probably because he spent most of the fishing season up the north coast or off the west coast of Vancouver Island in exotic locales such as Bella Bella and Ucluelet – noticed us.

"For Chrissakes, here's another one. Better break out the milk and cookies, Vic. Time for a tea party."

At this riposte, one of the men on the packer's deck stopped flinging salmon, the wood-handled pick hanging alongside his high black gumboots like a lion tamer's whip. He was likely the shortest man on the river, not much more than five feet tall, with a large-featured oval face, a preschooler's exaggerated drawing of a face. His gumboots, black as the ripest blackberries, seemed to have swallowed him to his round stomach, making the suspenders hooked over his red-and-green checked flannel shirt pointless. His voice was higher-pitched than most of the fishermen's, and mainly cheerful, perhaps because he didn't have to set and pick up nets in all kinds of miserable weather.

"If Hector wanted to go north," Vic said, "he'd outfish every one of you cowboys. Isn't that so, Hector?" As usual, my father didn't bother correcting the name. Instead, he ignored the question.

"Have you seen Dan at all, Vic?"

The packer shook his head as he turned and unwound a long rubber hose off a hook on the side of the large cabin. He handed the hose to the older fisherman, who immediately began to shoot water over his drum and stern.

The younger fisherman laughed. "Danny? I saw him just now up on the main river on that bar of soap of his. Thought he was a muskrat."

My father drew a long breath on his cigarette and let the smoke out slowly. The sound of running water from two hoses – Vic's deckhand was also using one to clean the packer's deck – sounded like a spring creek in the pressing gloom.

The older fisherman untied his boat as the younger fisherman began to throw his catch onto the packer's deck. As we slid into the vacated spot, Vic grinned at me and made the same reference he'd make all the years of my childhood.

"So" – I could feel his face beaming, as if it was on fire – "how are you likin' being back at school?"

During the summer, he always asked me if I was looking forward to school. My answer to both questions was always a smile and a head shake, even if my opinion of school was more complicated than outright dislike. After all, once you had understood the rules, finding innovative ways to break them was great sport – and learning that lesson, especially for kids like Jay and me, interested in the arts, was invaluable.

But Vic clearly relished the belief that school was plain torture for all youngsters, and I did hate it often enough not to care to disillusion him. Besides, I was never very talkative in the fishing world, which intimidated more than attracted, at least when I was a boy.

Our little ritual over, Vic and the deckhand, Rosie – late twenties, six foot five, with long rusty hair and a bushy rusty beard, a Viking warrior who never spoke, or spoke so rarely that I took him for a mute – turned their attention to the other boat's catch.

Slap. Chunk. Slap. Chunk. Slap. Chunk.

In the thin shreds of fog drifting through the light, we might have been witness to a Victorian grave robbing. The fisherman flung the black shapes on deck, and Vic and Rosie speedily dispatched them to the aluminum coffin. Meanwhile, other boats gathered at the edges of the light, waiting their turn with the anchored packer. For a time, no one spoke, which rendered the scene even more cadaverous. Only the slightly harsh breathing of the three labouring men and the idling of some engines disturbed the silence.

At last, with much delicacy, as if he was knotting a tie in front of a mirror, Vic manoeuvred the scale bar with one finger to record the weight of the catch. "Thirty-eight for three hundred and thirty," he finally announced. Then Rosie slid back the metal bar and – with a whoosh – the bottom of the aluminum box opened and the weighed dog salmon sloshed into the capacious ice-filled hatch. Vic scurried into his cabin – which was as clean and trim as a display room in a prize home – to record the numbers in the fisherman's tally book as water gushed from two hoses again and my father started to toss our catch from his side locker.

After he'd thrown about twenty dog salmon onto the packer's deck, he stopped and lit a fresh cigarette. I wondered what he was doing, since I knew that we'd also caught several large spring salmon. They would be weighed separately, for they brought a higher price per pound, but usually all the catch would be tossed on deck and Vic and Rosie would separate them by species. This time, however, I sensed a mysterious purpose to my father's pause.

"That's it, Hector?" Vic asked as the last dog salmon slapped into the box.

"That's all the dogs. I've got a big white spring here though."

The box opened and the salmon clattered down like medieval armour.

Vic rubbed his hands together. "Come on, then. Let's see him."

With both hands, my father hurled a large slab of salmon, like a chunk of concrete sidewalk, onto the packer. It slid and bounced against Vic's gumboots.

Vic looked down. "What do you say, Hector? I'll go forty-eight."

"A tad more, I think." My father took the cigarette from his mouth and studied the lit end, as if weighing it. "Fifty-one."

Vic asked Rosie for his guess, but, as always, I didn't hear the latter speak. I thought perhaps he'd made some sort of sign with his fingers.

Rosie picked the spring and, with a grunt, flung it into the box, where it landed with a clunk.

Vic tied another knot in the mirror. He shook his head. "How about that? Spot on. Fifty-one."

Now the younger fisherman, finished with the hose, untied his ropes and slid away from the packer. A different engine revved up, and soon another gillnetter drew alongside.

Meanwhile, my father had heaved a second spring salmon onto the deck.

Vic bent over for a closer look. "This is the same one. How did you manage that, Hector? Did the young fella here dip into the scale and take it out when we weren't looking?" He picked the fish himself and, raising it, appeared to stagger under the weight before he used his whole body to hurl it into the box. "I'll go fifty-one myself this time," he said through a breath-cloud like blown glass.

My father suggested fifty-three.

Vic stepped back from the scale, bemused. "How about that? Fifty-one exactly."

Once again, my father disappeared behind the drum, emerging seconds later with the third big salmon held under the gill with two fingers. Small as he was, my father had arms like knotted oak. "This one's got to be heavier," he grunted as the fish smacked onto the packer's deck. "I'll say fifty-six."

Vic, grinning, hands on hips, guessed fifty-five.

"For Christ's sakes," a gruff voice sounded from the swirling fog behind them. "Get a move on, will you? Some of us have a living to make."

The grin vanished from Vic's face as if it had been gaffed and thrown overboard. All five foot four of him stiffened. His chest expanded and his lips moved, but he didn't speak. He just lifted the salmon and threw it with greater force into the box. Then he did something peculiar. He tapped the scale bar once, stepped back, cocked his head, then slowly approached and tapped the bar again. At first, even I understood that he was being as deliberate as possible to annoy the impatient fisherman, a fiftyish slab-faced loner named Kirkhoff with a reputation for avarice. But soon the scale itself became the clear focus.

Vic mumbled to Rosie, who lumbered across like Frankenstein's creation to move the bar on the scale with his thick index finger. Predictably,

I didn't hear Rosie's verdict or see his lips move in his beard like clotted blood.

Vic, however, spoke in a tone unlike his usual jocular one, a tone I rarely heard any adult use. "It's fifty-one," he said, and looked quizzically at my father. "Exactly fifty-one."

"Goddamn it all. Hurry it up." The impatient Kirkhoff spoke under his breath, but on the river no words ever stayed under the breath, except perhaps for Rosie's. Kirkhoff started hurling dog salmon onto the packer's deck. They slid around Vic's and Rosie's boots like shards of a broken window stained silver, black and purple.

"Not an ounce over or under." Vic stared at my father. "All three of them. Not an ounce."

My father held the stare. He kept holding it. I thought for sure that he'd crack a joke or even just give a lighthearted low whistle, as if to say, "Well, if that don't beat all?"

But after a few more seconds of silence – except for the sound of Kirkhoff's salmon striking the deck – my father told me to get the tally book from our cabin. It was always my job to hand it to Vic and then get it back while my father cleaned our stern with the hose.

Like so many men of his generation, my father included, Vic had a graceful, even delicate handwriting. I stood right beside him in his wide, comfortable cabin as he wrote "White spring, 3" and paused. Finally, he shook his head and put down under total weight "153," a number which, of course, didn't begin to tell the whole story. "Exactly the same," he muttered, "like peas in a pod," and gave the tally book into my hands.

Taken aback by his uncharacteristic distractedness, I emerged onto the flood-lit fog-shrouded deck with some relief. What I found was a curious vibrant stillness, Rosie and my father holding the hoses, the dim black shapes of waiting boats at the fringes of the light (so many wolves circling a campfire), all the violence and humour and mystery in suspension, poised to break out again at any second. It was as if I'd come upon the cigarette-smoke-darkened canvas of an Old Master done in salmon oil and blood, the world briefly in adoration of the divine puzzle of three identically weighted large fish.

I had time enough to notice my brother's strange craft attached to the stern of our boat, his thickly bearded face a faint shadow of our father's grizzled one in the foreground.

But before the relief I felt could spread, before my eyes had quite drawn back to the hanging thick hook that, I was on the verge of remembering, was only used to weigh giant sturgeon, an explosion shredded the canvas. The standing figures jerked like marionettes, and then jerked again. Then they froze like actors in a Noh play. A cackling laughter flowed out of the darkness, seemed to come from all directions at once, even from the hidden stars and the river bottom. A frantic half-bark, half-yip accompanied the laughter – the two sounds might have come from the same throat.

"Jesus H. fuckin . . ."

"You crazy goddamned sonofabitch . . ."

The echo of the explosion and of the laughter and barking died at the same time. The Old Master hung in tatters, and the splash page of a superhero comic took its place, Edgar Winterbourne and his seal bomb as maniacal and graphic as the Green Goblin on his jet-ski hurling exploding pumpkins at Spider-Man. The shift from one world to another, from life to art and back again, the shift from the salmon at sea to the salmon dead under a motionless drum, the shift that haunts me still, at fifty-six, with my father's grease-stained tally book for 1975 in my hands, containing the graceful cursive recording three white springs at 153 pounds, provided the main narrative of all those vanished years, but the plot, of course, contained as many strands as the dissolving impossible-to-hold fog.

Then it was fully the season of the steady rains. The days dripped like melting licorice ice cream – off the telephone lines on which big crows perched like smudged clefs; off the eavestroughs of all our decrepit neighbourhood's mouldering and vacant Edwardian houses; off the unpruned, little-picked apple, pear, cherry and plum trees in their last windfall; off the blinking faces of loved ones and strangers (though there were few strangers) and the muzzles of stray dogs, off the handlebars of my bike as I pushed against great currents of wet and wind like a salmon en route to the spawning grounds. At the side of our bungalow, a gnarled Gravenstein apple tree with branches as black as a smoker's lungs slowly, sodden day after sodden day, gave up its last shrivelled fruit. Sometimes, in the middle of the night, a dropped apple would wake me again to time and consequence and calculation, as if some slow-motion abacus kept track of the inevitable changes no child ever really notices until childhood is long over.

I recall one escape, and one cold chore, above all others.

In our crushed gravel driveway sat a 1956 pale green Ford with whitewall tires and a bubble-domed cab and front and back cracked vinyl seats so covered in comic books – *Richie Rich*, *Little Lulu*, *Uncle Scrooge*, *Archie*; Illustrated Classics of *The Swiss Family Robinson*, *Treasure Island* and *The Count of Monte Cristo* – that you couldn't move for reading. Here, I retired from the fierce demands of being a child at the whim of adults, and even from my own nascent comic book collecting and writerly selves, to luxuriate for hours in the rainbow mulch of the then-much-maligned graphic art.

That my father never drove the car – that, in fact, its engine probably wouldn't have turned over in an emergency – made the old Ford an intermediary stop between my bedroom and the Haunted Bookshop two blocks away, across the vacant lots of thigh-high blue-joint grass intersected by flooding ditches over which muskrats slid like the gloved hands of undertakers along the lids of mahogany caskets. In those years – when I was between six and twelve – my mother worked part-time at the drug store in order to supplement my father's unreliable income, and she would bring home comic books from time to time. It was always a random selection, but, oddly, not superhero comics, not *Batman* or *Superman* or *The Fantastic Four* or *The Amazing Spider-Man* (perhaps because they appeared too violent), but kiddie comics, Gold Key and Disney (in the days long before Disney owned the superhero movie franchise and aimed its content at a much older audience than ten-year-olds) and, my early favourite, *Casper the Friendly Ghost*. Did she simply open the driver's-side door of the Ford on her way down the driveway and add a few glossy leaves to the dulled mulch? I like to think so. Parents didn't make so much of parenting in the

1970s, and besides, she would have trusted that I'd know where the new comics had come from.

    I can see her again, in her late forties (I was her last, and second surviving, child, born in her late thirties), her thick black hair bobby-pinned up under a rayon kerchief pearled with rain, her lipstick red as salmon blood, her pale-blue work smock stained with ink and perfume samples just as my father's white Stanfield T-shirts were stained with the blood and brine of his labour. She opens the heavy car door in the dim one-bulb light of our side porch and gently places rather than throws the comics on the front seat.

    Does she ever dream of climbing behind the wheel herself, of imagining another life, the one she might have lived in the heart of Toronto if a war hadn't come, bringing a shy blue-eyed sailor from the west coast into her dancing, factory-working days of rare freedom? Who doesn't have regrets, after all? The Gravenstein doesn't want to relinquish its sweetness to the killing frosts. The old Ford longs to speed along the highways again. The ghosts in the gloomy Edwardian houses (who tap me on the shoulder when I explore the musty rooms with their mouldy faded-rose wallpaper) drift away with all the ardency of flesh. But my mother's longings, such as they were, remain incommunicable, except in the way she always used the red-winged blackbird's song to call me in from play. The scarlet bangles on those wings, my working mother's made-up lips – these were the colours that inked my autumns' ordinary blacks and greys; these, and the colours of the pages in my hands as I lay back for the long drive that ends only at death.

    There was joy in that escape, but the cold chore never let me forget my family's place in the mundane wage-earning order of the world.

    Truth be told, my father didn't love fishing as much as most fishermen did, haunting the waterfront in the less productive seasons. Once the summer with its more lucrative sockeye bounty had passed, he continued to go out for every opening on the river, but he had mostly begun his winter hibernation by October, choosing to let the net repairs and boat maintenance slide. One memorable winter, in fact, he let things slide so far that his gillnetter sank in its moorage, only the cabin and mast showing above the harbour's murky surface.

Having decided to avoid all forms of authoritarian rule and scheduling after being ordered about in the navy, he appreciated fishing for the freedom it afforded him. The anxiety of the work, its unpredictable income, even the killing: these were the unavoidable trade-offs for escaping the nine-to-five world, the same trade-offs I have made and continue to make, minus the killing, unless you count the creative spirit that dies and must always be, sometimes against all the odds, resurrected.

So in the heaviest autumn downpours, usually after supper when the night was at its blackest, a knock would come on our side door, and my mother would open it to reveal the dripping, anvil-sharp face – with its full Biblical rain-diamonded beard – of Edgar Winterbourne.

Without preliminaries, as if reciting a prepared speech, he'd say, "Hecky'd better get down to the wharf and pump out his boat." Then Edgar would vanish, slipping back under the teeming onslaught like a seal, his exit silent and complete, leaving only the faintest wake of oil, sweat and river mud on our threshold. Bullet, who was always at his side, never made a sound.

By the time I was eight, I was regularly deputized to act on Edgar's warning, for it wasn't a complicated task to pump out the boat. My father, perfectly sanguine about leaving me to it, sometimes had to wave away my mother's concern that I might lose my footing on the slippery planks, bang my head and be swept away unconscious on the tide. She had never forgotten – how could she? – the five-year-old boy twenty years before who'd pedalled his tricycle off the upper wharf and drowned without anyone around to see the accident happen.

"You promise to be extra careful," she'd say as I pulled on my rain jacket and yanked the cords of my hood tight so that I really did resemble a tiny monk. "Take this flashlight. And be sure that you take Scooter with you."

And off I'd go, with our family's old springer spaniel at my side, and then ten feet behind me, and then twenty feet, and then I'd wait in the rain so heavy that it bounced up off the pavement as heavily as it fell from the sky as Scooter emerged out of his thick breath-clouds, his tongue lolling, his tail wagging, and we'd go on, past the Buckerfields grain store and warehouse at the corner, through the limpid splash of yellow light from one streetlamp, past the Seven Seas fish cannery on the dike above us, its tin roof rattling as if machine-gunned. Finally, once onto the dike at the blackberry-bush-shrouded entrance to the government wharf, after I'd used all my strength to lift Scooter up the last ten feet of the slope, I'd tell him to lie down and wait, because I was more worried about him falling into the river than me.

Unless you've lived through a real west coast autumn rainstorm, you can't know how the darkness itself seems to be wet, and how, if you're not careful about drawing the air into your lungs, you might just drown standing up. And when the wind blows the rain sideways, as it always seemed to do in those years when I pumped out the boat, you feel as if you're being whipped by invisible centurions. But how vividly the world comes to life in all your senses. Scooter, for example, was fifty pounds of steaming redolent fur when I walked away from him, his scent staying with me as if it too weighed several pounds, and the river was a glistening cauldron of hissing scents as I cautiously passed the main net shed and descended the steep cleated gangway to our moorage spot, moving from tiny chain-connected float to float like an anxious frog over lily pads.

A few nights after the miracle of the three white, identically weighted spring salmon, I stood again beside our drum, waiting to pump the water from the bilge. A hollow aluminum tube, round enough for a muskrat to scurry through and with an extension angled out to discharge the water, was all I needed to do the job. I'd push down the thin iron rod inside with the rubber cup at the bottom, then pull up as much water as I could and shoot it over the side of the boat. *Squeak, squeak. Squelch, squelch.* Even soaked and miserable, I found the job immensely satisfying and usually finished in a much better mood than when I'd started. I knew that my mother would have a hot mug of sugary Red Rose tea waiting for me, and, on this occasion, I knew I had the most recent issue of *The Amazing Spider-Man* to read in my bedroom. Everything, despite the tempest, was calm. Then I heard what I shouldn't have heard and, hearing it, began what I shouldn't have begun.

Muffled cries, faint at first, a little downriver, like what a lost kitten would make. Then louder, in a lull of the gusting rain, but still almost inaudible. I thought perhaps my imagination had gotten the better of me again. My fear of great white sharks had persisted, and I flinched at every sound. When a wharf rat plopped into the current as I had approached our boat, I had jumped back and almost fallen over a net some fisherman had unrolled off his drum in order to repair.

But it was more than sharks that worried me. I had all sorts of mythic subterranean and subaquatic monsters to fear, the creations of the twentieth century's most famous comic book artist, the one who'd inspired my best friend to become an artist, and the one whose war experiences and stressful economic life not only gave him a richly nightmarish psychology but also made him an honorary if only nominally present member of my neighbourhood's war-haunted river culture.

But all thoughts of sharks and Jack Kirby's monsters vanished as the strange cries rose and fell in the pelting storm. I stood still, straining to locate the source of the sound. All the fleet was in, which meant that each moorage spot had at least four boats, side by side, in it, adding up to at least fifty boats. But no cabin lights shone out of the blackness, not even any mast lights. Yet I swore the cries were coming from one of the boats.

I put the pump away and crept back along the floats the way I had come. Now my footsteps seemed more perilous, for even in the whoosh of rain and wind, in the Christmassy tinkle of the chains high up on the masts and the rubbing grunt of boats against the wooden floats, I heard my approach like gunshots. Finally, I reached a net rack halfway back to the gangway and placed my hand on it in an effort to calm myself. The noises, which had only seconds before suddenly rung out like gull cries, now came faintly again, at least three boats out into the channel. I took a deep breath and stepped onto the deck of the first boat. A sudden cough, deep and male, brought me up short. It was my chance to turn around, to ignore my senses and my curiosity, to listen instead to the instinct that was telling me to just go home. But some other instinct soon urged me onto the next deck. From there, I could tell that the sounds originated from the neighbouring unlit cabin.

By this time, I think I knew that no good could come from the knowledge of what I then only dimly apprehended. At ten in a working-class town, I knew the word "fuck" intimately – it has always been the anthem of my country more than any words written by a rum-sodden homesick Scot in the nineteenth century. But I didn't know what it was an acronym for. Even if I had known, I doubt I would have turned away, nor do I even now put much stock in most of the laws dreamed up by any group of men.

The night wasn't completely black. Dull orange wharf lights afforded some visibility in the gloom. And though I hadn't wanted it, the flashlight with its cold metal handle comforted me a little as, with breath held, I stepped onto the third deck as lightly as possible, so my weight wouldn't indicate my presence.

The cries had stopped, or else were too faint to hear above the storm. Very gently, I crouched and slipped along the gunwale beside the cabin until the open square window above the rain-streaked portholes was just over my head. Then I raised myself slowly, my fingers tightening around the flashlight.

Seconds passed. The current gurgled around the bows and the wind gusted like a bellows. I waited for what seemed like hours, and then finally worked up the courage to switch on the flashlight and train it at the square dark space.

A man's back and head showed briefly, moving in its position on the bunk, but the woman must have seen the light, for her face turned toward it, emerging from behind the man's head like a moon from behind a planet. Convinced that our eyes had locked, I reared away in a flash of recognition, banging the flashlight on the side of the cabin as I struggled to keep my balance. The sound rang out like a shout in the rain-whispery stillness.

Panicked, I switched off the flashlight and scrambled for the deck. As I leapt to the neighbouring boat, the cabin light came on like a burst of yellow flame behind me, and I heard a thumping movement at its source.

I slipped once, banging my elbow on the edge of a hatch cover, but soon was running along the chain-linked floats to the gangway. At the top, on the main upper wharf, I turned back, convinced of pursuit. But only the rain and wind followed me, and the current's hungry reaching for the sea. Far below, the vivid yellow cabin light trembled. I stood for several seconds, catching my breath, not even allowing myself to speculate over who I might have intruded upon. My cheeks were soaked, as if I'd been sobbing, and my hands felt numbed, heavy.

But I was free. I could turn the corner of the big dark net shed, bend down to pet my dog, whose smell still clung to me, and be home in minutes. So why did I feel chained in place? It was as if my body and mind needed extra time to absorb the change, as if knowledge was a chrysalis that first needs to crack the old self before the metamorphosis can proceed at its natural pace, which, it's clear to me only now, is the pace of a lifetime.

A thick shadow, moving swiftly in the wharf lights, snapped me out of my strange reverie. I ran onto the dike and almost right over Scooter, who lay faithfully in the wet dust.

"Come on, Scoots, come on!" I urged into his fragrant fur.

But he was an old dog and wouldn't be able to run beside me. I imagined a hand around my throat and felt almost too weak to move. Then I put my arms underneath the already-panting animal and lifted him to my chest. It was no good. He was heavy enough that I couldn't possibly run with him in my arms. In fact, I could only stagger forward.

I heard steps striking the gangway planks and made a desperate choice. As gently as possible, I put Scooter on the ground, and then I sprinted along the dike, heading for the shelter of the huge blackberry bushes in the vacant lot at the foot of my street. Once crouched there, trying to swallow the sound of my gasping breath, I looked back through the streetlamp's dim glow to where Scooter tried his best to follow me. But he hardly seemed to be moving at all as the thick shadow finally pulled up beside him.

I couldn't see the man's face or hear his breathing, yet somehow I felt the violence pouring from him. So when, after a few seconds of walking beside Scooter, he suddenly stopped and turned and gave one sharp kick into my old dog's side, I wasn't shocked enough to yell or run out or otherwise reveal my hiding place. Instead, I just clenched the flashlight even harder, imagining that I could swing it at the man's head and bring the same yelp of pain from him that he'd brought out of my dog. Scared as I was, however, I knew that if he did anything else to Scooter, I'd have no choice but to intervene.

But he just stood looking down as Scooter faithfully and slowly resumed his efforts to follow me. Then the man straightened up – I could see that he wasn't very tall, certainly well under six feet – but otherwise I had no clue as to his identity. At that point, I didn't really care about who he was; I just wanted him to leave so that Scooter and I could return safely home.

Finally, he turned and strode back in the direction of the wharf, and I was able to come out of the blackberry bushes and stand on the cracked sidewalk at the fringe of the streetlamp's glow. Scooter struggled slowly onward but he never seemed to come any closer and I didn't feel safe enough to walk through the light to go to him. I stood there, looking back. And the old dog (I feel this more viscerally now) was the past, my past, loving and warm, destined always to die but never to stop following me, and I cannot, even in this written return, go back and hold and carry and shelter even one single moment of time in my living arms.

II

The rain didn't let up for weeks. It beat an irregular rhythm on the rooftops and in the rusted beds of wheelbarrows and on the glistening oil drums standing like menhirs in the many unkempt tall grassy places around our neighbourhood. Even the great blue herons seemed weighted down with the moisture, flying so low over the town that I feared they'd smash into the telephone poles or get tangled in the wires. Normally, I didn't mind the rain; like most children everywhere, I simply existed in the weather without question, having more important matters on my mind, such as how much extra money I could earn collecting beer and pop bottles along the muddy riverbank at low tide to help finance my comic collecting habit.

Also – and I admit this now with some regret, thinking of all those wasted hours – I fretted about where I could play road hockey.

No doubt this problem seems an antiquated one in today's sedentary digital culture, but in the 1970s, even television provided limited viewing for children. Cartoons ran on Saturdays, and there were some early morning kids' shows during the week, but the rest of the time we had only reruns of '50s and '60s shows to watch, and they didn't always appeal. Opie's cuteness and Gilligan's idiocy would entertain for only so long, and inevitably the great outdoors became more attractive, especially when you could slap a tennis ball past your friend standing in the net with just a baseball glove and one of my older brother's broken goalie sticks for additional defence.

In the fall, when it got dark at 4:00 p.m., we played road hockey for hours wherever we could find a light source. Usually that meant under a dim streetlamp or under the freight entrance light at the back of our town's tallest building, the grain elevator of the co-op store. Darkness we could handle, but rain was more of a challenge. We did try to play in it, of course, but the fun didn't last, so we mostly waited out the rainiest times of the year.

That October, however, wore our patience thin, which meant we had to improvise. After being kicked out of an apartment building's undercover parking compound, Jay and I came upon the brilliant idea – brilliant because it was so obvious – to take shots inside one of my neighbourhood's many derelict buildings.

You see, I grew up in a period of economic decline in a town filled with ruins. Within a five-minute walk from my house, I could enter any of six condemned Edwardian houses, a boarded-up movie theatre, a half-block row of empty stores and an abandoned vegetable canning factory the length of a football field. Or if I preferred smaller shelters, I had my pick of rotting fish boats on the banks of the river, including a ghostly sternwheeler right out of *The Adventures of Huckleberry Finn*, and any number of rusting vehicles with missing doors and backseats clunky with empty beer bottles. Indeed, in my neighbourhood, the oldest and most decaying part of town, every yard had a junked car, a dry-docked boat and someone out of work. Most of my schoolmates, including Jay, lived in newer subdivisions a few miles south of the river, which made coming to the original townsite in the fall or winter rather like stepping into another world – a dark, drizzly world of foghorns, dim lighting and sometimes unsavoury characters. A very questionable pub, a half block from the Haunted Bookshop, contributed greatly to this disturbing culture, but history played a greater part, its wars still spreading terror and confusion long after the bombs had stopped exploding.

But all of that will be explained later.

For now, it's necessary to see another dark night of incessant sideways rain and two boys, one carrying an aluminum hockey net on his back like a set of cumbersome wings, the other carrying a coal-oil lantern and a flashlight. Jay and I didn't have far to go. We left the gravel driveway of my front yard and crossed the street to the soaked thigh-high grass of the vacant lot. Within a few minutes, we'd managed to force the net and ourselves through the glassless window of a two-storey house built sometime in the early years of the twentieth century.

Immediately I felt the presence of ghosts. Almost always, day or night, I sensed the presence of long-dead children in my neighbourhood's many vacant buildings, perhaps because I was a child myself and more sensitive to their departed energies. Regardless of the reason, I was chilled, not warmed, by the feeling. To compose myself, I asked Jay what he thought. My voice echoed up to the twelve-foot ceiling and slid toward the particularly ominous staircase leading to the second floor.

"I think," he said in his consistently upbeat and confident voice, "that we stupidly forgot the sticks."

Shining the flashlight at his face, I was met with the usual Joker-wide grin, dark and almost chestnut-sized restless eyes and flop of curls, like shavings of mahogany, emerging from under his vivid white bucket hat, which he wore as faithfully as Gilligan wore his own or as Jughead wears his beanie. For a twelve-year-old, Jay had a strikingly noble bearing – a large forehead, Romanesque nose and sharp cheekbones. But his ceaseless effervescence – always talking, always moving, even to the point of tapping his feet when reading comics – kept his physical appearance just childish and goofy enough to throw adults off. By the time they realized that this loquacious and regal child Caesar was just a loping, joking boy with a Grape Crush and a Crunchie in his hands who had read more books and seen more movies than they had, they'd already identified him as a threat. Only Mr. Edison at the Haunted Bookshop seemed to derive great amusement from Jay's overwhelming intellectual curiosity. After all, it was a rare adult, let alone a child, who had seen every episode of *Monty Python's Flying Circus* and read *The Communist Manifesto* and who wrote and drew

THE MARVELS OF YOUTH

his own versions of the Bazooka Joe strips found in packs of bubble gum. Mr. Edison must have felt at once astonished, grateful and bewildered to have a twelve-year-old customer as a break from bargain-seeking elderly Scotswomen. As for me ... well, looking back after almost fifty years, I can best describe Jay's effect on my intellectual world as a combination of Dr. Frankenstein and his creation at the exact moment that the corpse is jolted into life. That is, I experienced the scientist's thrill of discovery along with the monster's growing knowledge of the horrors of existence. If that seems like an extreme statement, then you don't understand the burden of critical thought in a world of violence and injustice.

"I'll go," I said, aware as always of my unwillingness to be alone in any abandoned house – or, rather, not really alone. If a swimming pool could potentially hold a shark, then certainly an ancient and decaying house could harbour ungentle spirits. I left Jay with the oil lantern and hurried back to the side yard of my house to collect the hockey sticks.

When I returned, no dim light shone in the living room of cobwebs and spiders, and there was no sound except the swishing rain.

"Jay?" My quiet tone sounded like a shout.

But only my own voice echoed back. For comfort, I took a tennis ball from my jacket pocket and bounced it on the floor. When my second call received no response, I tightened my grip on my trusty Sherwood and decided to wait a few minutes before letting fear drive me outside. Simultaneously, I heard a thump overhead and saw a wavering light approaching from another room on my level.

"I had to pee," Jay said as the lantern illuminated his grin. "And I thought I might as well take the light."

"Did you hear something?"

"When?"

"Just now. When you were coming in."

"Like what? The wind?"

I shook my head and slapped the tennis ball at the net, which Jay had positioned in front of the old brick fireplace. "From upstairs." I pointed the flashlight at the staircase as if forcing it through sand. "A sort of thump."

Jay bent down and picked up the goalie stick and baseball glove. "I'll go in net first." He somehow managed to carry the shimmering lantern and place it to one side of the net. "Unless you want to go upstairs and investigate."

"It was probably just a squirrel or something." I set the flashlight beside me and asked if he could see well enough.

Jay laughed. "Only one way to find out. Come on, let her go."

I blasted the tennis ball toward him and he didn't even move.

He laughed louder. "Okay. Any time you're ready." Then he bent into the net to retrieve the tennis ball.

After a few more shots, none of which Jay even moved for, I'd almost forgotten about the overhead thump when I heard someone coming down the stairs.

"Who's that?" Jay said, an edge in his voice.

Two blunt sounds – hopefully just footsteps – came out of the darkness. Then a third and a fourth. If someone was descending the staircase, they weren't in any great hurry. But then, killers always took their time.

"Shine the flashlight over there," Jay said under his breath. "Go on. Do it."

By the time I mustered up the courage, several more blunt sounds had ensued, followed by silence. I stared at the darkness exactly the way Richard Dreyfuss in *Jaws* stares at the surface of the ocean. No matter how desperately I wanted the tension to end, I couldn't bring myself to point the light at the staircase. By now, I could hear breathing coming from no more than twenty feet away. It was almost as if the old walls covered with peeling and mildewed flowery wallpaper had come to life.

At last, just as Jay began to speak again, I threw my arm forward like a wizard casting a spell. The light landed directly on a face that didn't flinch or even show an expression.

"Theo," I barely managed to utter. "It's just Theo."

"Who?"

For someone so intelligent, Jay had a remarkable capacity for being oblivious to his surroundings. Or perhaps he took interest only in what interested him, which is likely a key component of intelligence.

"You know. Theo. The little Greek boy."

"What? You mean that mute kid?"

I nodded as I slowly pulled the light down from Theo's broad face with its almond-shaped eyes and thick-lipped mouth. He wore only a T-shirt and trousers and a pair of big gumboots. I knew that Theo wasn't just mute, but also had some sort of – what we called then – mental handicap. Sometimes during the daylight hours, he followed me around if I was in the vacant lots near his own yard, which was half a block beyond this abandoned house. But I'd never seen him out after dark. Somehow this fact gave me a sickening feeling, one that I couldn't explain. I wondered why his mother or his older brothers had let this happen. Even though I thought of Theo as little, he was only two years younger than me, though considerably smaller in the body. His dark hair was always closely shorn and he seemed to wear his teenaged brothers' hand-me-down sweaters, jackets and boots. But it was his eyes – large and never blinking, as if some invisible force kept them open – that always made me shiver a little. They were as black and unyielding as a salmon's, and since a salmon's eyes are exactly the same in death as in life, I couldn't help but wonder what Theo saw when he looked at the world. Even worse, I had sometimes wondered whether he even closed his eyes when he slept.

"Theo? What are you doing here?" I said, forgetting as always that he couldn't answer, at least not in words. I trained the flashlight on his face again.

His eyes were still wide open, but now tears streamed down from the corners.

"What's the matter with him?" Jay asked, stepping up beside me.

"I'm not sure. Maybe he's just scared. He's not supposed to be outside after dark."

The three of us just stood there for several seconds, listening to the rain whoosh down in a house that had been vacant for as long as I could remember. Finally, I realized that there wasn't any other choice.

"We'll have to take him home, I guess." I moved slowly a few steps forward. "Okay, Theo? We'll take you to your house."

It might just have been my imagination, but he seemed to shrink back at the idea.

"You can't stay here. You should be at home. It's late."

By now, I'd taken him by the hand, surprised by how cold it was, as if he'd been plunging it in ice. But he didn't resist.

"I can take him," I told Jay. "It'll just take a few minutes. You can practice your shot."

"Yeah, okay. Maybe one of this house's creepy old ghosts will go in net. But I probably can't even put one past some ectoplasm."

By the time I'd led Theo outside, Jay was already whistling "The Lumberjack Song" from Monty Python and whacking the tennis ball against the mildewed wallpaper.

As we crossed the soaked grass of the vacant lot to the narrow cracked pavement of the road leading to Theo's house, he began to moan and shake his head from side to side. Not knowing what else to do, I just kept walking toward his house, encouraged by the fact that he hadn't let go of my hand.

The Vasilakis home was in complete darkness, without even the porchlight on. But the low sleek Chrysler, slickened with rain, sat in the driveway, and, more than that, I just had a sense that somebody was home. My sensitivity to the presence of ghosts carried over to a sensitivity to the presence of the living, which could be a little uncanny. Jay said that it was like I had my own Spidey-Senses. Besides, how could the family – the parents, and Theo's two older brothers and older sister – be away when he was out by himself in a storm?

For a few seconds, I stood at the foot of the four concrete steps leading up to the front door. I tried to will myself into seeing the bright blue and white colours of the house, which I knew was the colour of the Greek flag because Theo's older brother, Stevie – short for Stavros, he once confided, shaking his head – told me, and also because most of the Greek fishermen flew blue and white flags on their masts. But I couldn't will away the darkness, then or now.

Reluctantly, I mounted the steps and knocked lightly on the door.

THE MARVELS OF YOUTH

Getting no response, I knocked a little louder. Again, no one came. Theo, beside me, was snuffling and shivering, so I made the bold decision to enter the house uninvited. I figured the family wouldn't mind, considering that I was bringing Theo back to them.

Inside, I was immediately struck by a strange mixture of smells – an acrid smokiness, like what comes off the end of a punk at Halloween, plus a spicy aroma of cooking, some kind of meat and garlic and other scents I didn't recognize. In a large room off to the side entrance, there was a dull flickering light that now, against my will, drew me to it. Still I heard no voices, detected no human movement. Once inside the room, I stood, bewildered. A dozen candles flickered, and a few tiny electric lights mounted to one wall revealed several icons – I recognized Christ in agony on the cross and the Virgin Mary holding the baby Jesus, but only because my mother had sent me to summer Bible camp at the Dutch Reformed Church one year out of guilt for my lack of any religious instruction at home. Of Christianity, I recalled the key characters in much the same way that I recalled the key characters in the Marvel and DC comics. And I knew the "Jesus Loves Me" song and could still taste the weird Ribena drink on my tongue as if it truly was the blood of Christ. But I had come to resent the whole idea of a God that would keep me indoors during the most beautiful and free months of the year, a resentment I've never lost.

Still holding Theo's freezing hand, I noticed other candles that had either burnt out or been snuffed out by the wind blowing in through an open window. Just then, the wind, already strong, gusted powerfully, so that it seemed the house was suddenly adrift on the ocean. A candle went out. But Jesus and Mary didn't blink or adjust their positions; they were frozen forever, no matter what the weather did to the light.

This was so much worse than being in an abandoned house, even alone, that I quickly turned and pulled Theo back the way we came. Then I heard noises, very low beneath the wind, coming from a room down a narrow hallway. As I approached, Theo resisted, shaking his head and moaning.

"What is it? What's wrong?" I asked, forgetting again that he couldn't answer.

His jaw opened and closed, like a salmon's gasping for air. His terror raced along my nerves like an electric current. Jesus and Mary, together in death and birth, rode the great crest of the wind, staring straight through me. But I'd come too far to run away.

At the partially open door to the room with the murmurous sounds, I finally let go of Theo's hand. The sudden warmth that came from the release emboldened me, and I peered around the door into the brighter candlelight. All at once, I saw a woman's drawn face against a pillow, silhouetted by at least six figures, and heard some sharply spoken, though hushed, Greek. One of the figures turned toward me, but my eyes lingered on the pale female face, because I recognized it as Theo's mother's. Her name was Marina and she was my own mother's age, in her mid-forties, with the same large dark eyes and general air of kindness. But I had never seen her thick lustrous black hair before. It was always hidden beneath a black head-covering, part of the mourning clothes that Marina always wore because, as Stevie had also told me, the family had lost a child at birth, just as my own family had, three years before I was born. But my mother, if she ever wore black, stopped long before I was old enough to remember it.

Just as the figure blocked my view, however, I experienced a sudden sharp revelation that was somehow connected to the mystery of the icons, of the strangeness of that long-ago pregnancy and birth. For just the most fleeting of seconds, I saw the woman's face on the pillow and the woman's face emerging from behind the shoulder of the man in the boat cabin, and even though they were not the same face, just as Jesus's face was not Mary's, I was stricken by some obvious thread of connection, almost as strong as the current of Theo's fear that had jolted me in the larger room.

But there was no time to do anything except note the connection in my body before Stevie put his hand on my shoulder and, speaking a hurried Greek I'd never heard him use, gently guided me into the hallway.

Flustered, and anxious to defend my actions, I uttered Theo's name.

Stevie, whose handsome sixteen-year-old face I couldn't even see, just nodded. In fact, he didn't speak until the three of us were on the front porch in the darkness and drizzle.

"Sorry about that," he said almost sheepishly. "Only Greek spoken in the house. My dad's rules . . ."

He let the words hang in the air a while before he said something in Greek to Theo, whom he had pulled tight against his body. Then he thanked me.

"My mom is sick." A sob caught deep in his throat. "Very sick. We didn't notice that Theo was gone."

I didn't know what to say. In fact, for the rest of my life, faced with similar obvious moments of great emotion, I would respond with a silence that I allowed to be interpreted as tact but which I knew to be incomprehension in the presence of human suffering. That is, I could no more have consoled Stevie in his pain than I could have consoled Jesus or Mary, so I remained always as mute as Theo but as full and heavy as the surrounding storm.

With great relief, I returned to the abandoned house, eager to replace the ghost in the net. To take a tennis ball in the face seemed preferable to trying to work out why those two women's faces – the one in almost indifferent lust, the other in pain – should hang in the air like petals off a single stem. For the rest of my life, a glance from any woman – known or a stranger – will confound me, as if the plaster eyes of a candle-lit Mary had cracked open and I could see the whole other half of the world's suffering, for just a second, through them, before they closed again like a wound.

III

Dylan Thomas famously wrote that he wasn't sure if it snowed for six days straight when he was twelve or twelve days straight when he was six, and sometimes memory indeed plays such almost-logical games with us. But I know for a certainty that the revelation of Mrs. Vasilakis's illness occurred just a few days before one of Edgar Winterbourne's miraculous feats of madcap energy. Looking back, I think the purity of my recollection must have something to do with the flickering candles beneath the icons and that heavy smell of burning incense. Or maybe the gunshots of hunting season have somehow joined with the slapshots echoing in the mildewed rooms of that rotting Edwardian house. Perhaps my brother's resemblance to Jesus . . . But what is the past, really, except a dream that we can't help recalling because we don't require sleep to enter it? And what is a dream, as Charles Dickens asks, but the insanity of each day's sanity?

I didn't like hunting, but I loved my brother's company. So when he woke me on what must have been a Saturday morning and said, "Want to go for some pheasants, Champ?" I took in one deep breath of his stale-beer/Old Spice/wine-tipped-cigarillo scent and immediately pulled back my covers.

The rain had stopped, but that hadn't tempted the sun to appear. Shreds of fine mist hung head-high as we climbed into Dan's golden El Camino and drove west down a long scythe-curved road bordered with dripping weeping willows and monkey-puzzle trees and on out a few miles to where the wet, just-harvested acres of potato fields on the land side faced the black wire stacks of crab pots and the sunken grey net sheds on the river side. Scooter's strong breath wafted into my nostrils as he hung his head over my shoulder.

Dan laughed. "He still gets excited. But I can't remember the last time he retrieved anything. Usually just wanders off the wrong way now, good old fellow." He took one hand off the wheel and gave Scooter's muzzle a vigorous rub.

Soon we were driving over the small wooden swing bridge that connects the mainland to Westham Island, the largest of several silt islands settled like blood clots in the Fraser's final push to the sea. Out there, even the world of a sleepy 1970s town fell away. In the northwest corner of the island, a rum-running millionaire had left a bird sanctuary as a legacy, or perhaps as an atonement for the way he'd made his money, but the rest of the island was, in a manner of speaking, fair game. In those years, and in some families on the fringes of insolvency, pheasants and ducks stretched the food budget, as did the culls – the oddly shaped or slightly green potatoes that the farmers couldn't sell – in the drenched fields. That was why I carried two burlap sacks, one for the culls and the other for any birds we managed to shoot. Often, one bag remained empty, for it was much easier to find a cull on the ground than to flush a pheasant from a ditch.

It was cold. Our breath joined the strands of mist and a fine skim of ice often snapped under our boots as we mucked our way across the black acres toward a thick brimful ditch of inky water. Gunshots echoed around us, though not a figure was in sight, just a few farmhouses and barns that looked about as lively as the house I'd guided Theo out of a few nights before.

We walked for an hour, Scooter struggling so much behind us that my whole body kept shivering with the image of him on the dike, the brief abrupt kick he'd taken in the side. I stopped to wait for him, wondering for the hundredth time who the man had been. I knew the woman, all right, but the man definitely hadn't been her husband. An old man didn't move like that, didn't give off so much violent energy. Of course, as a boy in a small town, I knew enough – either by instinct or osmosis – not to let my wondering venture toward an active curiosity. Where would be the gain? Besides, I had papers to deliver, comics to collect, old houses to explore.

I picked up a few culls and stuffed them in my sack. Scooter huffed like a small boiler as he clumped along. The cold rose from the wet ground and pierced my flesh. Never, never in my almost sixty years, half of which have been spent in frigid Edmonton, have I been as cold as I was in those autumn years along or on the Fraser River.

Dan's long hair hanging below his khaki-green hunting cap was the only resemblance to Jesus that marked him now. The shotgun, held across his leather vest ribbed with cartridge pockets, was decidedly unchristian. Yet something about his silent confidence made his progress impressive in the same slightly chilling way. I knew enough about religion and hunting by the age of ten to know that both involved death more than life.

Just as I came up to him again, slightly behind on his left side, an amber flutter out of a furrow overhung with brambles broke toward the grey acres overhead. Dan swung around like a tank turret and heaved his shoulder heavenward. The wings made a sound like a collapsing skeleton in a classroom. I closed my eyes, afraid of the death I'd see when I opened them again. Pheasants are such beautiful birds that I dreaded the snapping of their necks, the staining of their soft plumage, the gutting at the kitchen sink as my tender-hearted mother sighed over the sad economics that made the entrails in her hands necessary.

"Damn. Winged him." Dan snapped the shotgun in half and popped the shells out. "Better to miss altogether. Come on. We'll have to try to find him." He sighed as he turned his lean, sideburned face down toward Scooter. "If you can, old boy, use that sniffer of yours."

But Scooter just wagged his stubby tail and smiled that maniacal dog smile that we always interpreted as happiness but was probably just exhaustion.

"There! Look!" I pointed at a darkness a few feet above the dark earth, perhaps fifty yards away. The bird moved across the louring sky as if being slid off a table. Then it plummeted out of sight again.

Dan ran ahead of me, his blazing scarlet hair swinging like a priest's censer, his wide-topped gumboots simultaneously cracking the skims of ice and making a sucking sound in the mud. I followed at a slower pace, half-hoping that the bird would escape and that some sort of natural healing would be possible. But you can't be a fisherman's son and truly believe in mercy, at least not from Nature. I knew that we needed to kill the pheasant for its own sake now.

All at once, the dark ground rose up straight in front of us, or so it seemed. We had come to a windbreak of scraggly poplars that divided one field from the next.

Dan turned back to me. "Damn. Did you see it go in here?"

I shook my head as the burlap sack of culls came to rest at my thigh like a club. "Maybe it flew over."

Dan put two fingers of one hand in his mouth and whistled, but Scooter couldn't move any faster, a fact I knew from recent painful experience. "We've got to find it," my brother said, and tightened both hands on the stock of the gun. I knew that he'd keep searching all day if necessary. Our father's gentleness with spiders in their webs was reflected in Dan's unwillingness to let a shot bird suffer a lingering death.

We entered the windbreak and stopped dead as soon as we stepped out on the other side. For as far as the eye could see, from the muddy shore with the pewter river flowing by to the road a half-mile to the west, the earth was covered with ripe pumpkins. Thousands upon thousands of them, their dull orange greasy with the rain. A strong gust of rot hit us full in the face, but it wasn't really unpleasant, nothing like rotting cabbage or salmon.

"Jesus," my brother said, and I almost laughed out loud. It was absurd that someone who looked so much like Jesus would use that curse, but then, no one in my family ever said the more common vulgar swear words. We were prudish that way. "Isn't it almost Halloween?"

"I guess so. Why?"

Dan didn't seem to hear me. "I forgot Ellis was putting pumpkins in. But they ought to be harvested by now." He let the gun dangle in one arm at his side. "There's no way we can track a bird through those things."

As he spoke, only thirty feet in front of us the wounded pheasant flew up with a terrific clatter and veered right at us before spiralling toward the river. Expertly, Dan whipped up the gun and shot. The dark smear exploded to the ground, somewhere among the faceless jack-o'-lanterns that ought to have been carved and set up on porches by now. Halloween was just a few days off.

The mist seemed to flow from the ends of a thousand invisible barrels. Scooter's barking played the concussive fatal shot again and again as my brother and I hesitated at the edge of the pumpkin field. Somehow, I had the feeling that we were being grinned at, mocked. The vines connecting all those unborn faces had an unnerving umbilical quality. It seemed wholly appropriate that we should have to step our way over those vines to find the death that we had caused. More than that, it seemed inevitable.

"Looks sort of like salmon roe, doesn't it? All packed together like that."

I followed my brother's gaze back to the field. The round orange globes under the vast grey sky did look like fish eggs stripped from a belly, but the image wasn't a cheerful one.

By this time, amazingly, Scooter had worked his slow way through the pumpkins and turned back triumphantly with the pheasant's soft body in his old jaws.

"Hey, how about that? Attaboy, Scooter! Good boy!"

Our dog's feat had been enough to brighten the hour for Dan, but I couldn't get the rot of the pumpkins or their invisible leers out of my senses as I picked up the bloodied mess that Scooter proudly dropped at our boots and placed it in the other burlap sack. Now I had an equal weight pulling at both shoulders, and stood still, like some sort of rural statue of Justice, as my breath swirled around my eyes. But I wasn't blinded, as Justice must be, nor am I now, for I haven't forgotten the hard lessons of those years, the knowledge of how fantasy and reality land eventually with the same heavy thud on the same cold ground, first the one sack, and then the other. Time in the left hand, change in the right.

We flushed nothing else that day and drove back home just as the rain resumed its slow months-long bleeding from the sunless sky.

IV

"You've got to see it," Keith cried, the pirate patch that should have been over his eye instead stuck in the middle of his forehead. He looked as if he'd been shot.

Normally our trick-or-treating didn't include the river. In fact, we always moved quickly away from my neighbourhood, which was the oldest and most ruined part of town, to where the newer subdivisions with their well-lit driveways and porches and houses packed closely together allowed us to fill our pillowcases more efficiently. But that year, my next-door neighbour and good friend, Keith, pounded on the door about an hour after dark (which came early on the last day of October) to tell me to come to the waterfront.

Even in the dim porchlight, his flame-red hair, much brighter than my brother's, seemed more vivid than usual, as did the freckles splashed over both cheeks – the hair and freckles joined with the black hole to intensify the look of violence, but Keith's whole demeanour was gleeful.

A year younger than me, and also a fisherman's son, our next-door neighbour was without question the wild alternative to my suburban, civilized temptations. Where I thrived in school, he kept the truant officers employed; where I loved to read, he loved to trap muskrats and build rafts and tree forts; where I played sports and had a paper route, he resisted all forms of organized and team effort; where I treated my parents with respect and civility, he often called his the most terrible names; where I relished Jay's company and the tight confines of the Haunted Bookshop, he avoided both like the plague. But when the wind blew off the river with its mulch of brine and fish guts and the gulls reeled screeching out of the overcast, or when the languid summer hours cried out for a meandering stroll through the tall grass to the Dairy Dell for a chilled grape Freezie, that part of me born to the best of childhood's freedoms always rallied to Keith's example.

It particularly amused my mother, after I turned to get my jacket as Keith waited on the braided welcome mat inside the door, that he should choose to be a pirate on Halloween. "What is he the rest of the year?" she'd say with a laugh later that evening.

Even their family house, a two-storey Victorian as thin and mouldy as a piece of Miss Havisham's never-tasted wedding cake, possessed a nautically aggressive quality. No doubt its piratical quality stemmed from the fact that Keith and his little brother Billy would sometimes fill thick brown paper bags with their urine and, leaning out of an upstairs bedroom window, toss them at the side of our house only thirty feet away. Why? For pure mischief. For the voluptuous pleasure of mocking adult forms of propriety. For the same reason that I can recall Keith only ever loving to read the backs of the Wacky Packages cards that he collected and kept in a tackle box under his bed. Sometimes, that family's world was so unlike mine that it was easy to imagine their house to be an anchored pirate ship that would be gone by daybreak, leaving only a slightly foul stench and a sinister laughter in its wake.

That night, Keith, barefoot as he so often was (the soles of his feet were like hardened leather) at all times of the year, ran ahead of me and refused to give any further information. By the time we reached the main net shed, I didn't need it.

"What about that, eh? Just look at that! How long do you figure it took him?"

I wasn't able to respond to these rapid-fire questions at first. But after a while, I dumbly said, "Took who?"

Keith punched me on the shoulder. "Who do you think?"

It was indeed a stupid question. Only Edgar could carve and light so many jack-o'-lanterns, hundreds upon hundreds of them. They grinned out at us from everywhere: on the upper wharf, on each of the small floats of the lower wharf, on net barrows and on the cabin roofs of all the boats in the harbour. At different heights, depending on whether they sat on top of an oil drum or a tarp-covered pile of net, they all faced the dike. It was like some sort of menacing beheaded army.

"Across the channel too. Look!"

Sure enough, other lights flickered from the net sheds and floats and even the derelict old stern wheeler half stuck in the bulrushes of the muddy bank. But I could only assume that these were also jack-o'-lanterns, for the lights were too far away.

As if reading my mind, Keith said, "Come on. I'll show you. There's even more."

I followed him down the slick gangway to where he jumped without hesitation into a listing old skiff heaped with torn web and corks and ungainly lifejackets (though I never once saw him wear one). By now, I could smell the same rot that had slithered up off the farmer's field, and, even more unsettling, I had noticed that every single jack-o'-lantern wore the same expression, the classic jagged grinning one with triangular eyes and nose. But the carving, not surprisingly given how much had to be done, was rough and inexact, so that the faces, rather than being identical, had merely a familial resemblance. Some of them, I noticed too, had shrunk back into darkness because their lights had flickered out. Even just to light them all, I thought . . . but Keith's quick rowing jerked me back to the moment.

We slid across the harbour channel in less than a minute (it was only a stone's throw from bank to bank), and I saw, with mounting astonishment and considerable unease, that all the jack-o'-lanterns along this bank were also the same. Sometimes three or four were clumped together, as if in a whispering conference, while others were set apart, as if exiled. Yet they

55

didn't look different other than the amount of space between them.

Our skiff bumped up to the edge of a float and we took a closer look. Some of the stemmed tops of the heads were missing, which made the candlelight brighter above and less vivid in the expression. Keith reached out to touch the nearest face and jumped back with a cry. A big rat flopped over the edge of the cratered skull and splashed into the current.

"Holy fuck, I just about shit myself." He touched the hole in his head with the fingers of both hands, as if he was afraid that a rat might suddenly emerge from it too. Then he pulled at the oars again and we continued downriver another hundred fathoms, passing dozens and dozens of the same skewed grin with every few strokes.

Now my recent fear of the water began to creep back in. The river surface was an oily black, impenetrable with the eye to any depth, so it was easy to imagine anything being below it, particularly when such a strangeness was above it, overlooking it, perhaps even in some way commanding the horrors beneath it. Once more, that terrible deep music from *Jaws* sounded through my whole body, and I scooched over to the very middle of the skiff.

Keith, meanwhile, continued hooting with admiration as we reached the last junk-laden and dilapidated float in the harbour, nothing beyond it on the far bank except bulrushes, mud and muskrat holes. Here, where Edgar always tied up his gillnetter, we came upon the final miracle.

His boat, the same twenty-four feet long and ten feet wide as my father's, crawled with jeering faces. The jack-o'-lanterns, bunched on the deck and bow and the roof of the cabin like mussels under a wharf, glared at us as we drifted to within a few fathoms. Keith rested on the oars, and all I could hear was the drip of oily water off the paddles into that horrifying surface. All at once, the night shrank into itself the way a spider does when caught in the rain.

"Let's go," I whispered. "We'll miss the trick-or-treating."

But Keith appeared to be frozen, his eyes never moving from the leer-barnacled boat, his arms extended as if nailed to the oars that were themselves nailed to the darkness. The seconds passed heavily. I imagined each of those slightly irregular faces counting them down under the breath of something I couldn't identify but which hovered so near to us that I was certain the tips of my hair trembled. The smell of rotted pumpkin, engine grease and stale fish slime drifted in gusts off the salmon net bunched as darkly as a monstrous spider on the wooden drum. For a split second, I thought the same mocking expression would look out from the bunched net.

"There's something . . ." Keith started, but his words vanished in the staccato burst that threw us both to the gunwale for protection. The river changed positions with the starless sky as the blood pounded in our chests and eardrums. I tasted the smell of rot as if it was blood at the back of my throat.

A piercing cackling as rapid-fire as the exploded firecrackers rippled out from somewhere behind the bunched and unchanging expressions on the deck. "Got you that time, goddamn ya goddamn ya. Hee hee hee."

"You fucking prick! You goddamned son of a bitch!" Keith started hurling corks and anything else he could get his hands on toward Edgar's still-invisible body. But another rippling of noise overhead made him grab the oars again and start slamming them into the water. Then a flash of light and a loud whoosh swept straight at us from the deck, as if one of the jack-o'-lanterns had done its master's violent bidding at last.

"The fucker's shooting Roman candles at us!" Keith began to row so fiercely that every third pull failed and he fell back with a jump. This whole time I just crouched as low as I could get without actually lying in the wet oily bottom of the skiff.

Finally, the explosions stopped but not the cackling. Edgar's glee was a kind of natural force, a human version of the freshet: powerful; unpredictable; awesome. It was unique and anarchic enough to leave even a wild boy like Keith in a desperate though short-lived recoil.

When we had pulled far enough from the source of danger, and the night had swollen to its normal dimensions again, we were able to relish the experience. I could even begin to see the parallels between Edgar's attack and, say, the hurling of jack-o'-lanterns by the Green Goblin. Except there were no costumes involved here, other than Keith's pirate patch, and no secret identities, unless you count the impenetrable layers of human psychology whose exposure might explain the creation of an Edgar Winterbourne out of a newborn, but probably wouldn't.

The candlelight flickered in the relentless gazes as we returned the way we had come. But more of the lights had gone out, more of the faces dissolved into the surrounding darkness, the black inside them just like the black of the air and the river. I could feel the presence of every face, though, and the gloomy and ominous relation between their staring and their rotting existence in Time.

By midnight, as always when Halloween wound down, most of the jack-o'-lanterns would be smashed on the wet streets by marauding teenagers. But Edgar's army was too vast for such a rapid defeat. Over the next few days, irritated fishermen would throw or boot the vigilant soldiers into the river, where they would bob along briefly before gulping down the last sight of sky and sinking to the muddy bottom. A few scattered survivors remained, however, their mocking leers becoming sadder and sadder with every week, until only a few holdouts – on the derelict sternwheeler and on the roofs of the sorriest net sheds – wore winter's first white grizzle on their sagging flesh.

V

Any childhood memories – yours included – will hold up under only so much scrutiny. Four and a half decades later, I cannot adequately explain why a man in his early thirties would spend an entire night transporting hundreds of unwanted pumpkins by boat to a small net shed, and then most of the next day rapidly carving and placing jack-o'-lanterns in places where almost nobody would see them in all their lit glory. The act, which seemed merely an impressive prank at the time, now strikes me as close to lunacy. Harmless, perhaps, but only because I didn't see it as a harbinger of the tragedy that would occur when such anarchic energy turned from pranks to uncontrollable rage.

Despite my friendships and family, I spent a great deal of each day alone, either reading non-collectible comics in my dad's never-driven Ford, reading collectible comics at my desk in my bedroom, doing my paper route by bike or else just wandering around the neighbourhood awaiting those serendipitous moments that a child believes in more than he believes in any adult god. For this reason, it's little surprise that my favourite Jack Kirby comic was *Kamandi: The Last Boy on Earth*. In the thirty-seven monthly issues that Kirby wrote and drew for the DC company between 1972 and early 1976, the hero — a boy with long, blond hair — tries to survive in a post-apocalyptic future in which humans have been reduced back to savagery in a world run by intelligent, highly evolved animals. My solitude, doubtless combined with my close proximity to the birds, fish, muskrats, seals, dogs and cats of my environment, made me especially sympathetic to Kamandi's wandering plight. By contrast, Jay — who loved Jack Kirby above all comic book artists — paid much greater attention to the intergalactic terror of planet-devouring deities that appeared in Kirby's Fourth World series, or to the grandiose and mythic verbalizing and soaring of characters like Thor and the Silver Surfer. In truth, I could understand *Kamandi*, whereas much of what went on in Kirby's creative universe flew — figuratively and literally — far over my head.

Not surprisingly, the comic that Jay and I began to work on more intensely over that fall of 1975 and the winter of 1976 took its greatest inspiration from the galaxies rather than the fields and rivers of Earth. Where Jay led, I usually followed, but then, it was easy to be swept up in my friend's enthusiasm for Kirby's dynamic grandeur.

"Can I see it?" he said to Mr. Edison, and leaned across the high bar-like counter in his enthusiasm. "My hands are clean. Honest."

The doyen of The Haunted Bookshop sighed so deeply that his salt-and-pepper walrus moustache trembled. "You've been eating ketchup potato chips. I don't even want you flipping through the *Archie*s."

Jay let his weight resettle fully on the floor. He licked his fingers and then rubbed his hands together fiercely as Lady Macbeth, but we both knew that he wasn't going to get his way. "Well, can you show *him*, then? Just open up to the spread. I'll stand over here." He shuffled closer to the big grey cash register.

Mr. Edison turned as slowly as a freighter toward the wall where all the most expensive comics were displayed. It took him so long that I caught the tiny smile that always peeped out, despite himself, whenever Jay displayed an almost manic enthusiasm for drawing. After all, Mr. Edison himself was an amateur cartoonist, and he published his own little mimeographed chapbook. It was called *Sunday Nite Special* and the first issue came out the summer before I started frequenting the shop. A second issue had yet to appear, however, mostly because Mr. Edison's general approach to everything was so laid back as to be almost asleep. "I'm the last of the hippies," he would say with a yawn, which probably explained why the most interesting part of *Sunday Nite Special* #1 was a strip drawn and written by another of the shop's artist-collectors, an older teenager named Nick Samaras. Entitled "Super Head," the three-page story involved a sort of pot-smoking Peter Parker who finds a weird roach on the sidewalk, smokes it and becomes a muscle-bound superhero who stands up for his scruffy peers against bullying cops and teachers, the arch-enemies of any self-respecting high-schooler, at least in 1975.

"If you don't mind, Sean," Mr. Edison said, carefully brushing the counter with his sleeve and laying the comic book down on the cleaned surface, "I'll turn the pages myself. This is mint."

In the world of comic book collecting, comics are graded according to the following formula: mint, near mint, very fine, fine, very good, good, fair and poor. Mint was, of course, the most desirable condition, especially for back issues, the term attached to any comic that was more than a few years old.

What lay before me in all its dynamic impact was not very old – only from 1971 – but it was part of Jack Kirby's Fourth World series, #4 of *New Gods*, to be exact. And it was mint, with sharp corners and white rather than off-white pages. In those days, anything mint by Jack Kirby from even just a few years earlier had shot up in value. So I was careful not to lean over the two-page spread for fear I might breathe on it.

Mr. Edison chuckled. "You won't wreck it by looking. Go ahead."

"See what he does with the perspective." Jay took a step sideways and pointed like Michelangelo's God. "It's almost 3-D. Look at that stick on the right."

But I was never any good at drawing, and so my mind always wandered to the dialogue balloons. There were three small white ones, like cumulous clouds, at the top of the page beside a volcano spewing lava. Two small figures (small in the perspective) on some sort of flying craft were discussing a fierce battle between prehistoric humans in the foreground. "One day, when their bellies are full," one figure says, "they will look up and see us. Then they will think and dream." And the word "dream" was in bold dark ink.

Think and dream. Already at ten, I knew that that was what the best comic books encouraged a reader to do, even if most adults scorned the genre as so much mental junk food. And what I thought and dreamt was usually about my own writing, or rather about the strip that Jay and I were working on. Our hero Blackstar needed an arch-enemy, but I hadn't worked up the courage to tell him any of my ideas yet.

"DC never gave anything Kirby did for them a real chance. No wonder he's coming back to Marvel." Mr. Edison took an HB2 pencil down from above his ear and started doodling on the foolscap paper taped to the counter.

"Why did he go there in the first place?" Without looking at him, I could see the distaste on Jay's lips. In 1975, Marvel was the only comic book company that really mattered. To prefer DC to Marvel was as wrong-headed as to favour Ford over Chevy if you were of driving age.

The top of Mr. Edison's pencil vanished under his moustache as he thoughtfully nibbled on the eraser. "Well, it's complicated. But I think it must boil down to money and creative control. DC must have made him an . . ."

"Offer he couldn't refuse," Jay cut in, doing his best Godfather mumble. Then, his voice suddenly dropping to a sort of serious in-church tone, he said, "And you're sure he's coming back? It's not just a rumour?"

Mr. Edison took the pencil down again and darkened a couple of eyebrows of the '40s mobster he'd sketched. "I read it in *The Comics Journal* a while back. Of course, in the comics business, there are no guarantees. I never thought he'd leave Marvel myself." Mr. Edison's tone clearly indicated that *he* certainly wouldn't have left the house that was responsible for all the great superhero comics of the 1960s. "After all, they don't call it the house that Jack built for nothing."

In truth, I always began to zone out whenever Jay and Mr. Edison delved too deeply into the mechanics of drawing or the politics of comic book publishing and personality. My friend was twelve going on twenty, while Mr. Edison, as far as I could guess, was in his late thirties or early forties and about as youthful as any middle-aged adult could be. In their presence, I often felt exactly like a ten-year-old, a ten-year-old who might never catch up. Now, on many of my late middle-aged days, I wish I could be back in their presence, standing at that high counter, daydreaming. But Mr. Edison is dead and the Haunted Bookshop has long since been demolished. Whatever there is to catch up to in life, I caught up to years ago, for better or worse.

I looked down at the spread again. The prehistoric humans in the foreground were fierce and so alive that they seemed to be pressing against the very edges of the book itself, ready to spring out into the so-called real world. Even a kid who wasn't much into drawing could tell that Jack Kirby's art had something uniquely dynamic about it.

"You probably ought to get going, Sean," Mr. Edison said. "Before the rain starts up again."

As always, I had gone to the paper shack to pick up the thirty papers I had to deliver and had then pedalled a block over to the bookshop to shoot the breeze before I carried on with my day's labour. Sometimes, I found it very hard to leave, but it helped to know that the last house on my route was, in fact, Jay's. I planned it that way so I could stop there, maybe watch an episode of *My Three Sons* or *Leave It to Beaver* or even to share any creative ideas I'd had while biking through the streets. Sometimes I'd go up to Jay's room and he'd show me his current work in progress on his big slanted drawing board, exactly like the one Jack Kirby had at his home in California, at least according to the large photograph of the master that Jay had pinned up on the wall. My friend's knowledge of "King" Kirby or "Jolly Jack," as he was known in the biz, was surprisingly deep and often arcane. But much of Jay's knowledge was like that. He had a particular obsession with, as he put it, "old stuff" – Warner Bros. gangster movies from the 1930s and '40s, Golden Age comics and even the earliest years of the NHL (he was always hoping to find a Montreal Maroons sweater somewhere).

THE MARVELS OF YOUTH

I mumbled something praiseworthy about the Kirby spread and looked at my friend. He must have touched the brim of his Gilligan hat at some point because two dried bloodstains of ketchup potato chip dust soiled the vivid whiteness. Just as I was about to point the stains out to him, the little bell over the door tinkled and an older teenager stepped into the shop.

Much to my chagrin, Jay immediately sniggered. "Behold, the Grim Warper," he said, not quite low enough to be inaudible.

Mr. Edison – who, after all, was running a business – scowled at Jay, but the look was either missed or ignored.

"You're out of luck," Jay said, frowning in mock sympathy. "*Anthro*'s still cancelled."

The newcomer – sixteen or seventeen years old with a head of tight black curls and a face empurpled with acne – didn't even look in Jay's direction. He nodded to Mr. Edison, who reached under the counter and brought out the customer's order. On top was the latest issue of a DC strip called *Tor*. I didn't know much about it, except that its hero was some sort of caveman who lived at the same time as the dinosaurs. The Grim Warper – so named by Jay because he committed the cardinal sin of rolling his comics into a tube shape for easier carrying – only seemed to buy the most unpopular comics. Obviously, he was a reader and not a collector, which Jay, and I to a lesser extent, found ridiculous. Why be one when it was just as easy to be both? After all, it was possible to read a comic book with pleasure without harming its condition. Or you could simply buy two mint copies of each new issue and put one aside to preserve it perfectly. Then again, as Jay often said with an almost world-weary sigh, who would buy an extra issue of *Tor* or *Shazam*?

"I have to get going," I said to Jay. "See you in a bit."

But I didn't really need to leave, not right away. I had simply noticed the angry red colour seeping out of the purple acne on the Grim Warper's face, and I didn't want to be around if Jay decided to continue with his needling, as he often did. For some reason, the Grim Warper, whose real name was Brent Harms (naturally, Jay often would step back in his presence and mutter, "Best to stay out of harm's way"), really brought out the cutting edge of my friend's wit. Other imperfect comic book buyers, such as Bill Bumstead, in his early twenties, bespectacled and lumpen, who collected Marvel comics but not the "right ones" (those made by the dream team of Jack Kirby and Stan Lee) received more good-humoured jibes. Naturally, Bill Bumstead was tagged with "Dagwood," the male hero of the long-running *Blondie* comic strip, and Jay sometimes would ask if he was getting along okay with Mr. Dithers. But Bill took these references in the affectionate spirit in which they were delivered. He would jut out his thick lower lip while pushing his black-framed glasses up the bridge of his nose, and say, "Oh, he's not giving me any trouble," and then ask Mr. Edison if the new issue of *X-Men* had come in yet.

On the sidewalk, I paused and looked at the sky. Dark, gelatinous clouds slid like octopi eastward over the condemned block of shops across the street. The light had not yet become twilight, which explained the low thudding of shotgun blasts coming from the direction of the marsh beyond the harbour to the north. I didn't like duck and pheasant season, in part because I knew the hunters would keep shooting until it was almost completely dark, a dedication that I had suffered from when out with my brother and wanting to go home.

"You're Dan Simpson's little brother, right?"

Her voice was surprisingly deep and raspy, incongruous with her almost exaggerated feminine appearance. She leaned against the maple tree, her jean-jacketed shoulder a couple of feet above where the frame of my bike rested. But the leaning didn't dispel her anxious manner. Within a half-minute, she had lifted and lowered a cigarette to and from her lips so often that I thought she was trying to break some personal record. The motion made me stare at her face, which was, unlike the last time I'd seen it, deeply rouged and eyeshadowed. Her long eyelashes seemed to shiver like spider legs with each puff on the cigarette.

I mumbled an affirmative that took all the breath I had.

"Danny's a good friend of mine," she said, and smiled. For the first time I saw the wide gap between her front teeth, but it quickly disappeared when she raised the cigarette again. Exhaling, she added, "And of my husband's. Of Hurry's." She nodded toward the pool hall doorway.

The charm bracelet with its tiny marine mammals and zodiac signs jingled. The shotgun blasts kept thudding away, like part of some distant war. Her shoulder-length black hair seemed as full and rich as the rain clouds. I had absolutely no idea what to say in response.

"You like hockey cards?" With her free hand, she lifted a pack out of the back pocket of her tight mussel-blue jeans.

I nodded.

"Here." The jingle of bracelets increased in volume as her long-fingered pale hand stretched out to me. "I'll have a bit of the gum if that's okay. I've had enough of this smoke taste." She tossed the cigarette to the sidewalk and ground it with a quick twist under her calf-high leather boot.

Even as I fumbled to open the pack, I sensed that I was making a mistake, that I was entering into a kind of pact for which I wasn't at all prepared. By now, I knew exactly what was going on, but I couldn't find a way out. I almost said, "You don't have to do this. I won't say anything," but the thought of addressing the subject of what I had seen on that boat was too embarrassing. It was one thing to understand each other without words; it was quite another to broach the business verbally. As it was, I couldn't even hold her gaze for more than a few seconds at a time. Despite the daylight and the makeup, the face was the same curiously indifferent face, except now the indifference was obviously feigned.

"Get any good ones?" She extended her hand again, and I almost gave her the Guy Lafleur card before I remembered about the gum.

She took the stick from me, snapped it in half and gave me a half back. Then she cracked her half between her teeth, chewed ferociously and blew out a quick pink bubble. "Ah, that's better."

The bookshop door opened and slammed shut. The Grim Warper, his face darker than the sky, pushed forward like a ship's figurehead into the gloom.

"Someone's having a worse day than me," she said. "I'm Vicky, by the way."

Her hand in mine was as warm as Theo's had been cold. It surprised me that I didn't want to let go of it and that I also desperately wanted her to go away.

"You?"

"Me?" I felt my mouth dropping open.

Her laugh was like a beer bottle breaking after midnight. "Your name?"

Blushing, I told her, and the gap appeared between her front teeth again. "Well, Sean, I'm glad to know you. Like I said, your brother's a good friend of mine." With both hands, she pulled her jean jacket together at her throat. Then she flipped her hair and sighed, her eyes looking away from me toward the pool hall. "I'd better get back."

Then she did something terrible, something that, from then on, I imagined her doing as I looked at her face through the open cabin window in the rain. She winked. And her long-lashed eye shrank to the size of a bullet hole.

"See you around?" The questioning tone meant exactly what I feared: that she didn't trust me enough not to go on bribing me, and that I lacked the courage to prevent her from doing so.

When she had gone, in a wake of sweet flowery perfume and cigarette smoke, I stood under the sky's reaching and withdrawing tentacles, my heart beating fast, and tried not to see the faces of Mrs. Vasilakis and the Mother of God also winking at me with the same piercing swiftness. Then I pulled on my bike, heavy with the day's quota of the world's violence, and pedalled away in the starting rain.

VI

Besides a few forgotten toys and pastimes, such as Klackers and Spirograph, nothing seems more representative to me of a '70s childhood than a paper route. It was the first job for many kids – including some girls – and it brought us into contact with our communities in a regular and often intimate way that seems rare in our more efficient and detached age. Of my thirty regular customers – from whom I had to collect payment at the end of each month – half were elderly residents of rather dismal four-storey apartment buildings built in the centre of town in the 1960s. And almost all of this half were women, mainly in their eighties and widowed, who had pictures of young men in WWI uniforms on their mantelpieces (I was often invited in for milk and Peek Freans when I was collecting). To go from the often dangerous mayhem of the paper shack, where the bullying of older teenagers was more the norm than the exception, to the antic creativity or musty studiousness of the Haunted Bookshop, was a mild adjustment. But to step into an eighty-five-year-old widow's tiny apartment was to step so far back in time as to step outside of time altogether.

I neither resented nor disliked the journey. For one thing, old people were alive and therefore not nearly as old or unsettling as the ghosts I felt around me in the abandoned houses of the neighbourhood. For another, my father was fifty-two in 1975 and my mother forty-seven, and my mother was the last born of eighteen pregnancies. To put it plainly, age was the theatre in which my childhood was performed. And with age came the very heavy shadow of pain, suffering and war, but also the quieter presence of courage, perseverance and dignity. Besides, my old ladies, including even the parsimonious Mrs. English, were generous tippers, especially at Christmas, and generous tips could easily be translated into gratifying purchases at the Haunted Bookshop.

So I delivered the *Sun* in the rain to the past. And I was all the better for the experience, even when one of my customers died or had to go into a nursing home and a son or daughter quietly gave me the news as if I was the one who had to be treated gently. No decade – certainly not the 1970s – is a Golden Age, but certain kinds of decorum existed then that no longer appear to be common, as did certain opportunities to confront the range of human experience if not to absorb its lessons.

One of the real peculiarities of my paper route, especially in light of my family's main profession, was that it was almost the same route my father did as a teenager in the late 1930s and my brother did around the same age in the late 1950s. Neither of them had the apartment buildings, of course, but they had the same long miles of cycling in the rain and snow and heat and the same responsibility of collecting money and signing up new subscribers. They might also have had some of my elderly customers when they were young (in my father's case) and middle-aged (in the cases of my brother). Having a paper route in that sort of town created that sort of pattern, just as the salmon returning to their birth streams each year was once such a vibrant and multi-strand pattern all up and down the coast.

November was always the wettest, darkest, gloomiest month of any year, but the 1975 version was particularly trying. I had to fight to keep my papers dry and I had to go down to my father's boat constantly to pump it out. Each time I made the perilous descent of the slick gangway, I heard

THE MARVELS OF YOUTH

the throbbing bass notes of the *Jaws* soundtrack. It didn't help that a few of Edgar Winterbourne's jack-o'-lanterns always watched me out of the rotting eyes in their sagging faces as I repeated to myself again and again, *Don't hear anything, don't see anything, don't look for anything.* I didn't want to come upon another scene of illicit behaviour, so I kept strictly to my task. The only other person I recall seeing around much, and then only from a distance, was Edgar. Mostly he appeared as a shadowy figure across the channel, passing briefly in and out of a cabin light or stern light. Once he stood for several minutes against the open slid-back doorway of his net shed, a thirty-foot-wide by ten-foot-high wall of light like a drive-in movie screen. I almost expected him to start acting, to make a speech or to turn and address another character. But only the low, fleet figure of Bullet ever emerged from the surrounding darkness, and the only sound was of corks and web splashing into the river or of an engine starting up.

One night, however, when my father's boat was the third out from the wharf, so that, standing on the deck, I was twenty feet into the black channel, I felt rather than heard a motion at my back. Turning quickly, my heart fluttering like a moth in two cupped hands, I saw the bulk of Edgar's gillnetter, all lights off, glide past me like a chunk off a huge black iceberg. His boat engine idled so low that I could hear it above the rain only by straining. Bullet, standing on the main hatch and looking straight at me, passed so closely that I could smell his wet fur. But he didn't bark. Looking up from the dog, I had a greater shock. Edgar also stood on the main hatch, a long pike pole in one hand, the other on the outside steering wheel. He was grinning, but – and this is the strangest part – apparently not at me. If I had stared at one of our town's several church steeples and seen a demon clutching on to it, I couldn't have been more amazed.

The image lasted but a few seconds, and normally I would have dismissed it, but it made me shudder the whole length of my body. The ensuing wake of gasoline, engine grease and fish slime intensified the foreboding and encouraged me to finish the pumping job and get home as quickly as I could. But not before I stood still for a full minute, watching Edgar's boat glide farther and farther down the channel, like prey in a boa constrictor's body, out toward the fishing grounds. Where was he going? The river wasn't open. And what was he doing with that long pike pole? Why were all his lights off, including the mast lights?

I mulled these questions over as I walked home along the dike, but could find no satisfactory answers. Something about that pike pole, his grin, the jack-o'-lanterns he had carved so obsessively: I couldn't shake the more frightening image of his head stuck to the end of the pike pole while its twin stared through crumbling black eyeholes at me from the top of his cabin.

With relief, I turned onto our crushed gravel driveway and glanced toward my father's stationary Ford. Full of comics, it might have been a beached whale stuffed with colourful intestines. As I wondered if my mother had tossed the latest issue of *Little Lulu* inside, Scooter greeted me by sniffing at my pant leg and then guiding me past the side door toward the backyard.

The rain had stopped again. In the thin light off the bare bulb over the door, I saw three mallards hanging by the necks from a branch of the apple tree. My brother had obviously come home from wherever he'd gone after the afternoon's hunting. The early evening dripped and sighed. I took a deep breath of the wood smoke spreading through the darkness from the yard, and watched the ducks' blood drip off their webbed feet into the soaked grass.

Then the side door opened with a creak. My mother stuck her kerchiefed head out. She was still wearing her smock from the drugstore and was dabbing her lipstick off with a piece of tissue. "I thought I heard someone out here. Why don't you go out back? I'm just making tea for your brother and your dad."

Fifty feet beyond the house, under the knobbed black branches of a large Queen Anne cherry tree, sat a clutch of lawn chairs made out of wood salvaged from the Fraser's treasure-unearthing currents. My father, in black skullcap and mackinaw jacket, poked at a pleasant orange heap of flame with a long stick carved from a cherry branch. My brother, his earflapped hunting cap turned orange-side instead of khaki-side out, stretched his long legs almost into the firepit. He was talking of the day's hunting. From several feet away, I could smell the beer wafting from his body. He must have gone to the pub straight out of the marsh.

My father turned his head from the fire as I stepped into the light. He smiled, and I sensed he was grateful for the interruption. Hunting had long been distasteful to him, ever since the time, many years before, when he'd looked into a deer's wet black eyes and been sickened by the idea of shooting it.

"Hiya, Monk. How's Old Betsy tonight?"

"Pretty full. I had to pump a lot."

"There's been more rain than usual. It ought to ease off for a few days now, give her a good chance to dry out a bit." He asked me if anyone else had been around.

At first, I wasn't going to mention seeing Edgar. In a way, I felt protective toward his privacy, or else the strangeness of his silent gliding appearance and disappearance seemed more delicious if kept to myself. But Edgar was rightly more a part of my father's world than my own, so I mentioned what I'd seen.

"The crazy bastard," Dan said, and belched softly. "Always up to something." I looked at my brother, and was startled by the sight of a drunken Christ. He lay as horizontally in his chair as possible without falling out.

"Running without lights?" My father lifted the stick from the flames, then deftly adjusted a charred bit of bark. Two clumps of ash hung in the smoke stream and disappeared in the surrounding dark. "Heading downriver?"

"Sounds like he's going poaching," Dan said. "I didn't think Edgar –"

"He doesn't. At least, I've never known him to."

My father, after a long silence, added, "It's that sturgeon he's after."

Dan uncrossed his legs. "What sturgeon?"

"That big one that keeps tearing through our nets. He said he was going to catch it. Remember, Monk?" My father leaned back from the flames, his face flickering in the hot light. "You know what he's like," he said to Dan. "When he gets an idea about something."

My mother emerged from the shadows carrying a tray with four cups of tea and a plate of cookies on it. "What who's like?" she asked, settling herself in a chair.

Dan laughed. "I guess he gets nothing but ideas, because he's always just like that."

"Edgar," I said to my mother. "I saw him at the wharf."

"Oh, Edgar." She raised the steaming cup of tea to her lips and took a sip. "I always remember my first Christmas on the coast because of Edgar. Christmas morning, and I was homesick for Toronto and the snow. Never been away from home at Christmas before. And what do I see when I look out the window? Rain. And little Edgar and his brothers running around barefoot in the streets." She seemed to shiver as she wrapped her hands around her cup. "Barefoot. In December. I knew then that I was a long way from home."

I was surprised by the mention of Edgar's brothers more than by the barefoot story. My friend Keith and his little brother often ran around barefoot in all seasons. The truth is, it wasn't always very cold in the winters. But any mention of Edgar's family was always surprising, because he never seemed to have anything to do with them. And though his two brothers were also salmon fishermen, they plied their trade in distant waters, far to the north or on the west coast of Vancouver Island. Highliners. He spoke as an honest lawyer would about an unethical one.

"He won't rest until he catches it," my father said. The sadness in his tone was unmistakable, but inexplicable to me. "Unless something more interesting comes along."

"Like booze, you mean." Dan yawned and rubbed so fiercely at his beard that I thought sparks would emerge from the gingery mass. "It's been a while since –"

"Yes, well," my mother said. "You ought to drink your tea before it gets cold."

"If there's room for any more liquid." I could imagine rather than see my father's scowl as he returned to poking at the fire.

"Oh Sean's old enough to know that people get drunk. Hell, that comic shop's right beside the pool hall. I'm sure he's seen a few guys stumbling out of there in the middle of the day. Besides, a drunk Edgar's not so different from a sober one. Only a bit more . . . I was going to say unpredictable, but he's always that." He took his hunting cap off and began to turn it inside out. The orange vanished as if he was some sort of magician performing a trick. "Violent. That's the only word for it."

My mother reached down and then gave Dan his cup of tea. "You ought to be more charitable. You ought to know what sort of life he's had. After all . . ."

"Yes, yes, I know. He's like a big brother to me." Dan reached out to touch my arm but missed and slumped awkwardly sideways. "But you've got to do more than live with someone to be their big brother, eh, Spud? I don't remember Edgar taking me to the movies."

"For Chrissakes!" my father said. "He was just a kid himself. You have no idea. If you can't keep your common sense when you drink, then you shouldn't drink."

My father's outbursts were always few, as he generally expressed his displeasure either by withdrawal or silence, so whenever one occurred, it had the effect of a commandment. Dan, at least, made no rejoinder.

The fire crackled and whooshed. A few bats flitted invisibly overhead. Beyond them, the stars were like old nailheads weathered by the centuries. I took a deep breath and plunged in.

"Lived with? What do you mean?" I spoke softly, more to my mother than anyone.

Still holding her cup in both hands, she leaned diplomatically toward me. "It was a long time ago. And didn't last long. Your father and I just took him in for a few weeks when things were, well, difficult at home."

My father pulled his chair forward, and was so close to the fire that I couldn't see any light between him and the flames.

"Difficult?" I whispered.

Dan suddenly pulled himself into a sitting position. He hadn't touched his cup of tea, but he raised the beer can in his left hand to his mouth, took a last gulp and dropped the can to the wet grass. "The old man liked to beat him. Beat all of them. Beat Eddy to within an inch of his life that time."

My mother shushed me.

"Aw hell, it isn't any secret. Everybody knows. But the one I always felt sorry for was Wendy. Beating's one thing, but –"

"Enough!" My father jabbed at the fire as if he was trying to kill it. "That's enough."

Just then, Scooter, who was lying behind my chair, gave a low growl.

My mother put her cup down. "Who's there?"

At first no sound came back out of the darkness. Then I heard something, a sort of shuffle on the grass. We all turned toward the sound.

After what seemed like a full minute but was less than ten seconds, a figure emerged into the light, as if conjured.

"It's Theo," my mother said. "Hello, Theo. Come and sit by the fire. Dan?"

"I'm going out for a bit anyway. Here you go, Theo." My brother pulled himself to his feet.

My mother whispered to my father, "What's he doing out at this time of night?"

Only I seemed to notice that Theo hadn't come any closer and that tears were rolling down his plump cheeks. His hair had grown like a dark tide farther down his large head, and shone as wet as a sandbar. He was trembling from head to toe. And though he wore a too-large sweater this time, he had only socks on his feet.

"Mom?" I pointed.

"Oh sweetie, you're shivering. Come here to the fire. Heck, build it up a bit."

But Theo didn't step forward. He didn't even lift his arms from his sides. Having come this far, he seemed determined to make a statue of himself.

"You'd better take him home," my father said. "They'll be frantic when they realize he's not there."

I wanted to explain to my father, as I had to my mother, about the night in the abandoned house and about Mrs. Vasilakis's drawn face in the darkened room, but I didn't have the chance. Besides, in the '70s, children's and parents' lives didn't run in such tandem; secrets were kept as a matter of some courtesy, as if there were a mutual agreement to respect our different worlds as our own.

"I'll do it," Dan said. "Hey, Theo, come on with me. I might even have a stick of gum in my pocket. Would you like a stick of gum?"

In her hurry, my mother knocked her teacup off the arm of the chair when she stood. "No, I'll take him back. You were going out."

I could feel rather than see my brother's grin. "Yeah, can't go calling on the neighbours with a little beer on the breath. Pretty shocking in this town." He bent down and gave Scooter's head a vigorous rub. "Sorry about the gum, kiddo," he said to Theo as he walked by him and disappeared into the dark.

"Can I come with you?" I said.

My mother hesitated, but eventually said yes. "We won't go inside. I imagine that they want to keep to themselves just now."

Whatever knowledge my mother had about the Vasilakis family remained unspoken, but I could sense it, just as I had sensed the motion of Edgar's boat at my back.

"Come along, Theo." As she took him by the hand, somehow I could feel its coldness in my own hand again, even through the warmth flowing from the teacup. I pulled my hand away, as if from the fire. Then I felt my body grow colder as the darkness swallowed the three of us whole.

The Vasilakises' house was in darkness again, and the same slick Chrysler seemed to be parked in the exact same position in the driveway. My mother knocked on the front door. After a minute with no response, she knocked again, louder. I looked at Theo's profile in the darkness, but could make out no features. His silence, as always, had a strangely explosive quality. It was easy enough to believe that his tears formed a kind of long wick that just needed one word or movement to spark a reaction that would change everything.

"There must be someone home." My mother, still holding Theo's hand, seemed momentarily lost, as if he was holding her hand.

Listening closely, I heard a faint sound coming from behind the house.

"I think someone's out back. I'll go and see."

When I rounded the corner of the house, I saw a figure moving swiftly back and forth in the light of a single bulb hanging off a clothesline on a rope. And I heard the gasping breaths and the heavy thumps a few seconds before I realized it was Stevie going hard at the punching bag hanging like a slab of beef from a thick branch of a squat apple tree. Shirtless, wearing only a pair of shorts that reached almost to his knees, he heaved himself into punch after punch with such ferocity that I was scared to interrupt him. Stevie had been a Golden Gloves champion for several years, achieving a minor sort of fame that he rarely spoke about, so it was always something of a shock to see him in action. Because he looked so much like the young Elvis, with his high cheekbones and sleepy-eyed smile, it would have been more natural to see him strumming a guitar.

I almost had to shout his name to get his attention. When I did, he turned, his red gloves raised, and for a second I thought he was going to heave himself at me. Instead, he just started untying one glove with his teeth. Then he threw that glove to the ground and untied the other.

"Theo?" he said, and it was like all the blood drained from his body.

"He was in our backyard. Without any shoes on."

Stevie straightened up. "Where is he now? You didn't go in, did you?"

I shook my head. "He's out front with my mom. We knocked, but nobody answered."

Stevie picked up his T-shirt from the hardened earth near the punching bag and wiped his face with it. "Yeah. My mom's still sick. She won't let us call the doctor."

I didn't know how to respond, so I just waited until Stevie pulled the soiled T-shirt on and headed for the front porch.

My mother held Theo close to her side, probably to warm him, but their hands were still clasped. "Oh, Stevie," she said as he came up, "is there anything we can do? Do you need anything?"

He shook his head fiercely, in the way that you do when you're fighting back tears. "No, thank you, Mrs. Simpson," he said. Then he held out his hand, which looked so tiny without the boxing glove, to Theo. "Let's go in, buddy, okay? I'll stay with you." Then he spoke, more softly, in Greek.

A moment later, they had closed the front door behind them, and the whole blackened house, like a cliff face to a retreating boat, rapidly subsided into itself.

"I'll send a meal over," my mother said, and I could tell she was doubtful in the presence of another culture, falling back on food as the most unobtrusive way of offering sympathy. "Marina must still be sick."

On our way back home, my mother paused outside the blackened house where Jay and I had tried to play hockey.

"There was a boy who used to live there." She pulled distractedly at the headkerchief knot under her chin. "Must have been . . . let me see . . . not long after the war. Your brother was just a baby." In the streetlamp light her face possessed a strange underwater quality, and I heard her voice, too, as if through several fathoms of moving current. "He died. Of polio." Then, as she began to walk away, she said, so quietly that I barely made out the words, "It was very sad."

The last word rose a little in volume and flowed out over the neighbourhood, like a butterfly with wings dusted in ash. I let my mother walk on ahead of me for a while, as I knew, from experience, that the sadness of such a death carried so much meaning for her. It wasn't only the stillborn child, a son, whom she'd lost a few years before I was born, but also all those faded ink names in the family bible that she'd inherited from her mother. I had looked into that thick tome once and seen the recorded infant deaths as well as, more poignantly to me, the death of an older sister, from diphtheria, at the age of ten, when my mother was just a baby. Even as a boy reading comic books, I understood that my mother's grim family history of urban poverty and infant death (only five of my grandparents' eighteen children reached adulthood, and the two boys died in their forties, one from tuberculosis and the other when, driving to one job after working a full shift at another, he fell asleep at the wheel and crashed into a train) was a kind of anchor to the reality of history that my peers would never have to hoist.

I looked at the abandoned house, its sagging verandah like a pouch for forgotten corpses, its widow's walk bearing only a ghostly patient attendance now, and suddenly I felt the darkness of everything – the night itself, the unseen scud sliding far above me, the roiling mud and silts of the great river emptying its burden into the sea, even my mother's ineffable heart – as connected, a part of the flow of time that couldn't find its way between the pages of a book, but instead carried words, painting, all ambition and accomplishment, with it to the same gulf where the bones of whales and gulls and men made a ceaselessly shifting cemetery of no purpose.

I looked beyond my mother's head to the peak of our own modest house, its orange-lit front window offering a gleam of comfort in all the surrounding blackness. But beyond the peak of the house, a few miles to the west, I sensed his presence, newly cast in my own blood now, of the brother who wasn't a brother, his arms extended, divining the river bottom with a pike pole like a lightning rod for any sign of the sturgeon's scouring appetite. Edgar's manic gaze should have shared the hearth light of home, should have glimmered like struck matches in the abyss, being human and longing, but what it longed for, in communion with so many others, long dead and not-yet born, I couldn't understand then and do not carry with much equanimity now, these many years with all the houses, shops, boats and most of the people gone.

The feeling left as quickly as it had arrived, a shiver of intuition that marks every childhood at its most serious, before the joy and wonder and confusion of ordinary time rush back in. Soon, I was back in the living room, with its hardwood floors the same ruddy gold colour as the breasts of the ring-necked pheasants mounted on the wall above the mantelpiece. The TV was on, the dates deepened on the calendar. I was returned once more to the world of the world.

THE MARVELS OF YOUTH

*

Of course, life's patterns persist beyond childhood and nature. Why else should I have spent my childhood living within a three-minute walk of a comic shop and my middle years in another province almost the same distance from the same kind of business? I didn't plan it this way. While looking at apartments and houses to rent, I didn't ask, "Where's the nearest comic book shop?" In fact, by the time I was fourteen, and until very recently, I gave no thought to comic books and superheroes at all.

But then my mother had to go into a nursing home, her house had to be sold and its contents, including all my comics collected in 1975 and 1976, removed to Edmonton, where I had moved in the mid-'90s for work. Here they are in cardboard boxes around me now, like the blocks to some monolithic jungle temple drawn by Jack Kirby. What am I going to do with them? Selling them makes good sense, yet each time I think of packing them off to the shop up the street, I open a box, take out an issue of, say, *The Avengers* and I become one of the characters in those fanciful tales, touching an object endowed with the power to cross galaxies and collapse the boundaries to the parallel worlds that exist all around us, worlds including childhood and old age, for what world can be more lost, mysterious or terrifying to those unprepared to enter it with eyes and heart wide open?

VII

November, not April, is the cruellest month, or at least it was in my hometown in the 1970s. The days were short and dark and so silent that you could hear the blood moving in your veins. To stand on the dike at midnight, when the rain and wind had let up briefly, was to hear the nesting heron untuck its head from its body and the sturgeon on the river bottom slowly translating the oxygen out of the muddy water as it waited a month, a year, a century for the carcass of some creature to descend the black fathoms. I liked to crawl into the comic book car with a flashlight and a bag of chips and listen delightedly to the rain splat on the roof and windshield. It was a relief not to be careful turning these uncollected pages, a relief to be free of all observation, either by peer or adult, a relief to live only for the present word and image that didn't have to be studied for homework.

Outside, the world wasn't merely dark and hard, but rather a mixture of opposing textures and colours, like an anvil dripping with silver rain. The people were that way too: sharp and black-featured, but often with soft words and kind eyes. They hurried through the streets just as the muskrats slid more quickly along the black brimful ditch that divided the half-dozen vacant and two inhabited properties across from my house. If one of the old ladies – so many with quaint English names, such as Woods or Lord or Hatt – should look out from under their dripping hoods and see me coming, they would always say hello, ask after my parents, ask about my schooling. And the more erratic bachelor fishermen, with names like Mackenzie and Leary and Stillwell, even when drunk, would lift a hand in greeting as they staggered past. Sometimes I even imagined that the weeping willows along the slough banks and the giant poplars on the dike, carrying on a polite conversation as I ploughed by on my news-laden bicycle, whispered an affectionate admiration of my work ethic.

But November wouldn't let even a child be innocent. The potato harvests were either in or else rotting in the flooded fields, and the fishing season, even if it wasn't officially over, was never going to salvage a year of poor income now. Whatever danger or deceit or outright evil existed in that place at that time might not emerge in those thirty dour days, but you always had the feeling that the worst of the species was being bred then.

At least I couldn't escape an uneasy sense of increasing tension that month. Mrs. Vasilakis, who had been a friendly non-English female face in the streets for as long as I could remember, didn't emerge from her house, and even Edgar and Bullet, so reliably and sometimes jarringly nomadic between the harbour and the outskirts of the old part of town, seemed to have been swallowed up whole by the unrelenting darkness. As for the Haunted Bookshop, it should have been a haven, as always, but when I stopped in one drizzly late afternoon, Mr. Edison's son, Stuart, was behind the counter, which was unsettling enough, for I always felt the weight of the physical stigma he bore on his mouth. What he said to me, too, should have been a delight to hear, but it only filled me with dread.

"It's your lucky day."

His nasally voice was straightforward and clear enough this time, with no sign of a lisp, but Stuart had more than his cleft palate to overcome. He was short for his age, with a small face made tiny by the frame of long brown hair that dropped almost to his shoulders. No matter how hard I tried not to, I always thought of E.B. White's Stuart Little when Mr. Edison's son appeared in the shop.

"Oh yeah?" I wasn't exactly indifferent, but I didn't like the sound of the word "lucky." In fact, it made me even more anxious. So I tried to switch the subject.

"Where's your dad? You're not on your own, are you?"

Stuart frowned and then chewed on his thumbnail, something he did often. "Not really. Well, yeah, I am, but only for a bit. He had to go to the bank." He held his thumb out and started picking at a hangnail he'd made. "Don't you want to know why you're lucky?"

"I guess so."

"Someone got you an early Christmas present. Look."

He pulled out a comic covered in a protective Mylar wrap. As I stared at it, the initial rush of excitement quickly congealed to dread.

"It's number seven. The one that's been hanging on the wall."

"Yeah. I know."

"Well, aren't you happy? You don't have anything that early, do you?"

I admitted that I didn't. And then, more to fend off Stuart's confusion than out of pleasure, I carefully slid the comic from its protective sheath. The cover, while not fresh and bright, was still in very good condition. On it, Spider-Man was in mid-air about to be attacked by a villain named the Vulture, a balding, skinny old man in a suit with green wings. I stared at the villain for a long time, unable to believe my eyes.

"There's a card too," Stuart said, and handed over a white envelope.

But I already knew who had paid for the comic and left the card. I also knew that the comic cost more than I earned from my paper route in a month. The villain seemed to be looking past Spider-Man and straight into my eyes, mocking me. I couldn't believe I'd never noticed the resemblance before. The Vulture could have been the twin brother of Mrs. Hurry's husband.

"Aren't you going to open it?" Stuart's voice was wheedling now, and I could tell he was greatly disappointed. Before I could say anything else, the door opened behind me. Mr. Edison stomped in, blowing air like a sea lion. His greying hair, almost as long as his son's, was stuck to his rounded cheeks, and he had dark smudges under his eyes, as if he'd rubbed charcoal there. "Okay, Stu," he said. "You can go back to sorting those paperbacks."

"I gave him the number seven," Stuart said quietly as his father passed him at the cash register. But Mr. Edison merely grunted as he sat in the swivel chair and took up a new issue of *Fat Freddy's Cat*. Then he smiled at me, said hello and added, "You want to be extra careful to keep that one dry."

Something in his tone, an almost aggressive edge, only made me more uncomfortable. It wasn't exactly out of character. After all, Mr. Edison had a full-time manual labour job, which Jay and I could tell he didn't much like, and he was prone to occasional sullen silences. Sympathetic as he was, he lived in the adult world, a world that only the most obtuse of children don't at least dimly apprehend as fraught with inexplicable trials and sorrows. At the moment, I didn't even have the nerve to ask him if Jay had been in. Instead, I took a long dry swallow and opened the envelope.

A folded piece of paper – in fact, a used score sheet from the local bowling alley – rested in my open palm. The handwriting on the clean side was in purple ink and crabbed and small rather than floral, which surprised me a little. I had expected something more feminine, even though I well knew, from hearsay and our one conversation, that Mrs. Hurry was no retiring violet. What she wrote, however, was predictable. *Hi, Sean. I know you must love comic books because I see your bike outside this place every day. So I asked the owner if there was anything special you might like. He suggested this one. I hope it's a good choice because I don't know anything about comics. I sure didn't know how much an old one could be worth! I should see if Hurry has any hidden in a desk somewhere! Those could be really old ha ha! Anyway, I just wanted to thank you again for keeping our secret. Your friend, Vicky.*

When I looked up, I saw Mr. Edison staring at me out of his sleepy eyes, the same soft blue of the cue stick powder from the pool hall. "Everything okay, Sean?"

For a few seconds, I seriously thought of unburdening my secret, for Mr. Edison seemed the safest repository, not being a resident of our town and hardly having any connection with locals other than those who entered his shop. But it was too embarrassing to have to explain what I had seen that night on the wharf, and even more embarrassing to admit that I'd already accepted one bribe to keep quiet. So I simply nodded and stuffed the score sheet into my coat pocket. With the ice broken, I felt confident enough to ask about Jay.

"Haven't seen him. Maybe he's sick. Even Jay must get sick sometimes." Mr. Edison reflected on this point and then his thick walrus moustache trembled with delight. "But I sincerely doubt it."

Relieved by this return to his characteristic good nature, I laughed as I prepared to leave and get on with my route. But Mr. Edison suddenly became serious. The swivel chair creaked as he stood and stepped across to the counter, lowering his head closer to my level. "It isn't any of my business, of course, but those people" – he nodded in the direction of the pool hall – "Well, I don't know that you'd want to be getting mixed up with them. At least not without your parents knowing about it."

I didn't know what to say, so I said nothing, and Mr. Edison, after a pause, rubbed his beard and retreated to the swivel chair. A minute later, as I stood beside my bike in the drizzle, staring at my brother's glistening El Camino angle-parked in front of the pool hall, I wished that I'd asked Mr. Edison why he was so concerned. Perhaps he had just experienced the inevitable conflicts that must occur when a used bookshop and a pool hall that serves liquor sit side by side. Or perhaps he knew secrets too. Either way, the opportunity was gone, and I was left with the by-now familiar unease in the pit of my stomach, made heavier by the knowledge that my brother might at this exact moment be sharing a laugh with Hurry's wife.

Then I had the same feeling I so often had when roaming through the neighbourhood's abandoned and derelict buildings: that someone was watching me. I looked both directions down the rain-darkened street, and across to the row of empty shops, but I saw no one. Over me, in the gathering gloom, a peal of gull cry fell toward the west. Closer, the bellhose of the Brownlows' garage dinged twice, though no cars had driven by me. Slowly, I turned and glanced up at the second floor of the pool hall building, just in time to see the two sides of a parted curtain in the window shiver into stillness.

Before I could fully take in this image, the door to the pool hall opened and my brother almost literally leapt out. I could see at once that he had been drinking, not only because of his animated movement but because his heavy silver belt buckle dangled loosely at the crotch of his jeans. Presumably he hadn't closed it properly after using the bathroom.

"Hey. Hiya, Champ. I was just on my way home for supper. Want a lift?"

His voice was low but only slightly slurred. He took his keychain from the pocket of his almost threadbare peacoat and started looking for the car key, the way a small child picks the petals off a buttercup.

"No thanks. I've got my bike."

"Oh yeah, so you do." With his free hand he pushed a long sweep of hair out of his eyes. Then, brightening, he said, "Did you hear? Kent's back in town."

"Kent?"

"Sure, you know. Kent State."

I must have looked bewildered, because Dan frowned and closed his hand over the keys to make a fist. "The draft dodger, you know. He was here before. A nice guy. I just bought him a couple of beers. He says he's going to stay in the clock tower again."

A vague memory began to surface, but it was only of someone living inside the squat stone tower of the town clock, or maybe just of hearing about someone living there. I certainly had no recollection of a draft dodger. However, given my brother's condition, I thought it best not to pursue the matter. Instead, I watched him as he gave a sort of Queen Elizabeth wave and, in three nimble hops, reached the driver's-side door of his car.

Dan had been a star athlete and top student in high school, destined for a scholarship to the University of British Columbia, but even at the young age of twenty-seven he already carried an aura of glamorous self-willed failure. It wasn't talked about much in the family, but my brother once confided to me that he just couldn't see a life for himself that didn't involve the river and the marsh and the fields. For nearly a decade, he had lived an itinerant working life doomed to extinction by the end of the century, a life of boats and tractors supplemented by a whole variety of part-time jobs, including sawmill worker, door-to-door dog licence salesman and even carnival roustabout.

But his real work, his successful career, was people. He had a gift for popularity. Everyone in our town of five or six thousand seemed to know Dan, or at the very least to know of him. Babies to centenarians, wharf rats to aldermen, drunkard fishermen to brothers at the monastery connected to the Sacred Heart Catholic Church: they all responded to his presence with delight. In this natural gregariousness, he took after our mother, who always said that her own "way with folks" came from her Irish mother, a woman who, during the height of the Depression, would often go without a meal in order to offer the ice man or the bread man a little something to eat. Our mother, however, lived the more restricted life of a woman of her generation, while Dan, as the Irish might say, lived the life of Riley, coming and going as he pleased, staying out all night and sleeping the day away, behaving as if he hadn't a worry in the world.

Part of that life, I knew, involved drinking, but the larger part, which I also knew but only vaguely, involved women. Though my brother technically still lived at home, he spent many nights away, and it was obvious that our father, in particular, disapproved. I didn't know at the time, but Dan wasn't fussed about the domestic status of his partners, accepting the maxim that "while the cat's away, the mice will play" as a kind of sporting invitation. He possessed, in other words, the sort of shoulder just made to be cried on.

I must have picked up some sense of his bed-hopping, perhaps through osmosis during especially tense exchanges between Dan and our father, because once I had watched him pull his car door shut behind him, I lifted my eyes to the pool hall window again, as if my brother's movements and the curtain's shivering were intimately related.

The idea turned an already bleak day into a prematurely black one. By the time I had neared the end of my route, with Jay's house in sight, it wasn't just the rain that encouraged me to pedal harder. I needed the distraction of my best friend's madcap enthusiasm.

THE MARVELS OF YOUTH

As always, he didn't disappoint me. I found him in the carport, on his knees on the cement, positioning a GI Joe in some sort of jungle diorama, complete with dirt, branches and what looked like a papier-mâché mountain.

"Finally," he said, turning with the usual crooked grin as I rode up. "I've been waiting for you before I shoot this. Here."

He held out a butane lighter and told me to ignite the diorama at a specific point. "But not until I give the word. And *don't* put your face too close. I've put some gas there, and some other stuff."

"What?"

"You'll have to get on your knees, and then sort of throw yourself back. You know, like a commando roll."

When I just stood there, the lighter flat in my open palm, Jay said, "I'd do it myself, but I've got to run the camera."

I had forgotten that Jay owned a Kodak home movie camera and projector, but then, it was impossible to keep track of all his possessions. While he didn't have a paper route or any kind of job, his parents, both lawyers who worked in the city, gave him an allowance for monthly chores, and he had two sets of generous grandparents as well.

Because I still didn't move toward the diorama, Jay said, "I just need to get this one shot. While there's still some light. Then I'll show you the latest drawings I've been doing for *Cosmos*."

Finally, I went down on my knees beside the GI Joe and held the lighter out. "Where, exactly?"

"Right at his legs. Get as close to his pants as possible, then light him and get out of there fast."

I looked over my shoulder to ask for more instructions, but Jay's head had already vanished behind the camera. All I could see was the white top of his Gilligan hat. There was nothing else for it, so I flicked the lighter and threw myself into a roll as a loud whoosh seemed to come right out of my hand.

"Perfect! Perfect! I got it in one!"

Jay hopped back and forth as if his own feet were on fire, the camera held in one arm like a weapon. GI Joe was now engulfed in flame and gruesome crackles. Within seconds, the mountain also caught fire, and I wondered whether Jay had set it up as a volcano that would burst into more glorious violence. But if so, I realized, he'd still be filming.

Silently, standing side by side, we watched GI Joe's plastic features melt as the light in the carport grew brighter and brighter against the increasing darkness crowding in, just the way a jungle darkness might surround a battlefield.

"What's this film for? School project?" I asked.

"School?" Jay looked at me as if I had rolled the spine of a new comic. Then he pointed at the burning set, which must have taken him hours to make. "Nah. For fun. Why else?"

A few minutes later, after I had helped him to hose down and clean up the mess, we bounded up the stairs in his typical three-level new subdivision home and entered his bedroom. Though I had been in it dozens of times, it was rarely the same room, because Jay constantly rearranged the posters on the walls – of Original Six hockey teams and '40s movie stars like Humphrey Bogart and Jimmy Cagney – and the plastic superhero figures on his shelves and desk. Quite often, he had moved his bed and desk, too, adjusting them according to the changes in both sunlight and moonlight that poured in through the one large and uncurtained window. But the telescope on the tripod never moved, nor did the metal foot lockers where he stored his comic collection. His drawing board and wooden easel almost always stood in the middle of the room, with a maximum watted light bulb inside a goose-neck lamp attached to the side. Pencils of different colours and lengths, as well as pens and nibs for inking, covered a small side table nearby. On a large metal desk against the wall, I noticed, sticking out from the typewriter, a page on which the words "euphony" and "egregious," with their definitions, were typed. Overlooking all this setup, from the same wall, was a large photograph of Jack Kirby himself, his hunched back to the camera, sitting at his own drawing board. I always had the unnerving feeling, perhaps because of Kirby's penchant for the magical and fantastic, that everything we said and did in that room was somehow heard and seen by the real Jack Kirby living and working directly down the coast from us in California.

In my naive way, I once asked Jay about his love for Kirby over all other artists. While I loved *Kamandi* and the 1960s era of *The Fantastic Four*, I mostly favoured *The Amazing Spider-Man* drawn by Steve Ditko and then John Romita. But really, it was the stories that mattered to me, and when they dealt with the world on Earth in a more recognizable manner, as in *Conan the Barbarian* where humans mostly clashed with other humans, my interest grew. Even Spider-Man stayed close to the streets and offices and ordinary workaday concerns of almost regular people. But Jay had a hunger for the galactic and the mythic, a hunger only Kirby could satisfy. New worlds, new gods, new eras: everything about Kirby's world was epic and explosive, and especially the way he drew.

"The first comic I can remember reading," Jay had once confided in a reverent tone, "was *New Gods* #1. My mom brought it home from the drugstore because she knew I liked drawing and she thought it looked different from everything else. I guess this was in grade two. Anyway, I had read hundreds of other things by then, but *New Gods* just wasn't like anything else. It was . . . I don't know . . . *huge*. Not even like a comic book. But it wasn't just the cover, which was a collage, really cool. I remember seeing the words at the top: *Kirby is here!* And I thought, who is this Kirby who gets announced with an exclamation mark? And if he's here now, where was he before?"

Jay nudged me on the shoulder. "Yoo-hoo, are you looking?"

I brought my attention back to the art on the drawing board. By a curious coincidence, it was a collage à la Kirby, of our hero Blackstar hovering in space and looking toward the Earth in the distance. The Earth had been cut out of a magazine or a textbook.

"This isn't the cover," Jay explained, "but since our first issue can't be too many pages, I want all of them to pop as much as possible."

I nodded, struggling to think of something useful to say, but my friend's talent and confidence, not to mention Jack Kirby's godlike presence in the room, were too intimidating.

"It looks great," I finally mumbled. "Really, really great."

"Hey! You want a ham sandwich and a pop?" Jay had jumped to his feet and pushed his Gilligan hat back on his prominent forehead. A spray of ebony curls hung below the brim. "Then we can watch *My Three Sons*."

An hour later, I forced myself away from the TV set in the basement and back into the rainy darkness. Only when I reached my bike in the carport, and saw my canvas delivery sack – inside of which, well-insulated by my own family's copy of the paper, rested the copy of *The Amazing Spider-Man #7* – did I realize that I hadn't told Jay about my good fortune. For a few seconds, I wondered if I had simply forgotten, but receiving an expensive old comic wasn't something I'd ever forget to mention to Jay, not if I'd been excited about the acquisition.

The smell of charred plastic and plaster-of-Paris still drifted on the damp air. Jay's black-and-white cat, Chaplin (so named because he had two strips of black fur under his nose that formed a Little Tramp moustache – "I couldn't exactly name him Hitler, could I?" Jay once explained) meowed and came out of the shadows to rub against my leg. The touch disgusted me, and I pushed the cat away. The forced affection reminded me too much of my new and unwanted "friendship." Besides, with cats, you can always feel their skulls through their thin fur, as if you felt a pool ball through the foot of a nylon stocking.

All the way home, in and out of streetlamp lights blooming every block like hothouse orchids in the slanting storm, I felt the cozening, sensuous, steel-cold touch of something I didn't understand on the back of my neck.

VIII

Wallace Stevens once titled a section of a poem, "The westwardness of everything," and I suppose that sentiment has come to define my own life. After all, childhood is origin, dawn and the east, and The Haunted Bookshop was a block away in that direction from where I slept each night as a boy. Now, a half-century later, the comic shop in my Edmonton neighbourhood lies a block to the west, while my childhood, like the setting sun, sinks on that same horizon. Even the rivers – for I have always lived beside two major rivers – speak of different times, longings and mysteries. The North Saskatchewan, without tides, flows east into the sunrise. The Fraser, with greater force, rushes westward out of the Rocky Mountains into its tidal estuary sunset 850 miles away in the Gulf of Georgia. So I can perhaps be forgiven when I hear again my father's whistling of the famous song from *Fiddler on the Roof*, and turn my blood toward its beginnings, where even the west still held a mysterious and romantic appeal.

It was, after all, where the fresh water turned into the salt, where the salmon disappeared for years in the deep ocean, gathering strength for the return journey inland, where, finally, the west travelled so far that it became its opposite. Why else did fishermen sometimes catch the large glass buoys of Japanese fishermen in their nets? Why else, when standing on the dike or building a tree fort high in the branches of a Douglas fir, did I always look toward the sea instead of toward the massive bulk of my own country standing at my back like some great tomb of history? The westwardness of everything, including the heart and the mind. Even the ghosts of the widows on the widow's walks of the abandoned houses directed their sighs into the sunset. To go west, I intuited early, was a dream that extended beyond life and even beyond death, but not at all an easy dream.

That black November, in the few days before old men and schoolchildren would wear the poppies of remembrance on their collars (which happened only on the actual day of the Armistice), my father seemed unusually distracted. He often lifted his face from the backyard fire and looked over his shoulder to the west. Or he stood on the kitchen side steps, gazing in the same direction, as if he had heard a noise inaudible to the rest of us.

When he finally asked me, early one weekend morning, if I wanted to go for a ride on the boat, I wasn't surprised but I was curious. We weren't the sort of family who could afford pleasure trips, so if my father wanted to go out on the boat, in the middle of November when the river wasn't open for fishing, I knew that he had some serious purpose. I also knew that we wouldn't be heading upriver, to the east.

At the kitchen table, while my mother packed some lunch for us, Dan, who had just come in reeking of beer and smoke from wherever the night had taken him, said, "There's no point, you know. It'll just be a waste of gas."

My mother didn't look up from the cutting board where she was spreading butter on slices of bread. "He's worried. Aren't you?"

"About Eddy?" Dan slapped his hand on the table. "You might as well worry about the moon."

"It's been weeks this time, not just days."

"Ah well, maybe he's got a girlfriend on Galiano."

My mother paused, the butter knife against her flowery apron. "Don't be making jokes when your father comes out. You ought to know it isn't just for Edgar that it matters."

My brother's face sobered immediately. He spoke more gently. "I'm sorry. I wasn't thinking."

"No. You weren't. And you haven't been."

Dan blinked as slowly as an owl, but he didn't look wise, just debauched.

I struggled to process this vague information, but made no headway before my father appeared, in the usual black skullcap, black floater jacket, cotton work trousers and black gumboots. He hadn't shaved for a while, and his later-than-five-o'clock shadow had more grey than dark in it. He slid a cigarette out of the Player's pack in his left hand, put the pack in his jacket pocket, then took a wooden match out of another pack from the other pocket, struck the match and lit the cigarette. Somehow he managed to do all this in seconds while seeming to take minutes.

"We won't be long," he said, taking the lunch bag and Thermos from my mother. As always, whenever they parted, they exchanged three quick kisses on the lips. It was the only sign of physical intimacy I'd ever see between my parents, but it was as reliable as the sun coming up. Years later, my mother would explain that the three-kisses-on-parting rule had been inherited from her own parents, who, doubtless, had suffered enough tragedy in their lives to feel keenly the foul breath of random fate on their skin. The kisses, I suppose, were meant to ward off regret in case of the unexpected, and no trip on the Fraser River could be undertaken with casual expectations of a safe return.

Ten minutes later, under a ceaseless assault of gull shrieks and a black scud squirming like amoeba on a microscope slide, we stood on the deck of our gillnetter as it idled downriver out of the harbour channel. By this time, I was excited, not just by the prospect of searching for Edgar, but by the intoxicating musk of brine, mud, mulch and rain that was like a weather system inside the weather. As we rounded a narrow point of tan bulrushes as tightly compressed as August cornstalks and headed northwest, I thrilled as always at the first sight of the Fraser estuary's silt islands.

There were at least a dozen of them, and all but one unpopulated, at least officially. The largest was Westham Island, where Dan and Scooter and I had gone pheasant hunting. It was home to a couple of dozen farming families, who mostly grew potatoes and strawberries, and to a bird sanctuary whose western edge looked out across a vast gill-like marsh to the Gulf of Georgia. Scattered within a few miles all around it, like poorly affixed postage stamps, the other islands were bordered with poplar, willow, spruce and maple trees, and nothing but mud and marsh grass and unnavigable criss-crossing sloughs otherwise. On the larger of these islands, which could be walked around in an hour if the footing wasn't so muddy and treacherous, was an abandoned hunting lodge once owned by the lumber baron H.R. MacMillan, who, wealthy as he was, once hosted there the silent film stars Douglas Fairbanks Jr. and Mary Pickford. But by 1975, only the occasional squatting hermit fisherman who wanted to get drunk in peace ever landed on these corpuscular accretions of silt. I had never set foot on any of the unpopulated islands myself.

Soon, we were among them, steering clear of the ominous deadheads that bobbed up and down with the current as if they too longed to go west. My father had chain-smoked several cigarettes already, and now drew down a half inch of another with one breath. He stood at the outside wheel, his concentration so fixed that it seemed to hurt him. The gulls kept streaming seaward, hundreds of them, crying louder as if offended by our journey. The day looked black around their pure white bodies.

Suddenly, my father turned to me. To my astonishment, his eyes were wet. But he smiled, and rubbed at his eyes with one hand, saying something about the wind being sharper as you move outside the islands.

"You don't remember your grandmother very much, do you?"

The question took me so unawares that I could only blink in return.

"Well, I'm sorry about that. Sorry that you didn't have more of a chance."

The truth was, I did remember my grandmother, but not with great clarity. She had died five years earlier, when I was five, just old enough to be able to ride my bike to visit her in her tiny stuccoed house in a row of similar houses that constituted a more civilized kind of old folks' settlement. Strangely, I remembered only partial images of the inside of that little house – where the kitchen was in relation to the living room, what side of the house I leaned my bike against and where I entered from (the west), and, most vividly and poignantly of all, an empty wooden birdcage that still had seed and some feathery fluff in the bottom. Of the woman who lived there, I remembered only that she was very old and small, with wisps of white hair, a bony face and cat's-eye glasses that often dangled around her neck on a chain. But I could remember nothing of what she said to me, nor even the sound of her voice or her scent. The memories I had retained, however, were pleasant, as if I had been to the seashore to spend time with a mermaid in her advanced years.

"I liked going to her house," I finally said. "I think she gave me lemon cookies."

The moisture in my father's eyes quivered. "Yes, she always had those. And she made the best cups of tea I've ever had." He put up his hand that held the cigarette. "But don't tell your mother."

We were idling now along the dripping treeline of an island bank, and my father seemed to have forgotten that we were on the river. It was impossible for me to forget, though. The Fraser in November is like the liquid state of depression. You can feel the weight of the hearts of all the people standing on all the bridges to the east, feel the sadness in their westward-gazing faces. And the hammered sheet metal of the surface, when it suddenly darkened to oil, suggested nothing but an undertow of the last gulping breaths of the drowned. The ceaseless gull cry certainly didn't ease my mood. The sound crashed down from the roiling clouds like the cries of whatever animals the gulls pulled the intestines from rather than from the gulls themselves. It didn't help that no other boats were on the river. If I had let my imagination run free, I could easily have believed that we were drifting toward the edge of a flat earth.

But my father, despite his strange mood, gave off the usual aura of calm. So I took the opportunity to ask the question that had been on my mind for the past hour.

"Dad? Why are we looking for Edgar? Do you think he's –" Swiftly, I changed my mind, and said, "in trouble?"

My father exhaled at length, flicked his cigarette into the current and put both hands on the wheel. "Edgar can take care of himself. He just might need a little help sometimes, is all."

Before I even saw the entrance, my father turned the bow into the mouth of a slough overhung on both banks with weeping willows.

"Be careful of the branches," he said, as we drifted slowly through a long archway of willows whose branches looked like the wing bones of great black birds. The gull cry stopped. Now I could hear only the wind, the current and our idling engine.

"Your grandmother helped him."

My father's voice trembled in the strange new darkness. I could still see him in the rippling shadows, but it was as if he had gone a great distance away and left me on my own.

"Your mother told you that she and I took Edgar in for a while some years ago. His mother died, you see, when he was just little. And his father wasn't a good sort of father." The voice didn't trail away, but it grew more faint. "Your grandmother looked out for him. And before she died . . ." I could almost feel the swallow in my own throat as he hesitated. "She asked me to do the same. Your grandmother" – I had to duck to avoid one of the whip-thin branches – "she never asked for anything, you see. So I promised I would."

The grey-black day seemed like a sunrise as we finally drifted out from under the willows toward a lone black piling stuck in the muddy bank thirty fathoms ahead. Here, my father cut the engine and secured us to the piling with a thick oily rope. "I'll just be a few minutes," he said. "There's a sort of shelter over there. You see all those blackberry bushes? Edgar sometimes uses it when he wants to be off on his own."

As I looked across the rain-soaked marsh grass, I couldn't resist asking another question. "But where's his boat?"

My father's look darkened. He told me to stay in the middle of the deck, or else in the cabin. Then he smiled slightly. "I just want to see if he's been here lately."

At the time, of course, I didn't understand that the absence of Edgar's boat might have been either ominous or encouraging, depending on his state of mind and his actions. When I was ten, I wholeheartedly believed, despite evidence to the contrary, that the violent and unpredictable world of comic books existed only in comic books. I didn't see then that what Jack Kirby, for example, put on the pages of his explosive fantasies was only what he had taken from the gnawing and fearsome realities of the living human drama.

My father was gone, just as he said, only a few minutes. I was greatly relieved to see his black figure growing larger again as he crossed the treacherous marshy ground that, I feared, would suck him under at any moment. But the relief was even more apparent in my father's voice as he climbed back onto the boat.

"He was here. And not all that long ago, judging by the firepit."

Given my father's more relaxed state, I ventured another question. "Why does he go off on his own?"

It was a boy's question that a man couldn't answer, perhaps even to himself. Why did my father, for example, retreat to his backyard fires at almost every opportunity, and fish only on the least popular drifts of the river? Why do I, at age fifty-six, find any gathering of people larger than two to be a kind of torture? When my father finally answered me, I applied his words only to Edgar, when, if I had been even a few years older, I might have picked up an even more personal resonance.

"I don't really know, Sean. It's just what he needs to do. To cope with everything." He struck a match in the gloom, and it flared out of all proportion to its light, as if suddenly, one out of a million black salmon eyes blazed red in the depths of the river. "Everything" hung heavily in the damp air between us, unexplained, and, as I understand now, inexplicable.

The slough broadened as we progressed slowly across the island. A great blue heron rose in squawking progress from a clump of rushes and flew away with that peculiar motion of a clumsy person trying to close an umbrella. From the north came the slow bellow of a freighter in the main channel, warning smaller craft of its approach. I breathed in the rich and comforting smells of mud, gasoline and cigarette smoke, but the unease of the previous days was only increased by my greater knowledge of our family's ties to the missing and enigmatic fisherman.

For some reason unknown to me, I sensed that Edgar was alive, somewhere to the west, and that when he did come back, it wouldn't be the way that a bird returns to its nest, but, more fiercely and conclusively, the way a salmon fights its way back to turn its birth waters into the folds of a winding sheet. But how long that journey would take was as unknown as how long any such journey – yours or mine – will take.

We rode the boat toward the ocean, my father and I, standing close together and looking westward to where the sun that we couldn't even see, and hadn't seen for weeks, would set again. I suppose my father, in his discreet way, was looking for any signs of wreckage, any slight indication that his relief might yet be a travesty of the truth. But I didn't feel the weight of his effort or responsibility. In fact, for the first time in my life, I was aware of a spirit presence outside of the abandoned houses, and it was gentle and warm, smelling of lemon and Earl Grey and the lovely, lonely wake of irretrievable time.

IX

For the first few months of the Covid-19 pandemic, when most businesses other than grocery stores were closed, I couldn't do anything about selling my childhood comic book collection. Of course, like everyone else, I had more important matters on my mind, such as trying to secure some income and stressing over the geopolitical and biological condition of the planet. But then, five months into what the media and health professionals insisted on calling "the new normal," most businesses, at least those that hadn't closed permanently, had reopened and some semblance of regular daily interaction had resumed.

So, on a sweltering August day, with the temperature at thirty-two degrees Celsius, I took a small group of comics – including mint copies of the first issues of *Black Panther*, which Disney and Marvel had turned into a blockbuster movie success a few years earlier, and *The Eternals*, slated for cinematic release in November – up to my neighbourhood comic book shop only a five-minute stroll away.

I felt strangely apprehensive as the heat leadened my limbs and the incessant cries of ambulance sirens and the Spider-Man *thwip-thwip-thwip* of the police force's crime patrol helicopter turned Edmonton into Gotham or Metropolis during a supervillain attack. After all, I hadn't stepped inside a shop devoted to comics and superheroes since 1977, nor had I watched any of the multibillion-dollar film franchise commonly known by fans as the MCU, or the Marvel Cinematic Universe. Of course, I had passed the shop thousands of times, had glanced at the posters and action figures in the window, had even stopped occasionally to marvel at the price tag on some of the larger collectible toys. Even that limited experience had told me that I definitely wasn't in Kansas anymore.

But who expects the world to stay the same? I certainly don't, but neither do I take a superior attitude about the past, happily consigning it to irrelevance while embracing every new gadget and entertainment that the busy, connected world wants me to focus on. A man has a heart, and if he has lived in places he loves and among people he loves or finds intriguing, then nostalgia's not a pejorative word that substitutes for mawkish or unrealistic. It's perfectly natural to look back fondly on the past as one grows older, and such looking does not mitigate one's pleasure in the present or interest in the future.

The truth is, however, that I couldn't help seeing my eleven-year-old self stepping out of The Haunted Bookshop for the last time, pausing and turning back to put my fifty-six-year-old hand on the knob of the door to Warp One. Growing older, you see, is exactly like that; growing older is "the new normal" that we all must adjust to, pandemic or no pandemic. Which is to say, I could have sworn I heard Jay laughing as I walked in and old Mrs. English trying to get a deal on an "omni-boos" edition of Agatha Christie, except Jay wasn't in Edmonton and Mrs. English was a long time dead.

Just in time, I remembered to don my black cloth mask, which made me feel rather like Peter Parker pulling on his costume's headgear. The bell above the door was still tinkling – such a powerful auditory memory trigger, akin to Proust's tasting of the madeleine dipped in tea – as I moved toward the nearest tall glass display case and tried to appear inconspicuous, not an easy trick when you're wearing a mask.

Warp One was three times the size of The Haunted Bookshop, and yet it was absolutely crammed with stock, much of it not in comic book form. But before I could even focus on the items for sale, I immediately missed the one sensory detail that I had always associated with my comic book reading days: that musty, rich smell of old paper, a kind of reader's incense that still can be found in used bookstores. They must have all the older comics in Mylar covers, I thought, and in boxes. I moved farther into the store, into what could only be called the harsh fluorescent light, hoping to browse through the back issues.

Then I realized that I was carrying some perhaps valuable old comics myself, and should probably go straight to the main counter first. I certainly didn't want to be accused of stealing anything. Behind a large Plexiglas screen, a man in his early twenties sat gazing into a laptop computer. When I cleared my throat, he looked up as if waking from a dream, adjusted his own pale blue mask and asked if he could help me.

"Do you buy old comics?" I said. "From the '60s and '70s?"

"No."

"Do you sell them? Do you have back issues?"

He adjusted his weight on his chair while shaking his head. "Not really. We do have some that are a few years old, in the boxes under the current issues, but that's it."

I spoke with him for a few minutes, long enough to find out a few useful facts. The most popular items in the shop were graphic novels through most of the year, and board games in the winter – not Clue and Monopoly, but a variety of newer strategy games: one whole long wall of the shop was devoted to these. No kids under the age of fourteen ever came in without a parent. Forty percent of the regular customers were female, but they mostly weren't interested in mainstream superhero stuff. The most expensive items in the shop, at about two thousand dollars, were some rare *Magic: The Gathering* playing cards (the playing card section of the shop had its own counter at the back, as well as tables and chairs for weekly tournaments, though these were suspended due to the pandemic) along with some action figures worth close to a thousand dollars. Most importantly, he had heard of Jack Kirby, and he did consider him to be relevant, but he wasn't aware of anyone who collected those sorts of comics.

"You could try Ultimate Key Issues in the west end," he said after some deliberation. "They buy old comics. But I'm not sure they're buying right now."

This pointed reference to the pandemic's effect on business made me realize that I ought to look around to see if there was anything I could purchase. After all, I do try to support the independent stores in my own neighbourhood when I can. And since I was receiving Canada Emergency Response Benefit cheques, I wasn't as financially desperate as some.

But I didn't want to shell out three hundred dollars for Batman's utility belt or five hundred for a Hulk figure not even modelled after Kirby's drawings. I wandered over to the graphic novel area. Hundreds of glossy-covered books, all sealed in plastic, no doubt to discourage browsers, challenged me to choose among them. But the choice was so overwhelming that I decided to do a slow circuit of the shop – passing the large manga section, the racks of superhero T-shirts, even the small glass concession case that contained cans of pop and chocolate bars (many of these brands were the same as in the '70s). En route, I realized that not only had the whole world of comic book and associated media and collectibles become more lucrative and sophisticated, more aimed at adults than children, but also that this change wouldn't diminish the pleasurable sense of excitement and belonging that people who frequented the shop experienced. It wasn't my comic book world, of course, but I did feel something of the old thrill and curiosity again just by being in such a place.

Then I turned down an aisle and came face to face with an item that made me catch my breath. No, it wasn't a beat-up shelf of old *Archie*s or a wall shelf of Louis L'Amour and Zane Grey paperbacks; it wasn't even something old, though it referred specifically to the year of my own comic book origin story. Before me was a door mat or welcome mat, about thirty inches wide and twenty high, with a black background and large white letters that read:

THE MARVELS OF YOUTH

QUINT'S
SINCE (JAWS) 1975
SHARK CHARTER
AMITY ISLAND MASSACHUSSETS

The word "Jaws" appeared inside the open jaws of a great white shark. I stared at the mat for half a minute, trying to convince myself that here was no astonishing coincidence. After all, I had seen several young people in recent years wearing T-shirts with the iconic *Jaws* poster reproduced on it; the film was obviously well remembered in the popular culture. And yet, despite my best efforts to settle my nerves, I heard the deep bass of the soundtrack again, pressing against the walls like an orchestrated thunder out of one of Alberta's legendary thunderstorms.

Timidly, I reached for the price tag: $54.99. Judging by the cost of many items in the shop, this was a cheap trip down Nostalgia Lane, albeit still overpriced. But I had all the material nostalgia I needed in the boxes of comics back at my apartment. Keeping a few of my old favourites, such as *Kamandi* #1 and *The Amazing Spider-Man* #7, would more than satisfy my need for a physical trigger to my childhood collecting past.

Ultimately, I decided to buy a copy of *Comic Book Apocalypse: The Graphic World of Jack Kirby*, more out of courtesy than anything else. Since the young man at the counter had been good enough to answer my questions, the least I could do was contribute a little something to his wages before I left. It was a practice my mother had instilled in me, no doubt because she'd worked in retail and knew more than a little about the ungenerous behaviour of the public. But when I opened my wallet and saw two fifty-dollar bills, a rash impulse overtook me and I hurried back to grab the *Jaws* door mat.

"I've never seen that movie," the clerk said on my return. "Is it good?"

The question stumped me. Was it good? Its quality as a film seemed irrelevant. It simply *was*. He might as well have asked if a bag of ketchup potato chips was good. Or if the year 1975 was good.

I smiled as he pulled the debit machine back under the Plexiglas screen. "It scared me when I was ten. I remember I couldn't even swim in a pool without being convinced that a great white shark was going to pull one of my legs off."

"So . . . good then?"

"It's the *Citizen Kane* of shark movies. If there are any other shark movies."

He didn't respond, and I can't say I blame him. The wit of someone nearly sixty doesn't generally go over well with the young, or, to be honest, even with those who are nearly sixty. So, clutching my *Jaws* doormat and my book of essays about Kirby's art to my chest with one hand and holding my unwanted old comics in a plastic bag in the other, I leaned my shoulder against the door and propelled myself into the sun-dazzled Edmonton summer.

Except I landed elsewhere. The day was raw and grey and bleeding gull cry. I stood on the upper wharf, as close to my father as I could get without appearing to be a frightened little boy, and listened as a small group of fishermen discussed the scene on the tide below.

"That's over a thousand bucks right there."

"Why hasn't he winched the damned thing?"

"He ought to take it straight to the cannery."

"He's poached it. How's he going to sell it?"

"He'll have to keep it until there's an opening."

"Right sort of a pet for that crazy bugger."

I listened to these comments, delivered with a combination of amusement and awe, while never taking my eyes off the strange tangle of ropes and the one dark figure commanding them.

Edgar hadn't been seen in nearly a month, but his hair and beard had grown as wild as if he'd been cast away on a desert island for years. Wearing only a holey black T-shirt and grubby jeans in the chill morning temperature, he manoeuvred the ropes like some sort of deranged puppet master above the giant sturgeon somehow half-attached to the stern of his gillnetter, which had sunk from the weight almost to the waterline.

"Why has he tied ropes around it?" I whispered to my father.

"He's not tying them," came the response after several heavy seconds. "He's untying them."

The gulls were screeching in the dead-fish-belly sky over Edgar's boat, circling so frantically that they appeared to be sucked toward a drain. I knew what was driving them mad, for the stench of the great fish almost made me choke. Every time I took a deep breath, I seemed to swallow clots of river mud and a ground mixture of rotted cat flesh and bullhead bones.

All at once, Bullet ran up into the bow and started barking at the gulls. The harsher echo of this repetitive fury combined with the gull cry to make a terrible shuddering machine over which Edgar, his black beard like a congealed blood flow above the white of his T-shirt, scrambled, throwing gears and levers.

My father and the other fishermen, realizing what was about to happen, moved forward to descend the steep gangway to the lower floats. I had no choice but to follow, though I never took my eyes off the sturgeon. It wasn't a great white shark, but somehow, in both size and appearance, and especially in proximity, it was more frightening. Over twenty feet long, gunmetal grey and a sort of green-brown at the head, the white sturgeon had two rows of barbed scales running vertically along either side of its body, the latter shaped like a python stuffed with its half-devoured prey, and a spine of even more pointed scutes. But it was the prehistoric head, and especially the mouth, that I couldn't look away from. Tiny in proportion to its massive body, the head resembled a well-pounded anvil, and long whiskers, like blood-seeking antennae, stuck out from each side. Because this particular creature lay slightly to one side, covering the whole stern of Edgar's boat, its broad, vacuum-like slit of a mouth was plainly visible. Every few minutes, in fact, the mouth opened like a fist into a palm and sent the gulls into an even wilder frenzy of cries. It seemed that the gulls knew what drain was pulling them down from their safer sky to the unlit trenches deep at the bottom of the river.

Meanwhile, Edgar stood smiling on the gunwale beside his drum, the end of several ropes in one hand, a long knife in the other. Most of the tied ropes, I noticed when I briefly looked away from the sturgeon, still held his steeply slanted boat to the wharf and weren't, in fact, attached to the fish – although one thick rope formed a loop around the sturgeon's distended belly.

"He's going to kill it with the knife," one of the fishermen said. "The goddamned crazy bugger."

"He must be drunk," added another. Then, into the throbbing raw air, he cried out, "You going for the eggs, Eddy? Those'll buy a lot of pints at the Arms!"

No one else laughed. The other half-dozen fishermen, like my father, were in their fifties or sixties, and judging by their taut faces and silence, they didn't find either the economics or the ethics of the scene to be a laughing matter.

The mouth, like some sort of horrible fast-blooming flower, opened fully again. I imagined the force of that powerful suction, and stepped discreetly back. Jack Kirby might have created out of the wilds of his imagination a character like Galactus, who devoured planets, but that was fantasy. Here, only forty feet away, hanging like the bell-pull for the Apocalypse, was the real dark world within the world. I shuddered to think of what other terrors might be summoned when it moved freely through the murk of its underwater kingdom.

Yet, as Edgar dropped the ropes and bent to the sturgeon's vulnerable dirty-white belly, the knife poised in his hand, I didn't feel relieved, or even afraid of the violence that would ensue, which, based on the thrashing of much smaller examples of the species, would be terrible. But rather, I felt a sense of injustice, that the battle, or at least this last stage of it, was unfair. After all, a superhero doesn't tie a villain up and then murder him in cold blood. At the same time, I understood that the business of fishing wasn't sentimental and that the economics and ethics of the work ran on their own mercurial and fog-shrouded track.

"It'll break your fucking arm," the younger fisherman said, his tone no longer amused.

But when Edgar lowered the knife and began slicing, the great fish didn't move. Its mouth didn't even open. Suddenly the gull cry and the barking ceased. I could hear the low tide gurgling at the base of the creosote-blackened pilings of the upper wharf. My father and the other fishermen, their bodies thick with cigarette smoke and engine grease, closed around me like the sides of a cave.

Then the scene exploded with a huge splash. The stern of the boat flew up so swiftly that Edgar seemed to leap at the circling gulls to tear them down. I saw the sturgeon thrash once in a spasm that lasted several seconds before its twisting bulk plunged below the surface of the river. Bullet ran to the disturbed water and barked fiercely into it as Edgar's laughter pealed across the jaw-dropped faces on the wharf beyond him.

"What the hell d'you do that for, you fuckin' lunatic?" The younger fisherman whirled around to state the obvious. "He just let it go. He fuckin' let it go."

Edgar stood with his hands on his hips as Bullet bounced around him like a boulder tumbling down a mountain slope. "I told you I'd get him, Hecky! You saw him. Over a thousand for sure. It took a while, but I told you." And he laughed that nasally, rapid laugh the likes of which I've never heard come from any other throat.

I stared at the river where the sturgeon had gone under. The river in the channel was grey and cylindrical, like a greater fluid version of its most unusual denizen. Suddenly the water opened and closed, opened and closed, just like the great mouth it really was, the mouth that had, and would, suck in innumerable human victims. So though I felt, as I knew my father did, pleased by Edgar's decision, there was little comfort in the morning's return to normal, or, indeed, in Edgar's return to the town. Without saying anything, and, in my case at least, without fully absorbing the significance of the startling event, my father and I left the wharf as if we'd walked away from a burning church.

X

November drifted along in a slow chiaroscuro flood. The whole town lay at anchor, riding it out, as the surrounding farm fields and the river blackened and swelled and the six-foot-wide ditch that cut behind the Vasilakises' property rose almost level with the ground. Even the weeping willows looked cried out, their branches dripping like hoses attached to taps that hadn't been properly shut off.

I did my paper route with grim determination, riding my bike with my head down toward the darkly glistening pavement ahead of me. More and more, the Haunted Bookshop became a lighthouse in the storm. Its ripe-pear light and the gutted-salmon red of my father's backyard fires formed twin points of refuge, even though the tension I'd been feeling for weeks never really lifted but became like the weather: so ubiquitous and constant that it had to be absorbed to be withstood.

As always, Jay's madcap enthusiasms lifted the gloom. He was rampant with ideas for our first issue of *Cosmos*, encouraging me to create a super-hero team like the Fantastic Four, the X-Men or the Avengers, and then to think about the first story. "We can do it like Lee and Kirby," he said. "We'll brainstorm a plot, then I'll draw it and you can put in the dialogue."

THE MARVELS OF YOUTH

But I wasn't entirely convinced that I could meet Jay's high standards. Trying, however, was an all-consuming activity that helped to brighten the endless November darkness, at least until one idea after another died weakly on my writing pad. The breakthrough, when it finally came, arrived unexpectedly.

I was pedalling furiously down Delta Street after finishing my paper route, hoping to reach the bookshop before it closed (Jay had stayed there, as he sometimes did), when a wall of music and a spill of light made me stop. The wooden door to the squat granite clock tower was flung open, and, from inside, the Doors' "Light My Fire" played at a volume not quite loud enough to drown out several voices.

Leaning my bike against one of the street's many empty shops, I walked through the light and stopped at the doorway of the tower.

"But I'm more of a patriot than most guys," a tall, skinny young man with square glasses and a dark beard with sideburns but no moustache said as he brought his skeletal hand down off a gear of the clockworks. "I know my history at least. Go on, man. Name a state and I'll tell you what major Civil War battle was fought in it. Any state. Go ahead."

Another youth, long brown hair to his shoulders, sat cross-legged on the tower's cement floor, intermittently smoking a joint and drinking from a stubby brown beer bottle. "Alaska," he said, and grinned as he flipped his bangs out of his seal-wet eyes. This was Nick Samaras, author and illustrator of *Super Head* and fervent reader of *The Fabulous Furry Freak Brothers*. I rarely saw Nick, as he was in high school and only came into the bookshop occasionally, probably during the day when he was skipping out, but he was hard to ignore when I did see him. Just as *Peanuts'* Pig-Pen was always accompanied by a cloud of dust, Nick Samaras, in his torn and faded denim, moved in a permanent fog of pot smoke.

"Alaska didn't become a state until 1959," a familiar voice said.

"Okay, Hawaii then." Nick tossed a bottle cap and Jay blocked it with his forearm.

"That's just it, that's just it," the youth with square glasses said. "Most guys my age don't even know their country's recent history. They haven't got a clue how many states there were during the Civil War. Worse, they don't even care. Yet here I am, a traitor and an exile, all because I didn't want to kill some poor guy in a rice paddy just trying to get his crops in."

"How about Arkansas?" Jay said.

Nick took a long toke and, reaching the roach out to the American, lazily said, "Why isn't it pronounced like Kansas? Ar-kansas instead of Ar-kan-saw? Hey, answer me that."

The American turned to take the roach and I got a vivid look at his face in profile: a long, bony nose, a broad temple with a pulsing vein and a small chin. "That's easy. The Battle of Pea Ridge – 1862. Ask me another."

"Aw" – Nick groaned and studied the mouth of the beer bottle – "you could say anything and we wouldn't even know if you're making it up."

"But that's exactly the point. That's what I'm saying, man. I don't make things up. I know my country's history. I can tell fact from fiction. I can tell when I'm being sold a pack of lies. Why else would a fellow like me – a top scholar, no criminal record – want to leave my home?"

"No criminal record? That's nothing to brag about."

"Vermont," Jay said. He sat on the third step of a wooden staircase that ascended to the upper part of the tower. His eyes narrowed, a sign that he was deep in thought.

Meanwhile, Jim Morrison sang bravely on, something about not being able to get any higher.

"Vermont? Let me see." The American stroked his cuff of beard as he handed the roach back to Nick. "That's a tough one. I'll have to think about that one. I'll get back to you on that ... uh, what did you say your name is?"

Jay looked up just then and saw me. "Hey, Sean, come on in and meet Thomas. He's an American."

I knew that, for Jay, "American" basically meant "a person from the place where everything interesting comes from." After all, what comic books did Canada produce? What movies? What books? What pop bands?

"Thomas Plum," the American said, ushering me inside with a wave. "But is it right to call me an American? Better to say I'm a man without a country." He sighed, and then, as if he'd insulted us, quickly added, "But

I'm grateful for this country, man. Don't get me wrong. In any case, Vancouver's more like Portland than it's like Washington, DC."

Nick, busy rolling a fresh joint, didn't look up. "Tom's a draft dodger, if you couldn't tell."

"Aw, man, I hate that word. 'Dodger.' When else do you ever hear it? The Artful Dodger, in Dickens. He's a criminal. I mean, he's just a kid, but still . . . I prefer *resister*."

"Or you could be a baseball player from LA." Nick licked the rolling paper and, looking up with his eyes half closed, added, "But that's about as American as you can get. Unless you're Captain America, eh, Jay?"

"Now you're just fuckin' with me, man," the American said, but wearily rather than with anger. "But how are you supposed to get it? It's not like your government's ever going to draft *you*."

The needle of the record player got stuck and kept repeating the same six words. No one moved for a full minute. Then Jay, his brow still furrowed and his eyes distant, asked, "How many states were there during the Civil War anyway?"

Nick rose slowly and unsteadily to his feet. He reached down and placed the beer bottle on the floor as if he was touching a flower. "I get hassled enough by the cops. We'd better not push our luck. Old Splinter Dink might just cruise by, after all."

I turned, already convinced that Officer Woodcock's patrol car would be sliding greasily toward us.

The American smiled. "It's cool. I've got diplomatic immunity. Pretty funny under the circumstances."

When we all just stared at him in response, he walked over and lifted the needle off the record. The sudden silence quickly filled with the whoosh of rain and wind. "The clock. How do you figure I can stay in here?"

"I thought you picked the lock," Nick said.

"Nah. I'd find a better place to crash if I was going to break in. Your mayor lets me stay because of my expertise with the old guts of this time piece. It's 1912, you know. The Howard Company of Boston, Mass."

Faced again with our silence, Thomas Plum simply shrugged. "My old man had a clock-repair shop. But he wasn't just an ordinary fixer. He was a regular horologist."

Nick sniggered, then mouthed the first syllable of the strange word to the air, but the American quietly added, "You never know when the stuff you saw or did in your childhood might come in handy." For some reason, he sent a penetrating look, like a kind of comic book laser ray, straight at me.

I felt a strange sensation as I looked at the time on my wrist inside of the clock tower; it was like trying touch the tide without noticing the river. "I have to go. I want to stop at the bookshop before it closes."

"Good idea!" Jay said, springing off the staircase.

"Stop in any time," Thomas Plum said. "I'll let you know the answer about Vermont."

"I don't know about that guy," Nick said as he walked along beside us, face wide open to the rain. "There's something off about him. If he's so good at fixing clocks, why is that one broken already? Come to think of it, I can't remember it ever giving the right time."

"But he is a draft dodger?" Jay asked.

Nick stopped outside the pool hall and turned his amused face on us like a floodlight. "Oh sure. I don't doubt that. I've met plenty of others. Lots of them deal. And he's just the type. No matter what, they always want you to know that they're Americans. Well, fellows, say hi to Lari for me. I think I'll shoot a little pool."

Jay frowned at Nick's retreating figure. "What's wrong with saying that you're American?" When there was no answer, my friend turned his quizzical look on me. I just shrugged and hurried to park my bike.

Inside the shop, Mr. Edison took one deep whiff of us and shook his head. "Been talking to Nick, eh? You boys want to be careful you don't inhale too much when you're around him." He winked, and then told us he'd be closing in ten minutes, but that we could stay for another fifteen or so minutes until he was ready to leave. "I just got something in that you'll want to see." His soft blue eyes twinkled at Jay. "But it's definitely a handle-with-extreme-care item."

Then he reached under the counter and brought out a comic and laid it on the surface.

"Oh wow!" Jay said. "Where did you get it? How much is it?"

Mr. Edison chuckled. "Okay, okay, slow down, one question at a time."

He then explained that he had just bought a *Fantastic Four* collection from a collector in Richmond, and that most of the comics, like this copy of #1, were in at least fine condition. "I had to come up with a fair bit of cash, but when you buy a whole collection, you can usually get a bargain on the individual gems."

"How much?" Jay asked, his voice barely above a whisper.

Mr. Edison, gently but firmly, removed the comic from under Jay's hungry stare. "Too much. But I need a few big sales. I'm asking two hundred for this one."

"Whoa." Jay bit his lip so hard that I was sure it would bleed. "That *is* a lot."

"Don't worry. A lot of the others, in as nice condition, are more affordable. Here, take a look."

For the next twenty minutes, while Mr. Edison cashed out and locked up and busied himself in the back of the shop behind the hanging curtain, Jay and I breathlessly looked through dozens of precious Jack Kirby and Stan Lee creations. Every few minutes, my friend would point at a certain panel or sequence of panels, say something about continuous action or a photo collage. Meanwhile, because the Fantastic Four and Kirby weren't as much of a passion for me, I began to look up from the pages to think about my own superhero team, the Vengeance Squad. Already, I thought that a character based on an American draft dodger could be pretty good. Maybe I could even give him some kind of power having to do with time. Maybe he could make it pause, or go faster. Or maybe he could travel back into the past and try to prevent crime before it happened. But then how would the other team members be involved?

So the twenty minutes passed, with the rain slashing against the window and the yellow light in the shop growing brighter against the deepening night and the smell of musty paper mingling with the smell of the marijuana smoke. Out there, in the world that wasn't new, all my customers were opening their newspapers and reading about the great turmoil of nations and money, but here, in the fragile barque of the imagination, all the surrounding water and sky glittered with the astonishment of making and dreaming, as the great works of the river turned and turned again our hours like fathoms into the sea.

Out on the sidewalk once more, after Jay had walked away, I noticed the pounding bass of the jukebox in the pool hall, and the sound, louder than usual, made me hesitate. Then I heard the shouts coming from behind the window on the second floor – mostly male but with the occasional female tone breaking through. The shouts fell around me like mortar bursts, and for several minutes I just stood there, knowing instinctively that I was involved, knowing that I wouldn't escape my involvement. After a while, I was able to pick out two clear words in all the shouting, which was in Greek, a language that seemed to my inexperienced ear to be softer than the Chinese I'd heard spoken by local farmworkers but harsher than the French I took in school. The pool hall door opened and Nick Samaras stepped out in one long stride. When he saw me, he flipped his hair back and looked up at the window.

"The old bastard's really giving it to her this time," he said.

"*Pes mou!*" exploded the two words again. "*Pes mou!*"

Nick scowled. His lean left hand hanging out of the frayed jean jacket cuff opened and closed rapidly. "She's not going to tell him a damned thing. Why should she?" Then he seemed to really notice me for the first time. "You ought to get home. This is just Greek stuff. Happens all the time."

Even though I knew he was lying – because I'd never heard shouting like this coming from the pool hall before, except when a couple of drunks got into a fight over a pool game – I decided to leave. I put my hands on the cold handlebars and pushed my bike off the curb. The shouting immediately subsided as the wind gusted like a freshet and swirled a powerful aroma of smoked salmon out of the nearest backyard smokehouses all around me.

THE MARVELS OF YOUTH

It was an ocean smell, full of longing cut short by violence, and it turned the rain on the streets into blood. For comfort, I looked to the sky. A few dozen stars struggled to stay clear of the trawling overcast, flooding the earth like a night within the night. But already thin wisps of white were sliding in from the gulf, so by the time I began pedalling along the unlit street that passed the Vasilakises' house, I wasn't surprised to hear the mournful bellow of the foghorn out beyond the jetty. Two notes. Like the two words shouted behind the window. *Pes mou. Pes mou.* The foghorn had more of sadness than rage in it; though, when I consider these emotions in the context of all I know now of my kind and my world, are sadness and rage not merely brothers born of the same conflict, the one sweeping up the glass that the other has just shattered?

The fog gave birth to a surprise the next morning. Under a pearl sky, in a rare pause of the black rain, I saw Mrs. Vasilakis and Theo standing by the full ditch near their house. Mrs. Vasilakis was dressed all in black and wore a dark veil, and Theo, bareheaded but otherwise properly dressed for the cold, still hadn't had his hair cut; it looked as if he'd had ink spilled down his skull. On my way to school, I had coasted within thirty yards of them, just wanting to say hello, but at the sound of my approach, Mrs. Vasilakis stepped back from the ditch as if shot, pulling Theo with her. I saw that she gripped him by his left wrist with her right hand. I opened my mouth to apologize, but she moved so quickly toward the house, yanking Theo close to her side, that I couldn't bring myself to shock her any further.

Though her reappearance wasn't nearly as dramatic or disturbing as Edgar's a few days before, I couldn't put it easily out of my mind. Mrs. Vasilakis had always been so friendly to me. A few times, when I was just a little boy, she had even invited me into her kitchen to give me some delicious Greek cookies covered in icing sugar. I remembered the warm smells of unfamiliar spices and the sight of intricately braided strings of garlic and onion hanging above the kitchen windowsills. And her face, broad, red-lipped, kohl-eyed, possessed a vibrant earthy quality that made her halting English seem more magical than pained. She must have invited me over in the hopes that I could become a companion for Theo, but it obviously became clear that such would not really be the case, so in recent times I had mostly spoken to her briefly in the streets.

Now, I couldn't understand why the sight of her outside, recovered from illness, should be so unsettling. The mourning clothes and veil were not unusual, for as Stevie had explained to me, it was customary for Greek women to honour the dead in such a way, and they had many relatives, especially back in Greece. Thinking of Mrs. Vasilakis, in fact, often reminded me of my own mother and her family's tragic losses in the first quarter of the century, all those infant deaths. "The undertaker was coming in the front door as the midwife was going out the back," as my mother explained it. She also told me that different colours of wreaths for different ages of the dead would be hung on the doors to let the neighbours know what had happened.

Yet in my polyglot hometown along the banks of the Fraser, private matters of one ethnic group remained mostly within that community. This natural hermetic impulse was only heightened by the tensions still palpably lingering from the terrors of warfare, terrors from which no community escaped.

So when I came home from the bookshop that late afternoon, and smelled the smoke of my father's backyard fire and walked along the side of the house toward it, the strange figure hunched in a chair in the flickering fire light put me immediately on my guard. When the face – small, wrinkled, hard – of the Vulture turned its cold eyes away from the flames to look at my father, I had to resist the urge to spin around and run back the way I'd come.

"I wanted to give you a chance to talk to him first," Hurry said in a voice like a dog's growl. "I'm not saying he's all to blame."

My father didn't raise his head. "She said it was him, then?"

Hurry pushed his shoulders back, and looked even more like the Vulture perched high on the ledge of a skyscraper and glaring down at the embery city lights far below. "No. She won't say. But I've got other proof."

THE MARVELS OF YOUTH

When my father remained silent, Hurry said, "Your younger boy. She's . . ."

"Sean? What's Sean got to do with it?"

"I've seen her talking with him. Outside that bookshop beside my place. Why else would she be talking to a kid?"

By this point, I had shrunk back into the deeper darkness, hoping that the pounding of my heart would soften over the softer earth. Rapid calculations clouded my consciousness. What explanation could there be other than the truth that would explain her talking to me and also remove all suspicion of guilt from my brother at the same time? As for the truth itself, what I knew was only partial anyway. Yet I had kept it to myself. Even worse, I had accepted bribes to keep it to myself. And then, what did I even know of my brother's relationship with Hurry's wife? She had said they were friends. But she had mentioned her husband at the same time too. I tried to clear these thoughts and focus again on the conversation by the fire.

"It's out of respect, Hector, that I even come to you first. You know that. If it was anybody else, I wouldn't hesitate."

My father took the cigarette from his mouth and flicked it into the fire. "I think you're mistaken. But I'll have a talk with him. With both of them."

"We Greeks usually handle these things ourselves. It's only out of respect that —"

"I'll talk with him. And if there's any truth to it, I'll put a stop to it."

The Vulture unfurled himself and rose up against the firelight, his wizened face as small as a palm. Before he could move any farther, I turned and fled, my feet skimming the surface of the soaked grass.

I couldn't go into the house until I'd thought everything through carefully, so I kept on running, across the street into the vacant lots. My father was a shy and gentle man, but I already understood that, in his withdrawal from the world and its systems, he resented anything that intruded upon his almost-hermitage. I also understood that my brother's flamboyant gregariousness was a source of nearly constant resentment. That there was love, however, I didn't doubt, but love, as I had gleaned from comic books and the world around me, was not always a reliable piece of flotsam to cling to when the shipwreck happens.

The rain began to fall again and the town opened to it like a gill in a dying salmon. I made directly for the abandoned house where Jay and I had tried to play hockey. It looked even more like a neglected tombstone than usual, or, rather, it gave off a cemetery sound, the rain and wind both darkening and increasing in volume as they struck the moss-covered sides and broken shutters and fretted the gaps in the verandah railings. Inside, I couldn't bring myself to shut the front door, but merely stood in the opening, the present and future swirling ahead of me and the past, no more comforting or certain, conspiring in whispers at my back. What was I going to say?

My father, like most honest men, had a nose for lies, so I knew I'd have to be either very composed and creative, or else I'd have to tell the truth. Could I do the latter? That would mean returning the copy of *The Amazing Spider-Man* #7, which felt like too great a punishment since I hadn't really done anything wrong. Besides, the truth would betray Hurry's wife and wouldn't even prove my brother's innocence, for if she was having one affair, she could also be having more than one.

No, I would have to lie, I would have to come up with a convincing reason for Hurry's wife to talk to me. The solution wasn't long in coming, but I couldn't easily work out the morality of it. By saying that she had been asking me about Dan, I'd be leaving him on his own to defend himself. But then, there'd be no harm in that if he was innocent. And if he wasn't?

The house didn't creak and groan and sigh around me, but its silence was worse. I imagined that all the dead who had once lived there were also weighing my options and that they were judging me on my strongest inclinations. For I already knew that I was going to let my brother go it alone. "If he's made his bed," I heard my mother say, "then he's going to have to lie in it."

But I could warn him first. It would be a difficult and embarrassing conversation, for he was really more like another father to me than a brother in so many ways. But if he was fooling around with Hurry's wife, my warning would at least allow him to make his own plan.

So I decided to look for him in town, starting with the parking spaces outside of the Legion and the Arms. If I found his gold El Camino there, I could either wait for him or else try to get someone to bring him out for me. What I feared, of course, was that I'd find his car parked in front of the pool hall. In fact, I realized it would be better not to find it than to find it there.

To my great relief, the El Camino was parked outside of the Arms, its cargo bed, as usual, filled with heaps of snagged fishnet and corks, soggy cardboard beer bottle cases and hockey goalie equipment. The street was still and empty, except, at the far south end, for a stooped old woman carrying a grocery bag through the misty halo of a streetlamp's light. I looked up at the huge white face of the town clock. As always, the time was wrong. When I looked again a few minutes later, the minute hand hadn't moved. Nick must be right about that American, I thought. So why was he allowed to live in the tower? Or maybe he just broke in? I listened for the sound of music through the stone, but heard nothing. Time passed, but the sign of it remained the same.

Somehow the longer the silence lasted, the more my anxiety increased. I began to feel just like Peter Parker – alone and tormented by my secret knowledge, unable to confide in anyone, unsure even of my own feelings. I could see myself on one of those classic Marvel splash pages, my face encircled by the faces of everyone in my shivering web of connections: Hurry's wife, Hurry, my brother, my father, Mrs. Vasilakis, Theo, Edgar, even Mr. Edison and Jay. All I had to do was turn the page and let the rest of the story happen.

Several pub patrons passed before I worked up the nerve to ask a middle-aged woman if she could tell my brother that he was wanted outside. When I began to describe him, she said, "Oh, you mean Danny? Sure, darling, I'm always happy to talk with Danny."

Her long-lashed wink did nothing to comfort me; in fact, it only reminded me of the huge white sturgeon's horrible mouth.

After fifteen more minutes, just when I had assumed that the woman hadn't delivered my message, or that Dan had chosen to ignore it, he exited the pub. But not alone. A young woman with long blond hair and wearing a short skirt was leaning into him as they walked. Both were laughing and obviously drunk. I didn't recognize the woman, but that wasn't surprising, as people came from all around Vancouver to drink in our town, just as local residents frequented bars and pubs in the city and neighbouring towns. Alcohol and partying clearly had no geographical limits.

From where I stood, up against the clock tower, I could see my brother's every expression and gesture in the light shining from above the pub entrance. He moved as if shadowboxing in slow motion, and at one point, leaning to kiss the woman, he missed her face entirely, which sent her into peals of laughter. At another point, he dropped his keys on the sidewalk and almost fell over retrieving them. I knew it was useless to warn him in his condition, and I figured there was a good chance he at least wouldn't go home until the next day. But even so, I couldn't just do nothing. I had to try to warn him, if only for my own sake.

I hurried up to him and shouted, "Dan, it's me! Listen! Just don't go home tonight! Okay! Don't go home!" Then I ran off down the gleaming sidewalk past the row of abandoned shops, feeling both absurd and relieved.

Back home, I told my father when he asked that Hurry's wife wanted to know where Dan was because she hadn't seen him in quite a while. I congratulated myself on that last part, for it suggested that they might not be having an affair. It was the best I could do, and I pulled the lie off with a convincing nonchalance – at least my father didn't analyze me with one of his penetrating silences.

At long last, I found myself in my tiny bedroom, comforted by the stacks of Mylar-covered comics on the shelves, the posters of Spider-Man and the Hulk on the walls, the bedside lamp with the tall-masted schooner pictured on the lampshade, and the manual typewriter on my desk. I could breathe easy again, maybe even do some work on my superhero team, the Vengeance Squad, with its new addition, the time-travelling Dodger who, when he wasn't fighting villains, liked to relax by reading Civil War history and listening to the Doors. Slowly, without really being conscious of the process, I had begun to blend fantasy and reality, to translate through the imagination what had been recently encountered through living. I had started the clocks moving in parallel worlds, just as the salmon hundreds of miles out in the deep shivered to their own ancient chronology and journey, and as the people around me, too, followed their circuits of blood toward all the un-illustrated and un-inked panels. In the world of comics – at least of the superhero genre in the 1960s and '70s – these panels would fill with violence, chaos and an almost ecstatic sense of grandeur. Somehow, despite my relief, I couldn't be certain that the world of reality wouldn't also proceed via the painstaking labours of the same dark draughtsman.

The next night, I learned that my brother had denied all carnal knowledge of Hurry's wife. "We're just friends," he said. "For Chrissakes, give me some credit."

My mother, in a voice so calm and quiet that I had to strain to hear it from my position in the hallway, said, "It might be more sensible to choose unmarried women for friends. If you must have women friends."

"Well, it's 1975, not 1955. As far as I can tell, the only people who have a problem with men and women being friends are people your age."

"That's because," my father said, "it isn't possible. I don't know what sort of world you think you're living in, but the only male friend a woman ought to have is her husband. That's why she gets married in the first place."

"Good God! And you think I've got sex on the brain. Listen to you. You sound as if you go around undressing every member of the opposite sex. It's ridiculous. I went to school with Vicky. I've known her for years. If I was going to sleep with her, wouldn't I have done so long before now, when she wasn't married?"

Then my father said something too low to hear. Whatever it was, the comment only made my brother raise his voice even louder.

"I'll spend my time with whoever I choose. If Hurry has a problem with that, tell him to come and talk with me."

"That might not be so pleasant for you," my father said. "If you get on the wrong side of him, you get on the wrong side of plenty of others."

"Yeah, sure, I know, don't ever fish in the Greek slough, don't ever talk to a Greek woman. Someone ought to tell Hurry that this isn't Greece."

Something – perhaps a cup – slammed on the tabletop. My mother said, "If you don't have any respect for yourself, you can at least have some for us."

My brother's voice softened. "Of course I do, Mom. You know that. But I can't exactly turn my back on Vicky whenever she comes near me, can I?"

"No, but you can draw clear boundaries at least."

"How am I supposed to do that?"

"Maybe you can stay away from the pool hall for a while. That wouldn't hurt you, for many reasons."

"Not the drinking thing again. How many times do I have to tell you that you're seeing trouble where there isn't any? Ask around. I don't have any debts. No husbands are out looking for me with shotguns. I'm clean. As clean as Sean."

"And it'd be better if your friendship with her," my father said, "didn't involve him either."

Dan laughed. "So, no more passing of rendezvous notes, then? Got it."

"Daniel!" my mother said.

Then the door slammed and my mother spoke in a hushed, hopeful tone. "Well, I believe him. I don't think there's anything going on."

My father grunted, and the subject was quickly dropped.

But I understood clearly, through instinct more than logic, two things: my brother hadn't been the man on the boat with Mrs. Hurry; and my brother was lying about the extent of his relationship with her. I didn't know why he was lying, but I wasn't under any pleasant illusions that I'd never find out.

As it happened, I eventually managed to discreetly extract some additional information from my mother and brother about Mrs. Hurry: that she had grown up very poor and had married Hurry for security and the chance to leave her life of deprivation behind, and that, as my brother said with frustration, she'd obviously had no idea that Hurry had so much money only because he was such a "tight-fisted old bastard." Dan then shrugged.

"You can hardly blame her for looking elsewhere when the bargain she'd thought she'd struck turned out to be a total con job. Hurry even does the shopping himself, just to keep her hands off his money. But she's resourceful, Vicky is. A lot smarter than people give her credit for."

XI

The rest of that year, as far as I can recall with any clarity, passed in an almost endless turning of my bicycle wheels through puddles that finally wore a thin sheath of ice as the dark and wet gave way to a greater dark with fog and the occasional snow flurry. The river and the fish in it were quiet, the fields softened almost to water and then hardened, and 1975 swam almost but not quite to a full stop, because, just like the great white shark in *Jaws*, time had to keep moving, despite the static hands on the face of our town clock, in order to stay alive.

Jay longed for the copy of *The Fantastic Four* #1 on the wall of the Haunted Bookshop and spoke of that and of our own comic book creation and little else as we took slapshots at one another under the dull streetlamps or lay under the shelf reading *Archie* and *Uncle Scrooge* as Mr. Edison fiddled with the channels on his radio, endlessly trying to find the one with the clearest reception. I still told no one about my contraband copy of *The Amazing Spider-Man* #7, and the skin at the back of my neck prickled every time I passed the pool hall or had to park my bike in view of its second-floor window. Dan barely came by the house, and when he did, he was often drunk or incommunicative, but that tension, too, seemed to be in abeyance.

Only Edgar, and sometimes my wild friend Keith, moved through the ash-end months of the year with much vitality. Edgar especially would appear on the dike or in the streets of town like a scarecrow made animate by a mad scientist – I often heard his cackling laughter even when he wasn't laughing, even when he wasn't visible. And Keith, who trapped muskrats in the ditches and sloughs all around town, sometimes emerged from nowhere, from right out of the earth, carrying a burlap sack and steel traps that made him resemble an escaped convict who had broken his shackles.

The Vasilakises' house remained a lightless, uninviting place. The same earth that had brought Keith to life seemed to have swallowed Mrs. Vasilakis and Theo whole. But Stevie sometimes appeared in the yard, his training assaults on the punching bag more ferocious than ever, his silences deeper. Most of the people in town, from the elderly women to the drunken bachelor fishermen, even to the draft dodger manning the clock tower like a remote forest fire station in a world without trees, had gone to ground like cautious foxes.

So I did my paper route and I drove whole galaxies of escape and wonder inside my father's undriven car stuffed with the comics that my diligent mother continued to deliver there after her long shifts of standing on her feet and having to be polite to those who didn't deserve her smiles. The wind rattled the windows and tried to lift the tires from the crushed gravel, and then the cold fixed the car in place and fogged over the rear-view mirror so that I could only look to the west when I sat at the steering wheel. I still had to pump the boat, my hands numb as I broke the thin ice and clutched the iron bar and looked over my shoulder at the slightest sound on the water or high in the mast chains. I heard my teachers from a great distance away, as if I had driven past them on some highway that rose off the Earth and plunged through the constellations.

All the while, the great blue heron and the white sturgeon, at the top and the bottom of our sighing human construct, carried on their ancient colloquy – an open pair of sexton's arms searching without hope for the buried casket of jewels.

XII

Am I a lonely man? Some might say so. The fact that I have no immediate family nearby or close friends, that I live alone in a small apartment in a city famous only for its cold and where I have no compelling past, is evidence for the prosecution. But then, why should I be convicted of so common a plight, if plight it is? Loneliness, as far as I can tell, is our fundamental condition. Perhaps I just choose to keep it closer than others do.

When I left Warp One and the present dissolved in the heat, I decided not to go straight back to my apartment. Instead, I kept walking as I remembered, the rhythm of the body and the breath and the heartbeat forming a kind of incantatory chant that repeatedly brought the past into more vivid relief. In this state, masked and passing many others in masks – as if we were all participating in some universal comic book convention – I eventually found myself on the Mill Creek overpass looking down into the shimmering green fathoms of the North Saskatchewan River Valley. Here, the cottonwoods and firs were thick, sheltering a narrow, paved trail that disappeared toward the skyline of skyscrapers on the northern horizon.

But what startled me, what assailed not only my visual sense but also – and it is curious to write this, my moral sense – was the large white, almost square, blank in the middle of all the green, as if the corpse of Moby Dick had finally floated to the surface of the ocean. But in the context of my memories, the image was much more familiar than that – it was as if the fully coloured and explosive action of a Jack Kirby splash had been wiped clean at the same time that my own most precious childhood memories had never happened.

Melville, in *Moby-Dick*, famously catalogues all the terrors associated with the colour white, concluding that "there lurks an elusive something in the innermost idea of this hue, which strikes more of a panic to the soul than that redness which affrights in blood." But what most disturbed me as I stared down through fifty feet of air at the rough white sides and bottom of the empty public swimming pool was the stark contrast with its pre-pandemic self. Less than a year ago, on a similar summer day, hundreds of people of all ages, but mostly teenagers and young adults, would have been almost shoulder to shoulder in the brilliant blue water and on the vivid green of the surrounding grassy slope. And the sound of public human joy – a diminishing commodity even before the pandemic – would have risen from the valley in an ecstatic and erratic chorus, loud enough to compete with and almost drown out the traffic noise on the overpass.

Now the high chain-link fence around the waterless concrete compound of white spoke more of prison than of freedom, and the sound of traffic behind me was like the sophisticated hiss of corrupt politicians. Dejected, I stepped away from the railing, the empty pool still flashing on my consciousness for minutes afterward, as if I had been staring straight into the sun.

Back in my apartment, I checked email, without much hope, to see if I'd been offered any work for the fall at my old school, and then, with the same impulse that makes a person probe a sore tooth with their tongue, I looked at my bank account. It was diminishing, despite the federal government cheques. Finally, with a glass of whiskey in hand, I settled in to read what the experts thought about the graphic world of Jack Kirby.

But when I opened to a random essay, and saw what it was about, I knew that an "elusive something" was turning me back again, with an increasing urgency, to the long war shadows and the psychic damage hanging over my lost coastal home.

From the opening sentences of "The Red Sheet," Glen David Gold essentially summarizes the twentieth and early twenty-first centuries:

> Here's something we tend not to think first when evaluating Jack Kirby's artistic intent: Kirby killed Nazis, and he did it in hand-to-hand combat... I think that experience, his time as a combat infantryman in WWII, charged his vision with a dark paranoia that fueled even the seemingly hopeful and innocent Silver Age stories of the 1960s.

Had I known this about Jack Kirby in 1975? I knew that he had drawn war comics, but these weren't of much interest compared to his grandiose superhero fantasies. Basically, despite the often apocalyptic subject matter of Kirby's graphic world, especially in the 1970s, that world seemed as far away from the ordinary grim realities of the newspaper headlines as could be imagined. That was why Marvel's legendary creative duo of the 1960s regularly presented themselves as "Smilin'" Stan Lee and "Jolly" Jack Kirby. Even when the comics tackled contemporary social unrest or delved into the angst of the zeitgeist, the editorials in each comic – the Marvel Bullpen page – remained outlandishly upbeat, even goofy, never letting the reader forget about the comic element in comic books.

As a boy, I had no idea of what Gold claims to be the central motivating factor behind Kirby's graphic world, especially post-1970 after he had left Marvel for DC and then returned to the fold: that he suffered from undiagnosed PTSD and, as he aged, increasingly explored that condition in his work.

To be brief, Kirby arrived in France in 1944 as part of a famous infantry division commanded by General George Patton. Deployed as a scout because of his sketching abilities (fellow comic artists always said he drew faster than anyone), Jolly Jack was part of an advance squad that entered towns and villages still occupied by retreating German troops. What he encountered there was, not surprisingly, violence, terror, exhilaration, sadness and deep trauma.

"There was one shell that had hit," he said in one interview, "and I saw these Germans lying in a perfect circle except the bottom half of their bodies were missing, see? The shell evidently hit right in the middle of this group. You see a lot of these nice designs if you're an artist."

In that last sentence, Jolly Jack steps right out of the pools of blood into the kind of necessary coping deflection that often defines a veteran's post-war life. In another wartime memory, Kirby describes coming upon three Nazi officers in the tavern of an otherwise-abandoned village. They forced him to his knees, from which position he observed what was right at his immediate visual level: "They have these great, beautiful riding boots that go up to here. Not only that, but the riding boots have a sheath for a dagger that fits perfectly in there."

But Kirby never goes on to explain what happened: instead, as he puts it, a "red sheet comes down" to block out the memory. According to his son, Jolly Jack either stabbed one German with his own knife and then shot the other two, or shot two first and then killed the other by throwing a knife. In another interview, commenting on killing men during wartime, Kirby said, "It's a strange experience. Some of it is even good. There have been times when I felt just great – it was almost like having sex. And you feel about ten feet tall if you can live through it."

Gold finds the admission that killing isn't all bad to be chilling, which of course it is. But I recognized, too, in my own limited way, the deep truth of the seductive nature of all violence, including the slaughter of other species and the destruction of the planet. That Kirby would link killing with sex not only made perfect sense to me, but the idea was another ticket home, to the mid-1970s and the "astonishing" (to use a favourite Marvel word) conflict between innocence and knowledge, fantasy and reality, and power and frailty that defines every childhood and therefore every human life.

As for Kirby, Gold claims that his PTSD was unleashed in his 1970s Fourth World work at DC, when he no longer had the goofiness of the non-veteran and very suburban Stan Lee to rein him in. And even when he returned to Marvel in 1976, Kirby's vision was darker, more apocalyptic, more intensely focused on ultimate battles. As Gold writes, by that time "Kirby was wrestling with such deep nuances about the intermingled natures of good and evil that they're only comprehensible when viewed through the effects of wartime experience." And he wrestled increasingly alone, as so many veterans do.

I thought of the men of my childhood, so often alone and drinking – fishing alone, living alone, suffering alone. I thought of the women, too, who had shared the trauma or were still sharing it, waking up in the night, as my grandmother and mother and Kirby's wife did, to comfort their husbands who had been screaming in their sleep. And what of the trauma of the private wars? The violence of the parent upon the child, the sibling upon the sibling, the husband upon the wife? I thought of Edgar Winterbourne then, who had never fought in a war that would earn him a government pension, but who lived alone and fished alone and suffered alone, except for his loyal canine friend.

I dropped the book of essays into my lap and took a deep gulp of whiskey when I read about Kirby's one fully developed war memory, or at least the only one he ever offered in an interview. Was this memory why I loved *Kamandi* more than all other comics, because the boy-hero was alone in a post-apocalyptic world controlled by talking animals? Was I picking up, without conscious awareness, Kirby's message about loneliness and the need for pity? That Kamandi was Kirby, and me, and Edgar Winterbourne, my father, Theo Vasilakis, even old Mrs. English – every masked character of the past who didn't wear a visible mask, and every masked citizen of this pandemic age – was neither comic nor fantastic, but was, in fact, a truth more real than what appeared and still appears at the top of the nightly newscast. Not long before he died, Kirby, when asked whether comics mirrored reality, answered that "no, comics transcend reality." His questioner then replied, "If you were to mirror reality, then perhaps others could begin to understand it." With a hard stare, Kirby explained that "when you mirror reality, you see it all backward. When you start transcending it, that's when you have a real good shot at figuring out what's going on."

Entering a bombed-out French village with his platoon, Kirby was sent out to scout for Germans. "It was like walking in on a movie set," he said, adding, "it was like a dream or nightmare" when he stepped into a charred hotel and was startled by a noise from behind a pile of rubble. Raising his weapon, he cried out in French and German to come out with your hands up. Receiving no response, he cried out again, this time certain that he was going to see some action. But what followed wasn't at all what he expected:

> This big dog came out from behind the pile. It was a great big hound that was badly injured. It was cut and burned all over. They must have blown the building when the dog was in it. It stopped in front of me and just stared. It didn't growl or whimper, it just looked at me with these deep accusing eyes; it was the most human expression I have ever seen on an animal. It was like he was saying, "You, you did this to me."
>
> Oh, I felt so guilty.
>
> I felt just terrible and so hurt, because to me it was like an accusation by a dumb creature that didn't care why I was there or anything about the Germans. All he knew was that I was there and he was hurting; that's all this animal knew . . . I lowered my rifle and it limped past me out of the wreckage and onto the road. He kept giving me these dirty looks, these terrible dirty looks.

After rereading Kirby's one complete war memory, I could see the eyes of my own real and symbolic animal, staring out, not just at me but at something that encompassed me and all the far-reaching purview of our senses and imaginations. By the time I finished, I had already collapsed the time barrier again, and returned to those intermingled nuances of good and evil that shift as continually as the dark silts on the bottom of the Fraser River.

XIII

In the 1970s, the daily newspaper was still a major source of information and analysis, almost rivalling the televised newscast. When I did my paper route in those years, Vancouver had two daily papers, one that came out in the mornings (called *The Province*) and one that came out in the afternoons (called *The Sun*). I delivered the latter, often, ironically, in the dark and rain, but both papers shared one thing in common: during the week, they ran a completely black-and-white comics section, and on Saturdays they ran a larger format full-colour comics section.

When I think of the dramatic transition from fall and winter to spring and summer that occurs on the coast, I'm always reminded of that pattern of the daily comics, with black ink and shadows and tight, constricted panels blooming into a whole spectrum of colours in much larger panels on larger pages, as if the characters themselves had burst into life. In short, the separate Saturday comics section – that contained *Peanuts* and *Beetle Bailey* and *Dick Tracy* – was as joyous and expansive as the summer itself. I remember that we used to take our Silly Putty and flatten it over the colour comics and then peel the putty back to show the image of the art transferred onto it. Even the gum that Jay and I chewed – Ton 'O' Gum and Bazooka,

THE MARVELS OF YOUTH

Black Cat and Dubble Bubble – seemed like confections lifted right off the comics section. In much the same way, the backyard swimming pools that we spent so much time in were nothing less than giant comic book panels; we flung ourselves across them as furiously as if we had been sketched into the brilliant water by the master Jack Kirby himself.

But all of this life and colour couldn't rival the summer's most electric and magical spectacle: the return of the salmon to the river. The salmon's homeward journey touched off a fever in the whole town, and in hundreds of towns along the coast, as if we had all suddenly tuned in to some radical pirate radio station all at once, as if we hadn't really experienced life before. Now the days simmered on the edge of violence, and the nights almost brought the constellations crashing down onto us. Even in the midst of a long, lazy spell of days with little to do but roam the fields and riverbanks in the sun or walk barefoot to a swimming pool with a towel as bright as a folded comic book around your neck, we could feel the low vibrating hum of an energy that transcended our lives. It wasn't spoken of or celebrated, but now that it's been gone for decades, that energy's absence has diminished us, made our ambitions and dreams smaller, inconsequential. If the world was a transistor radio – another vanished form of '70s life – the battery and all its coloured wires have been yanked out of it with the routine violence with which we'd once torn the guts from the salmon.

Yet on a still night like this, a thousand miles away, I can hear the faint throb of that energy coming from somewhere, perhaps out in Kirby's fantastic galaxies, and I can see, as close as the Nazi's boot in the eyes of the kneeling artist, all the faces as if they, too, for only a moment on their own journey to absence, had paused at the sound and, turning, resumed their places in my diorama of blood and brine.

My brother, barefoot and bare-chested, leaned his bronzed torso over the bottom of the *Driftwood* and gave a few whacks with the hammer in his right hand. He lifted his sweating, amber-eyed, full-bearded face into the sun, squinting up at me in my position on the wharf. "Give me a few of the big nails, will you?"

When I handed them down, I saw that the bottom of his boat was made up of at least five different panels of wood. A couple of them looked as if they'd been torn off a rec room wall. "Are you sure it'll be safe?" I asked.

"Nope." He swung the hammer for a moment, and then sat up and took a long swig from the beer bottle perched in the bow. Then he grimaced at the sound of an approaching vessel and deliberately turned his back on the channel. Noting whose boat it was, I understood. Kirkhoff was a highliner whose hunger had often been the subject of much rancour among other fishermen. My father hated the way he "corked" other boats, setting his net too close downriver from someone else's, reducing their chance of a good catch. He also didn't appreciate Kirkhoff's tendency to race his ultra-modern aluminum craft at high speeds past boats at anchor or with their nets in the water.

But I sensed a deeper emotion in my brother's response, no doubt a result of the upcoming strike vote. Because the canneries were refusing to pay what many fishermen considered a fair price per pound for salmon this summer, the union had been active all up and down the coast, trying to unite factions who, at best, were suspicious of one another, and, at worst, hated each other's guts. Soon, however, the decision to stop fishing would go to a vote. Kirkhoff and a few others, I knew from hearsay, opposed a strike. My father and brother supported the union's desire to apply pressure. Day by day, the tension had been rising.

Yet, in the languid days between openings, the harbour channel trembled slightly, like a hammock in a breeze, and even the gulls lining the net shed roofs and perching on every creosoted piling had stopped shrieking, their appetites perhaps sated for once. Now fishermen could mend their torn nets or, as in my brother's case, prepare their boats for the next time the government allowed them to head out to interrupt the salmon's fierce journey. The air, still drenched with the smell of fish and gasoline, seemed to breathe in and out slowly, and the few white cumulous clouds in the sky's swimming-pool blue hovered like jellyfish.

THE MARVELS OF YOUTH

Because the whole coast was divided into different commercial fishing zones with different opening times, the number of boats in our harbour had dropped considerably. Most of the more ambitious fishermen spent the busy summer months away, though some of the highliners often raced from one zone to another, depending on rumours and calculated guesswork as to where the catches might be best. Kirkhoff, I suspected, had returned to the Fraser River because the next opening was forecast to be an especially lucrative one. But that opening was still a few days away, so it was a surprise to see his high-hulled boat shimmering in the midday heat; highliners usually ran their boats all night to arrive at the river just in time to set their nets.

Kirkhoff suddenly revved his engine and lunged his boat ahead for a dozen fathoms, just enough to send an annoying wake toward our little wharf, and then cut in to a net shed on the other side of the channel. With little interest, I kept my eyes on him as my brother said, "What's Jerk-off doing here already?"

But once the wake subsided, Dan returned to patching up the *Driftwood*, and so only I saw Edgar and Bullet emerge from the net shed. Edgar made a dismissive gesture with one arm as Kirkhoff, standing on his main hatch, attempted to position his boat next to Edgar's. Bullet's rapid, hollow barking formed a weird staccato rhythm with the sound of my brother's hammering. The little dog stood right at the gunwales of his master's boat now. I could just see his jaws opening and closing, but the heat shimmer made everything a bit vague, just as, on the hottest summer days, it creates that effect of water on one end of a street when you're standing at the other. Kirkhoff, his black boots reflecting the dazzling sun, stepped away from his outside wheel and moved toward Bullet. Just beyond, still on the net shed wharf, Edgar had picked up a gaff hook and was holding it out at an angle from his right shoulder. I heard his voice but couldn't make out the words above the barking and hammering. Then, as so often seems to be the case in life, nothing happened and everything happened all at once.

Kirkhoff stopped, close enough to Bullet that the dog disappeared for a few seconds behind the man's bulky outline. I blinked rapidly to try to clear the heat shimmer from my sight as if it hung like a spiderweb in the fifty yards of intervening distance. Already, with a kind of dull, rising panic, I began to see the figures assume a familiar and almost-forgotten shape. Kirkhoff turned, his profile fitting perfectly into a profile I had seen before. But I didn't make the connection until he kicked out savagely at Bullet and the little dog, still barking, flew back sideways onto the deck. Edgar threw his gaff hook and leapt forward onto his boat in one motion. For a few seconds, Kirkhoff's profile hung in the heat shimmer before he raised his arm, and seemingly the middle finger of the hand, before his bulk dipped out of sight into his cabin, the engine roared and the boat jumped away from the net shed, a bubbling white froth at the stern.

But those few seconds had been enough. Now I knew who Mrs. Hurry had been with that night in October, and I knew who had kicked Scooter. It was a revelation of the body as much as of the mind; I felt the certainty of it race through my central nervous system as I tried to orient myself to the possible consequences of the information. My brother's intermittent hammering continued as the river shivered to a calm sheet-metal surface again. No matter how hard I tried to connect what I had just witnessed with the scene from the fall, I couldn't make the link. Mrs. Hurry and Kirkhoff? It was impossible, and even more disturbing than if she had in fact been with my brother.

Time rapidly contracted, the past several months flooding into the present. After buying me the copy of *The Amazing Spider-Man #7*, Mrs. Hurry hadn't bribed me again, so I'd gradually felt more at ease around the bookshop and pool hall, even though my guilt at accepting the bribes never really went away. But I'd seen Mrs. Hurry and my brother talking and laughing together on a few occasions, through the window of the pool hall and outside of the Arms. And though these meetings were innocent enough, they nagged at me, as if I had something on my own conscience to expiate. Also, I had caught Hurry staring at me a handful of times as I passed him in the streets, and the attention was unpleasant.

I looked down at Dan's muscled and sweaty back. His long hair swung with each strike of the hammer, making him resemble a freshly coloured drawing of Jack Kirby's Thor. How does a mere mortal, a boy, approach the Norse God of Thunder, especially on such a sensitive topic? I wanted to tell him what I had seen on the wharf that night, and I wanted to confess to taking the bribes, too, but somehow I understood that the knowledge might simply open a mostly closed wound. On the other hand, I also sensed, though at a much deeper level that was easier to block out, that my continued secrecy would come to no good in the end. But it was my own sudden taste for revenge against the bully who had not only kicked my dog, but who had also insulted my sense of the beautiful proprieties of the world, that should have disturbed me most. For now the fuse of that summer had been stretched across the ground and I stood like a match that the heat was trying repeatedly to ignite. I looked across the channel once more, and there was Edgar, looking back at me from the deck of his black gillnetter, as if he knew exactly how I felt and what that feeling would lead to. Our unspoken complicity was unsettling, but I couldn't deny the excitement of it either.

XIV

The heat intensified. Jay and I spent many lazy afternoons up at the Ashtons' swimming pool at the end of my street, revelling in the warm yet cooling rectangle of blue and talking constantly about comics. In that long-ago summer of 1976, with America celebrating its bicentennial and Jack Kirby finally back at Marvel, the comics world seemed like kids at the edge of a pool trying out dives: all headlong enthusiasm and creative daring. It didn't matter at all to Jay and me that we weren't Americans, or that we were perfectly content to be Canadians. Long before the age of twelve, a Canadian in the 1970s understood our country's relationship to our large brash neighbour. That is, we were paradoxically insignificant and superior, and so we could enjoy all of America's exciting cultural output while standing safely to the sidelines of its violence. It wasn't at all lost on us that Thomas Plum was living inside the tower of our town clock because he hadn't been able to stay safely on the sidelines in his own country.

The summer sailed gloriously on in one respect, and tensely on in another. The American TV, film and comics that constituted most of our entertainment made us raptly passive, while the local politics, at least for me and those in my neighbourhood close to the waterfront, thrust us into the centre of sometimes disturbing action. The stillness of the one world would eventually be revealed in stark contrast with the fury of the other, just as the corn ripening in the fields all around town stood at once separate from and part of the fierce motion of the salmon schools rushing in from the ocean to clog the Fraser's muddy mouth.

The heat and the sun became as constant as the rains in autumn. Each day shimmered, and we could almost hear the blackberries fattening on the thick bushes bunched like bison and the cherries and apples turning colour on the abandoned orchards all over the neighbourhood. The blue-joint grass in the vacant lots, waist-high now, swelled and waved and whispered like the sea, and we waded in, barefoot, bare-chested, wearing only cut-off jeans, Scooter moving as invisibly and slowly as a sturgeon somewhere at our sides. On the far side of the sea, on dry land again, we'd walk through waves of heat, past Thomas Plum suntanning outside the clock tower, which was as strange as seeing Abraham Lincoln suntanning, and on to the Daisy Dell, which used to be the Dairy Dell (no one ever explained the name change) where we'd buy our pop and chocolate bars before slowly reversing our steps and landing safely inside the Haunted Bookshop.

Mr. Edison had no air conditioning in the place, so the door was always propped open with an outdated textbook and a couple of large fans whirred like grasshoppers from opposite corners. Now, when Jay and I lounged under the shelf to read *Archie*s and Gold Keys, it almost seemed that the comics melted before our eyes just like the Pep-Chews and Kit-Kats in our hands if we didn't read them quickly enough.

Every day, with a kind of frantic anxiety that was hard to differentiate from his usual frantic enthusiasm, Jay would check to make sure that the copy of *The Fantastic Four* #1 was still hanging in its prominent place on the wall of honour above Mr. Edison's broad and, in the heat, gargoyle-still figure. Every day, Jay was relieved and surprised, for he was convinced that Jack Kirby's much-heralded return to Marvel would lead to a mad rush on everything Kirby had ever done. Yet quite the opposite was true, a fact that Jay eventually had to face.

One afternoon, when I stopped in the shop for a half-hour before continuing on with my paper route, I found Jay and Mr. Edison in deep discussion, almost bordering on argument.

"It's never the drawing," Mr. Edison said, turning the comic on the counter back to face him. "No one can draw like Kirby. Nobody fills the page or the panel with so much energy. I can't say anything against the artwork. But the writing, that's something else. The dialogue is . . . well, it's awkward."

"Come on, Lari, you don't think that?" As he often did when excited, Jay took his Gilligan hat off and worked it like bread dough in his long-fingered hands. "How's he going to talk about gods and myths without using . . . without at least trying to . . . without . . ."

Mr. Edison (unlike Jay, I never felt confident enough to call our mentor by his first name) unfurled his thick forearms and leaned forward with a mad glint in his pale eyes. "Exactly. How's he going to do it without sounding just a little . . . I won't say silly, but strained?"

Just then, the little bell over the door tinkled and we were all smote with a wave of marijuana fumes.

"No way, not when you've been at it, Nick. You know the rules."

"Give me a break, Lari. There's no one in here. I'll leave if one of the old biddies shows up."

Nick's expression and manner, so respectfully on the edge of mockery, won Mr. Edison over. Or else the argument with Jay was of greater import to him at that moment. Softly, he said, "You know how much I like the Fourth World stuff. This is just the same territory, but not as good."

When Nick passed behind me and hung his head like a bloodhound's beside Jay's to look at the comic, the pot smoke felt like a hand on the back of my neck.

"How can you say that?" Jay spluttered. "It's just the first issue. He has to set everything up. He can't give us the best stuff all at once."

Mr. Edison scowled. "I do know how comics work, Jay. I've been reading them for a long time."

"Ah, Kirby's new one," Nick said, his voice drifting like a wisp of smoke inside a fog. "He's losing touch a bit. Still a master of composition, though."

THE MARVELS OF YOUTH

"What do you mean, losing touch?" In his anger and bewilderment, Jay had dropped his hat on the floor, where it lay like the last blossom of some Amazonian plant. "Don't you wonder about the possibility that some superior race visited earth thousands of years ago? Doesn't the line, 'The gods are coming back,' raise the narrative stakes about as high as they can go?"

Nick's laugh was like Fat Freddy's cat stretching. "Is he still on that god trip? He ought to put his feet on the ground for a while."

Mr. Edison thrust his hand up like a cop halting traffic. Like me, he must have sensed just how upset Jay had become. "Of course you have to wonder about it. You have to think about these things, especially if you're an artist. I guess what I'd say is, even with his faults, Kirby's a risk-taker. He's ambitious. I'll always respect that. Better to fail than not even to–"

"Ike Harris turns out to be 'Ikaris'?" Nick looked up from the coloured page, pushing his brown bangs back. Then he dropped a hand on Jay's shoulder. "I sure wouldn't risk that one."

Jay knocked the hand away. "Yeah, well, Kirby isn't a head case. He isn't stoned all the time."

"Hey," Nick said in his lazy mock-offended tone before sobering up slightly. "I wish I could afford to be. Funds are so low I might even have to deckhand on my uncle's boat next opening. Nothing I like more than listening to old Greeks cursing their luck. Like Hurry, just now. He was really ripping into Vicky. I had to get out of there."

Mr. Edison exhaled heavily. "So I take it you won't be buying anything today? At least Jay and Sean are willing to open their wallets."

I heard my name as if from across a field, for just the idea of Hurry arguing with his wife still made me anxious. Now that I knew, or thought I knew, who'd she'd been with that night on the wharf, I couldn't be certain of the nature of her relationship with my brother. After all, Kirkhoff seemed to me to be the very bottom of the barrel, and I knew how attractive Dan was to the opposite sex. Yet I had allowed myself – or allowed the summer and its languorous seductive pleasures – to distract me from such worrying concerns.

Nick's voice at my ear brought me back, more violently than its softness should have. "He's not too happy with your brother, either, from what I could gather. Just what has Danny been up to now?"

Jay, obviously exasperated by the turn the conversation had taken, started to talk about Kirby again, but the little bell tinkled once more. An elderly man stepped inside and headed straight to the tall shelves of Louis L'Amour and Zane Grey paperbacks opposite. Mr. Edison put a finger to his lips to shush Jay, and then calmly asked us how many copies of the new Kirby comic we wanted. Almost simultaneously, he looked at Nick, wrinkled his nose and nodded toward the door.

Jay laid a two-dollar bill on the counter. "Eight."

Mr. Edison's caterpillar eyebrows lifted. "That many?"

"Everything Kirby does is going to increase in value."

Jay's petulant tone only made Mr. Edison smile. "I never argue with money," he said. "But how are you ever going to save up enough for the *FF* #1 if you buy eight copies of Kirby's new titles?"

"I'm not." Jay bent down as if punched in the side and scooped up his hat. He positioned it on his large skull with both hands as if he was gripping a steering wheel. "It'll be long gone before I even get close to that amount."

"Oh I don't know," Mr. Edison said, his tone deflated. "It's been here quite a while. Not that many collectors are willing to spend that kind of money these days." He looked at me. "You've been awfully quiet. Are you wanting multiples too?"

I wasn't as excited about Kirby's return to Marvel as Jay was, but I had great respect for my friend's taste and collecting acumen. Without his example, it never even would have occurred to me to speculate on the future value of comics. I would have just bought them and read them until their covers came off.

I put my own two-dollar bill on the counter, but had enough independence and self-respect to ask for six instead of eight. With the two quarters of change a little cool from the till in my moist palm, I decided that the time had come to finish my route.

THE MARVELS OF YOUTH

All was quiet at the pool hall. At her desk, Mrs. Hurry didn't look out the window into the street, nor did a face appear in the open window on the second floor. Up the block toward the river, the bell hose for the gas pumps dinged, once for the front wheels and once again for the back. I anticipated the second sound perfectly, for I knew by long experience exactly how much time that tiny interval of silence lasted. Caught there almost lovingly by Time in one of its million insignificant guises – as in those seconds when a too-ripe blackberry falls off its stem to the dusty dike, or when a salmon's gills open and close in slow succession in the unfamiliar element of the air, or when my parents' three quick goodbye kisses counted out their coming absence from my life – I stared at the row of empty shops across the street, unpopulated with human custom, and then, at the striking of the second bell, thrust the cold coins into my pocket and carried on.

XV

The union strike vote was held in the large net shed of the upper government wharf on a black silken evening with the orange wharf lights as soft as the candle glow in a Japanese temple. At least a hundred men, mostly middle-aged and older, crowded elbow to elbow together on the well-worn cedar planks outside the open net shed door, their cigarette smoke thick as salmon milt, their grizzled and heavily bearded faces rigid at the jawline, their black skullcaps like ashes blown off a bonfire of the driftwood they'd brought home all season.

On a wooden fish box as long and wide as a coffin stood the president of the United Fishermen and Allied Workers Union, a giant of a man, dark-skinned, ink-eyed, so clean-shaven that I thought I could see blood through his cheeks. Of mixed heritage – with a Greek father and a Coast Salish mother – the president commanded respect right across the industry, even though his political beliefs were mostly dismissed as either extreme or crackpot. As proud of their working-class status as most fishermen were in the 1970s, few, including my father, brother, uncles and cousins, ever considered communism to be a better option than capitalism. But the union president had run in provincial elections on the communist ticket, and he spoke against the "bosses" with thundering and credible authority.

"They're trying to screw us again," he shouted. "We know it, and they know it. The only question is, do we have the balls to call their bluff? Jesus Christ, on what they're offering for the Adams, you can barely cover expenses for the gas you'll burn."

He paused to let his gaze settle on every corner of the crowded wharf. When he resumed, his voice was lower but no less firm. "It's simple. I've been all up and down the coast this week, and guys aren't happy. But it's in our hands to do something about it. We're not just going to roll over and accept their latest bullshit offer. And there's no way in hell we're going to sit back while a bunch of scabs come up with their own goddamned outfit." He gave a snort of laughter. "The Pacific Gillnetters Association. What the fuck's an association? A fancy word for company men, that's all that is. Brothers, even the kids around here can tell a slimy from a sockeye. I don't have to tell you this, but as soon as you think you're too good for the next guy, as soon as you think you can make it on your own, then the companies have got you by the balls. I know I don't have to ask for your support on this. Most of you have fished these waters too many times before. But I just wanted you to hear it from me that, everywhere I go, we're united, we're strong. We're ready to shut the whole coast down if we have to."

The black gumboots shifted on the planks. The fiery ends of a few cigarettes plunged through the dim light into the inky current below. Keith and I, seated out of sight on a flat, wooden net-mending wagon behind a tall black piling, grinned at each other. It was after dark on a summer night; the tension around us was more exciting than worrying; and we had the added thrill of knowing that we weren't supposed to be present.

The fishermen didn't form a line so much as they gathered like salmon at a fish ladder up the valley, somehow managing to enter the net shed individually to place their vote in yet another wooden fish box. Near us, I heard a man say, "If it lasts more than a week, it'll hurt us more than help us." Another voice replied, "Oh I don't know, depends on the sort of offer we can force out of them. As long as there's two cents more before the Adams really get here."

I knew about the Adams River run of sockeye, the largest return of salmon to the Fraser River, that happened once every four years. The anticipation around it made everyone in town look more often toward the sea. Boats that had gone north to the Skeena or west to Ucluelet and Bamfield suddenly returned, and fishermen that hadn't been seen in months appeared in the grocery stores, loading up on food and ice for the expected long, hot hours of labour ahead. Even Keith's father, who was away so often that he'd become almost a mythical figure, raced home for the Adams run. When those sockeye hit the Fraser, a man's living for the entire year, and his ability to withstand the following lean years, could be made if his luck held out.

Under the constellations, as close and heavy as lit iron candelabra, the fishermen slowly dispersed. Even my brother, one of the few younger men in attendance, wore a resolved, almost grim expression as he walked with our father onto the dike.

"I'd better get going," I said.

Looking the other way, over my shoulder, Keith pointed. "Isn't that Edgar?"

I turned and saw the familiar char-black boat gliding along the channel in the faint glow of the far wharf lights, Bullet stiff in the bow like a figurehead.

"Doesn't he vote?" Keith asked. When I said I didn't know, he added, "Maybe he's a scab."

"I doubt it," I said, but without real conviction. If anyone seemed less likely to participate in any sort of group action, I couldn't imagine who that person might be. Yet it was just as difficult to picture Edgar crossing a picket line. Though he stood apart from the town and the fishery, he was, in essence, the town and the fishery.

I ran alongside the main net shed, but before I could even reach the gravel dike, I heard my brother's raised voice.

"This is all because of Hurry, isn't it? You'll question everything I do because you're that worried about his opinion? It matters so much more to you than your own son's? Stop and think about that. You care so much about that greedy old bastard's opinion that you'll believe I'm capable of anything. What if I asked you the same question? How would that make you feel?"

The breeze, blowing from the west, gusted the rich elixir of ripening cherry and blackberry in my face. A tomcat crept out of the tall grass of the roadside vacant lot and sat in the fringe of the streetlamp's glow to lick its paws. I could hear the bootsteps ahead of me still crunching the gravel, so I moved forward cautiously.

"I'm a scab who sleeps with married women. All right. You've done a great job, then. Agh, why should I keep my voice down? You scared some useless old drunk of a wharf rat's going to think badly of you now?"

The bootsteps stopped. I could see their two figures in the streetlamp's glow, etched like iron weathervanes in a dead calm. My father's voice was much lower, but I thought he said, "You'd better watch how you talk to me." At first, when he lifted his arm, I flinched, but then saw that he was only taking a drag on his cigarette.

"I'll tell you what," Dan said, his arms loose at his sides. "Let's put your mind at ease. Then I'll stay right out of your hair, okay? And you stay out of mine. She was in trouble and she needed my help, right? Money and sympathy, got it? She wouldn't tell me who the father was, but the bastard refused to have anything to do with it. I'm her friend. She needed help. Even if she wasn't my friend, I'd have helped. That's the point, isn't it? That's what you're so worried about? My values. Whether I'm a good person. It's like you don't even live in this town, or you live with your eyes closed. A good person? Here? What makes you think that Hurry's a good person? How do you think he made his money?"

The tomcat suddenly appeared in the middle of the street, as clearly visible in the light as if it was the middle of the day. Orange fur like wax paper barely covered his skeleton.

"Or Tanner next door. Try looking there if you want to find a scab. In fact, just walk up and down the street and pay attention. You think Vasilakis's wife wears a veil all the time because she's grieving? You think Stevie's bruises are all from the ring?"

My father tossed the cigarette onto the gravel and started to walk away. But Dan continued, his voice growing edgier.

"Just ask Mrs. Hatt about your own father sometimes. You should hear what she has to say on the subject of him. She calls him Bluebeard. Ha! At least I *like* women."

My father stopped dead, but didn't turn. I couldn't see Dan move, but I imagined him trembling, because even from my position thirty yards back I knew how angry my father had become. Then the tomcat, who had also been still, started to walk across the light. I counted the seconds in time to the silent fall of his paws. By the time the cat had vanished into the darkness on the other side of the street, my father had begun to walk away again. Much to my relief, Dan didn't follow or shout after him. Instead, he rubbed his face with one hand in a semicircle from temple to temple, and then, dropping down to the street, headed purposefully toward town.

I stayed in the shadows until he was gone, and then hurried home. My father, as I expected, had gone into the backyard, likely to make a fire. Choosing caution over curiosity, and needing to process what I had just heard, I slipped into the house.

I said a quick and furtive greeting to my mother in the kitchen, and then entered my bedroom and oriented myself with the familiar loved objects – the manual typewriter on my desk, the sheet of doodled-on foolscap torn off the bookshop counter and taped to my wall, the lampshade with the image of the tall ships, the shelf of comics, the desk with the mint copy of *Eternals* #1 unopened on the surface, the bed covered with a quilt patterned in colours of rust and the deep blue sea.

Still dazed with unexpected knowledge, I threw myself on the bed and lay on my back, gazing at the cracked ceiling. As boys in small towns went, I wasn't exactly street-smart, but my naivety had its limits. That is, I understood what "being in trouble" meant for a woman, even if I had absolutely no idea of the ramifications of that particular situation. Hurry's wife had become pregnant, and not by her husband – that much I grasped. But that my brother needed to give her money and sympathy wasn't something I quite followed, nor did I understand why she couldn't identify Kirkhoff as the father. For I couldn't imagine the guilty party being anyone else, despite what my brother's other revelations should have taught me about the duplicitous nature of appearances as they pertain to human behaviour. That Mr. Vasilakis, for example, might be physically abusive to his family, or that Keith's father might be a scab, seemed truths that needed greater evidence before I'd accept them, whereas I believed Kirkhoff was guilty because I had been a witness not only to his involvement with Hurry's wife but also to his general foul nature. For in my innocence, I couldn't connect evil to friendliness or popularity. As for my grandfather's mysterious wrongdoings, since he had died before I was born, I couldn't even begin to assess the fairness of the accusation. But I both saw and felt how the words had struck my father, and that was upsetting enough for me to shelve those particular intimate speculations in light of all the other unwelcome news.

By the time my mother knocked on the door and came in, asking me if I wanted to have tea out in the yard, I had resolved myself into such a state of confusion that all I wanted to do was fall asleep and wake to a cleaner, more clarified world of coloured images in panels and chlorinated rectangles of water and old men and old women without histories walking slowly through the songbird-shadowed streets. It was the dream, of course, of a child, but does that childhood dream ever cease to hover before us? I closed my eyes then, and the dark over the river and the town was the same dark over the human heart and between the galaxies. Even as I fell asleep, a part of me, the part already stepping toward the next stage of life, knew that the darkness would never really dissipate, but would remain in shifting shades, like a ground mist, even in the fullness of summer's carnival brilliance.

XVI

I reached into one of the cardboard boxes and pulled out the entire nineteen-issue run of Jack Kirby's *The Eternals*. On the top of the stack, as expected, I found six mint copies of issue #1 in protective Mylar sleeves. These comics hadn't been looked at in over forty years, and I wondered, as I began to flip through them, if my fingerprints still remained on the covers. Or perhaps Mr. Edison's were there on the edges, from when, with a bemused expression, he counted out the six copies as the radio sang softly behind him and a beam of sunlight played through the plate-glass window, casting the battered copy of Christopher Morley's novel into a bright relief that would last for hours rather than years. Somewhere, that worn, jacketless edition of *The Haunted Bookshop* probably still made its silent and inviolable way through the world, for hardcover books, unlike comics, rarely get destroyed.

Meanwhile, outside in the great world of event and consequence, cases of the deadly coronavirus were on the rise, and parents had become increasingly concerned about sending their children back to school. But significant numbers of people, especially in the United States (and including its president), believed the health risks had been greatly exaggerated and that the measures taken to control the spread of the virus were an infringement on personal liberties.

I knew as much about the virus as I had known about the world of adult news in 1975, but I did what I had always done: I acted on faith, believing in a firm division between reality and fantasy even as I acknowledged the seductive appeal of the latter. Who doesn't want to believe that everything is all right? But I wondered, as I checked eBay to see what ballpark value had been placed on copies of *The Eternals* #1, if perhaps the movement toward fantasy in the world of entertainment simply reflected the same desire to escape the reality of empirical evidence rampant among so many politicians.

I didn't wonder long, distracted as I was by the prices of my six old comics – between two hundred and one thousand dollars depending on various minutiae of what constitutes "valuable" condition. For the truth was, I couldn't afford to be a fantasist. Just like Jack Kirby, who never escaped the fear of running out of work and therefore money, I had to face the real world of getting and spending. But unlike Jack Kirby, I had to do so during a global pandemic, and alone.

Early on in Akira Kurosawa's *Seven Samurai*, there's a scene where the aging lead samurai explains to his young would-be apprentice what he can expect from life. The dreams of youth don't materialize, he says, and you find that your hair has turned grey, that your parents are dead and that you're all alone. The actors in the scene – samurai and village farmers – all look down for several seconds in silence, and the viewer feels the full weight of the human condition settle like a tide of ash over everything. I didn't know if the films the Disney Corporation had made out of Kirby's comic book creations contained such scenes, but I didn't need to know. I needed to know only how much money I could expect for my *Eternals* on the open market because money was draining out of my bank account and not even the federal government's benefit programs could stem the flow. The time had come to visit another comic shop.

But the memory of watching *Seven Samurai* wouldn't let me stay in the present, nor would the musty smell of the cardboard box and its other less-than-mint contents. For my childhood years were as much defined by the movies as by comic books, and I had to accept that I was no different than the escapists of the age, for what is the past but a fantasy that borrows from reality to weave its cold magic?

I had never known Stevie to come to our house before, and though his visit was for an entirely innocent and delightful reason, I could no longer look at him without seeing blood and bruises, even though they weren't there.

As a champion boxer, he rarely got hit hard in the face, and besides, amateurs always wore protective headgear. Physically, Stevie resembled the young Elvis and moved like the young Ali – lean, supple, tightly muscled, with his crewcut dark hair and large eyes and high cheekbones, he always made me think of a clean-cut greaser, mostly because he preferred to wear blue jeans and plain white T-shirts. But Stevie was serious about his sport, so you'd never find a pack of Marlboros rolled up inside his sleeve. All that ever dangled from between his cherry-red lips was a long stalk of feathery bluejoint grass plucked from the vacant lot beside his house.

He stood at our side door, on the top step, moving the stalk easily from one side of his mouth to the other with his tongue and then taking the grass down between two fingers to ask if I wanted to go to the drive-in.

"I just got my license," he explained, beaming. "And I promised Theo that the first thing I'd do was take him to the movies." His tone saddened. "He really misses the old theatre."

That wasn't news to me, as I remembered seeing Theo standing outside the building's boarded-up entrance, staring into the streaky strip of ticket-booth glass, on more than a few occasions. I'd done so myself, until the sense of lost wonder just became too depressing to face.

"Why don't you see if Keith wants to come? We'll leave from my place in half an hour."

"What's the movie?"

Stevie stuck the stalk of grass into his mouth again, his grin even wider. "What difference does it make?" he said.

THE MARVELS OF YOUTH

A half-hour later Keith and I sat in the back seat of the Vasilakises' rattly Chrysler, with Stevie casually slouched at the wheel and Theo sitting far up on the passenger seat beside him as if the movie was already playing through the windshield.

Twenty minutes of driving down narrow roads between acre after acre of head-high cornstalks as the day itself began to slide its curtain aside to feature the night brought us to the drive-in on the outskirts of town. Three dozen cars crammed together, all pointing the same way, like so many salmon schooling for their inland journey, and a giant screen – dark now – loomed over the landscape like one of Kirby's celestial monoliths. The scent of ripening corn that had been flowing through the open windows of the Chrysler was swept under by the more intoxicating aroma of buttered popcorn. Right away, Keith announced that he was going to the concession stand. I decided, of course, to go with him.

"Get a big tub of popcorn," Stevie said, handing us a two-dollar bill. "And an Orange Crush and some red Twizzlers for Theo."

The buttery air flowed silken and warm, alive with concealed images. The sun had dropped below the horizon and a pale bicep of moon flexed over the shadowy cornfields. Music played from various car radios, punctuated by laughter and low voices, as Keith and I walked on the beaten grass between the parked vehicles. All of them had wires hanging from the driver's-side windows connecting the speakers to the speaker posts, making the whole area look like some sort of neonatal ward for one of the alien pods that might show up in a grainy late-late feature.

But as soon as I saw my brother's El Camino and the two figures nestled together on the front seat, all my delicious anticipation drained away, replaced with the by-now familiar tension. Somehow, I knew that the woman laughing was Mrs. Hurry, and at the same time I understood that my brother was a liar. Friendship and support didn't mean going to the movies – going to the movies, past a certain age, meant a great deal more than watching the images on the screen. But what upset me most was Dan's brazen disregard for appearances. His car, after all, was the most recognizable in town, and the drive-in was hardly an inconspicuous rendezvous place. Might that still mean, then, that his relationship with Mrs. Hurry was as innocent as he claimed?

When the laughter stopped, and the bodies had moved so close together as to be one dark shape, I had my worrying answer. Quickly, I veered away in another direction to avert Keith's notice, and tried to forget what I'd seen. But all through the movie – which turned out to be an exciting spaghetti western – I kept playing another film in my mind, a docudrama that depicted the breakdown of two families. Not even Theo's frequent, silent bouncing up and down as the huge horses galloped toward the very edges of the darkened cornfields distracted me from the hard truth that my brother couldn't be trusted. It was as if the salt of the gathering sea to the west had filled my mouth and drowned the summer night's more appetizing flavours. Every parked car except ours seemed to shelter an unpleasant reality, made all the more sordid and grim by the majesty of the whitening moon over the vast screen of shifting kaleidoscopic colours.

Driving home in the shimmering darkness, the Chrysler's headlights dusty with the gravel-wake of all the vehicles on the road ahead of us, I understood that I wasn't going to be a passive participant in the summer's cruel unfolding, but rather an agent of the events that had to happen if I was ever going to rid myself of worry and return for good to the carefree patterns of bookshop, fields, reading and river that had defined my life to this point. I knew who had been with Mrs. Hurry that rainy night at the wharf, and who was the father of her aborted child; it was time that somebody else knew as well.

I was still only eleven years old, and cautious by nature. The thought of approaching someone directly with my incendiary information was too intimidating, and so, falling back on instinct, I struck upon the idea of sending Hurry an anonymous note. Of course, I realized that doing so would betray the trust that his young wife had placed in me, but I now resented – indeed, almost hated – Mrs. Hurry for her cavalier relationship with my brother. By going straight to Hurry with my revelation about Kirkhoff, I hoped to divert the old Greek's attention from my family altogether.

But each time I drafted a note on my typewriter, I couldn't see myself delivering it, in part because imagining Hurry's reaction terrified me. There was no telling what he might do. But a note couldn't be simply slipped through the pool-hall mail slot, for Mrs. Hurry might intercept it, and obviously she'd recognize me as the sender straight away.

So I delayed and plotted as the long days of midsummer came and went and the sunset-bloody month of August hovered above the massing schools of the great Adams River run on the near horizon. At home, my father calmly mended his one spare net in anticipation of the frantic fishing ahead, but I could tell from the number of cigarettes he smoked and from the way he massaged his temples and stared off into space that he was worried. The likelihood of a strike increased as August's promised bounty approached, and the creaking of the winch down at the waterfront and the revving of boat and pickup truck engines sounded more aggressive than usual. It was as if some great invisible machine was being tightened in readiness for an unpredictable conflict.

Meanwhile, the river opened again, and I went out with my father to the familiar drift. All the usual fishermen were there, including Edgar on his unadorned gillnetter that looked as if it had been dipped in tar. Its oily blackness against the turquoise sky and burnished steel water was always more comforting than alarming. But the general atmosphere, even on a slack tide, was tense. The salmon had largely vanished, and we were lucky to pick up two or three a set, a situation that naturally put even more pressure on the month ahead. So I wasn't surprised when, after hauling in a fifty-five-pound white spring, my father heaved it into a side locker. "That's one for Mrs. Nakatani," he said with palpable relief. Like most fishermen, my father conducted a few private sales, not usually because the money was better, but more as a symbol of independence from the canneries and as an inherited communal act. Mrs. Nakatani, I knew, always wanted the giant white springs, and paid almost double for them what the canneries paid.

The sweltering day ground on at thirty degrees with the surface of the river like a blinding mirror. In the heavy silence, every dog bark in town and every heron croak in the marsh sounded like gunshot. I looked downriver and saw Dan, standing shirtless in the stern of the *Driftwood*, his T-shirt wrapped around his head, shielding his eyes as he gazed toward town. There seemed to be nothing between him and the water. His vulnerability saddened me, for he and my father were no longer on speaking terms. But at the same time, I found the direction of my brother's gaze annoying, believing that he was testing the limits of human vision in order to see Mrs. Hurry at the pool hall cash register, pushing back her astrological charm bracelets with a suggestive shiver of her finely haired arms. For the hundredth time, I vowed to deliver my anonymous note, but then the champagne bubble–froth of a salmon striking right at the cork line distracted me, and I let the heat immerse my consciousness again.

Time was never slower than on a midday summer slack tide. When the packer appeared on the main river to the north, it seemed to take hours to reach us, crawling like some clumsy beetle through a pool of molasses. On deck, Vic and his deckhand Rosie stood as still as bulrushes as the packer idled into position alongside our boat.

"Ready for school yet, young fella?" Vic said, but even his characteristic good nature was dampened by the general anxiety surrounding the fishery. He took less of an amused interest from my scowl and head shake than usual, and immediately turned his attention to the few sockeye that my father had flung onto the deck.

"Slim pickins, eh, Hector?" He pierced the head of a salmon with his pick and deftly swung the fish into the aluminum scale box with a clatter. "Same everywhere today."

My father asked for any news about the canneries reacting to the threat of a strike, a question that only lowered the packer's spirits even further.

"Nope. Haven't heard a whisper." He looked down at his gumboots, glistening and black and reaching almost halfway up his squat figure. Then, as if he'd been searching for any sign of hope, he suddenly smiled and pointed downriver to where Edgar's boat rested against the skyline like a sated blowfly. "The only one feeling good about the state of things is Edgar. You heard about his new boat?"

THE MARVELS OF YOUTH

My father and I looked at each other. Vic might as well have asked if we'd heard about Edgar's new wife.

"He's paid some builder out of Steveston to get a start on it. Not anybody I know. Brand spankin' new engine, the whole shebang."

Rosie, who almost never spoke, who just stood by the scale box like a Viking who'd thrown his armour away and was ready to sleep until the next battle, became briefly animated. "It's those brothers of his. Down from up north, filling his head with big ideas. I don't trust them myself. Not their money being spent."

My father's face darkened. "What has he paid already? Any idea?"

"Not really," Vic said. "But it's got to be several thousand. Work's supposed to start next week, so I hear."

My father nodded and, more aggressively than usual, began to wash the blood and slime from our stern with the packer's hose.

An hour later, the tide began to move, and we drifted slowly downriver into a heat-haze clamped like a vise over the estuary. In order to keep the white spring as fresh as possible, we soaked a burlap potato sack in the current and covered the fish with it. By late afternoon, with our latest set a "skunk" (no catch at all), my father decided that we'd better take the spring in and get some supper before heading out again for the dark set.

The harbour was empty of other vessels and the smell of oil and creosote hung heavily in the air. It was so still that I thought I heard the eyeballs turning in the heads of the two bone-white gulls watching our every move from the tops of two pilings. And when I tied us to the wharf, the ropes in my hands were so sun-baked that dry shreds came off into my palms like heavy dust.

On the dike, the chemical smell dissolved into the sweeter scent of ripening blackberries and plums and the earthy musk of the bluejoint grass in the vacant lots. But then my father shifted the great salmon from one hand to the other, and a wash of blood and slime – the defining mixture of that time and place – flowed so heavily into my face that it almost swept the bangs out of my eyes.

"That's a real beauty," my mother said, coming down the side steps to look at the fish laid out in the thin shade created by the overhanging eavestroughs of the house. "I'll give Mrs. Nakatani a call right away."

The flies and the wasps had already started to hover over the salmon – which looked like nothing less than a thigh covered in chain mail – so my father found another burlap sack, laid it over the fish and soaked it with the garden hose. Already, through the open kitchen window, I could smell potatoes and eggs frying in the pan. Excitedly, I realized that if I ate quickly, I might be able to get a swim in at the Ashtons' pool before going back out on the river.

Two hours later, when I returned, the towel around my shoulders almost dried again and an invisible pungent coating of chlorine covering me from my wet scalp to my dried bare feet, I was surprised to see that the spring salmon was still there in the spreading strip of shade.

My mother said, "I haven't been able to get hold of her, so I just keep running the hose over the fish. But it's still drying out."

Frowning, she asked me to carry the salmon into the bathroom and to lay it in the tub.

"At least I can run the tap on it," she explained, "and it's a little cooler inside. Not much." As proof, she blew her damp black hair out of her eyes and wiped the sweat off her palms onto her apron in order to grasp the receiver of the phone. "I hope I get her soon."

But Mrs. Nakatani didn't answer, and I became aware, for the first time, of the severity of our economic life, and especially of the strain both my parents were under. One fish, one private sale, counted on but by no means guaranteed: such were the margins that my parents had lived with all of their lives, starting with their childhoods in the Great Depression. Perhaps that was why, on that early evening, as my father dozed fitfully on the living room couch and my mother, between frequent trips to the phone and to the bathroom to run the tap over the white spring, told me this story from her childhood. It was one of her earliest memories, and – I can see this more clearly now – it cast a darkness over her world, long before the war spread an even greater darkness like fresh blood from an old wound.

"I used to walk past this house on my way to school," she said. "An

Italian family lived there. Poorer than us, as they didn't speak much English yet. Their little boy – I guess he was three or four, just a few years younger than me – always came to the gate of their yard's iron fence – it was short, only a couple of feet high – to wave at me. He seemed, oh I don't know, to look forward to it. And I . . . well . . ."

She paused, and looked at me, her forehead and cheeks so damp with sweat that her pansy-sized eyes appeared oily. "I was what people called a pogey child, because my family always had to go on relief, and I got picked on because of it. When that happens, I guess it sort of makes you think less of yourself than you should. So this little boy – I suppose I liked his attention. I liked thinking that he admired me." She smiled and distractedly slid her thin gold wedding band up and down beneath her reddened knuckle. "He was a handsome little fellow. With a big round face, long blond curls and blue eyes – like a kind of baby angel you see in those old paintings. Not what you'd think an Italian child would look like. Most of the others in the neighbourhood were dark. Anyhow, he never spoke, just waved. A cute little boy, always wearing shiny black shoes and short pants and a sort of puffy shirt, like a blouse. My own private angel."

Her voice trailed off, and she stood up heavily from the kitchen table chair to go and check on the fish in the bathroom. Too impatient to wait, I followed her, and sat on the closed toilet lid as she knelt on the cracked linoleum tiles to turn on the tap.

"What happened to him?" I asked, the smell of river and blood again in my nostrils, as if I'd dived into a pool of it. As the tap water splashed over the solid slab of pewter flesh, my mother's cupped hands casting the liquid toward the great head with its one gaping black eye turned up to the ceiling, she continued, her back to me so that suddenly her voice was no longer softened by the congenital compassion in her face.

"One day he wasn't there. And even though it was just one day, I think I already knew. You see, it's what having so little does to you. You begin to believe that anything good just can't last. When he wasn't there, on the second morning – oh it's a strange thing – but something about the front of the house, how it was dark and closed, so opposite to his broad, bright, smiling face, told me that he was dead."

When she had spoken this last word, my mother stopped casting water from the stream under the tap. Her entire body went still.

"Death wasn't unusual then. I knew of many women who had lost babies. And, of course, my own mother had lost several, too, though I probably didn't know that at the time. Seeing a dead body wasn't unusual either. In those days, families had showings in their front parlours. Even the poorest families. A wreath would be put on the front door – black for an adult and mauve, I think it was, for a child – and anyone was welcome to come in and pay their respects."

The water kept streaming from the tap, and because the fish covered the drain, the water began to gather. But my mother paid no notice. Her voice was at once present and very far away.

"He had swallowed the lead from a pencil. Of all things. And it poisoned him. Even after the mauve wreath went up on the door, and the stream of men in black suits and women in black dresses and veils came and went, and all the neighbours, too, including my parents, I just couldn't bring myself to . . . maybe it was because I had heard the mother wailing from inside when I stood on the sidewalk, my hands on the cold iron of the top of the gate that I just couldn't open. I don't know. It all seemed so unfair. And stupid. Lead poisoning from a pencil. Not a disease, or being hit by a car – somehow those would have been easier to accept. Or at least that's what I must have told myself. Because, when you're as poor as we all were then, when you don't know when your next solid meal is going to come or when the landlord's going to raise your rent and force you to move on to an even more rundown house, you almost expect certain kinds of tragedies as a matter of course. Diphtheria, mumps, polio. They killed many children in those days. But I never heard of anyone else ever dying from lead poisoning. I felt that somehow the little boy's death, cruel as it was, was my fault, that because I needed him, you see, to feel just a little special, that I had brought such a terrible fate down on him."

Mechanically, my mother reached out and shut off the tap, but still she didn't turn or rise.

"I guess it was the guilt that finally made me go in. I wish I hadn't. Ever since that day, I haven't been able to bear the scent or sight of white calla lilies. They were all around his little casket. A heavy, heavy smell, thick as dirt. And though it was daytime, the parlour was lit with all these candles, so that the casket – it was a very nice one, and I imagine that the family must have gone into even more debt to afford it – gleamed with reflections.

"I never should have looked. He was in this dark suit that didn't quite fit him right, and his big blue eyes were closed and his curls had been slicked down with something. It was all wrong for him. Such a pretty, happy little boy."

She sighed deeply and at length, then placed both hands on the edge of the bathtub. "Not much bigger than this fish." Heavily, she pushed herself up into a standing position. With her back still to me, in almost a whisper, she added, "And just as dead."

Finally, she turned, herself again, and smiled. "That was such a long time ago. But it's funny the way some things stay with you. I'd better give Mrs. Nakatani another try."

After the phone call, which still did not succeed, and back at the kitchen table, I took a chance that my mother's confiding mood might have remained. I asked if Mr. Vasilakis was a violent man.

Her eyebrows lifted. "What do you mean?"

"It was just something Dan said. About Stevie's dad . . . that he hit him sometimes. And Mrs. Vasilakis too."

My mother looked beyond me, as if she could see through the wall to our Greek neighbours' house. "Your brother knows better than to spread gossip. Marina – Mrs. Vasilakis – hasn't had an easy life. But her husband isn't the reason for that."

I waited, the droning of blowflies on the windowsill and the ticking of the wall clock counting out the treacly seconds.

"Having a child like Theo. As loving as he is, it's very hard. I think sometimes it just becomes too much for her, loving him as much as she does and knowing what the world can be like, even for the strong and healthy. And, of course, she lived through the war, back in Greece."

In our household, I knew what any reference to "the war" meant:

unspeakable losses and suffering, so many that there was no need for further discussion. Consequently, my mother stopped fiddling with her wedding band and made yet another phone call to Mrs. Nakatani, this one, to my mother's obvious relief, a success.

"She'll be here in fifteen minutes. Sean, can you carry the fish into the kitchen? I'll lay down some newspaper. Oh, and I'd better get out the hand scale."

It was strange to struggle the slippery salmon out of the bathtub. I had to pull it close to my chest in a kind of awkward embrace before I could work almost my entire hand under one gill. The whole time, its smothering musk and silver-black colouring, once so comforting and familiar and ordinary, only put me in mind of the calla lilies and the lead poisoning of that long-vanished parlour in my mother's childhood. Even the salmon's wide-open, unseeing eyes, looking in opposite directions, were, for a few seconds, completely closed and yet still seeing whatever there is to see on the other side of measured time.

XVII

The hammering began the next afternoon, within hours of the bulldozer's arrival at the boarded-up cinema. On the mainland bank of the harbour, beside the main net shed on the upper wharf, construction began on the hull of Edgar's new gillnetter. But I didn't see him there. Instead, in the early after-supper hours, when the initial interest in the demolition of the old theatre had dissipated, he appeared amidst the splayed rubble of beams and plaster and tile and rusted plumbing, his head down, rummaging the way a seagull plucks at the intestines of a dead fish. Meanwhile, on the sidewalk where the ticket booth had been only hours before, Theo stood, tears streaming down his cheeks.

Keith and I, walking home from the candy store into the glaring new absence of building, which suddenly made the neighbourhood and the horizon larger, approached the mute boy cautiously. His hair, still not cut, spread unevenly and as thickly as molasses over his forehead and temples, and his bare legs and feet were pale and scratched red, probably because he'd been in the prickles of the blackberry bushes. He was blubbering, without sound, and tears dripped from his lashes and the end of his nose. I assumed he was so upset because he must have always imagined that the movies would start up again in the building, and I knew from his excitement at the drive-in just how much he loved the movies.

Of course, I felt sorry for him, but the faint buttery smell on the air – from decades of saturation into the wood and worn fabric and wallpaper – and the presence of Edgar, who had just vanished below the heap of rubble, attracted most of my attention.

"What's he doing?" Keith said, and slowly held a handful of chocolate-covered raisins out to Theo.

I shook my head. Nothing Edgar ever did seemed ordinary or predictable. Building a new boat on the eve of a strike, for example, was as unique as picking through the rubble of a demolished theatre.

The buttery sunlight drenched the new vacant space and all the surrounding ones, and the blue sky climbed away from the fresh openness like a gigantic screen against which some evening swallows performed their scissoring pirouettes and manoeuvres in pursuit of the termites rising dustily from the ruins.

The hour was strangely still, as if a projection had jammed. Other than the winch creaking down at the waterfront – some tardy fishermen changing nets – and a rustling of breeze in the tall grass, the only sound was of the occasional distant car, a sort of motherly hushing. Distracted by the altered perspective of the neighbourhood – for instance, I could now see the town clock a block to the west without the cinema in the way – I barely noticed that Edgar had risen from the rubble and staggered off, carrying something of obvious weight and bulk.

"What's he taking?" I asked, but Keith was busy picking up the raisins that Theo had let drop from his hand. "Come on," I said, and broke from the sidewalk into the razed lot, my eyes fixed on Edgar. He moved in a sort of crouch, like a hunchback with the abnormal growth in front, and, just like his old boat, his darkness seemed to leave behind a dark wake. Even at the height of summer, he wore a black skullcap, black boots and cotton work pants. The only concession he made to the heat was that he wore a bloodstained black T-shirt instead of a flannel plaid work shirt or, in the deepest cold of winter, a dingy green army surplus jacket.

THE MARVELS OF YOUTH

At the waterfront, Keith and I watched from the upper wharf as Edgar, on one of the lower floats, suddenly turned, a block of red at his chest startling us further into momentary silence. Then he straightened up fully with the bulky object and stepped across the gunwale of the first moored boat.

"It's a seat!" Keith cried out. "He took one of the seats!"

We rushed down the gangway to get a closer look as Edgar's boat slid into the channel and made a slow sweeping turn across the harbour. For half a minute, the cinema seat – a folding one, in two halves of crushed red with the black steel frame underneath – shone as vividly as the setting sun. It might have been my imagination, but I thought I caught a richer smell of butter on the briney air, just for a few seconds, while I stared at the seat propped up against the front of the cabin in the bow.

"What does he want to go and do a thing like that for?" Keith bent and picked up a chunk of bark from the float. Tossing it into the channel, he shouted, "You crazy bugger, Edgar!"

Only Keith's echoing voice returned over the water. Even Bullet, who had appeared in the bow to sniff at the strange new object, didn't bother to bark at the insult. As for Edgar, he remained at the deck wheel and simply lifted one arm in a mock salute. Though I couldn't see his thickly bearded expression, I knew he was grinning because, unless he was drunk, a grin was his only response to slander, whether it came from a boy or a man.

"Hey," Keith said, "we should get one of those for our tree fort."

It sounded like a great idea, except that, when we returned to the rubble, we found that the remaining chairs were still attached in rows far too heavy to shift, let alone pick up and carry. Edgar had picked out the one option, but we had no idea why. It wasn't as if the old seats had any value. Otherwise, the demolition crew or someone else would have taken them all away.

Up on the sidewalk, Theo was no longer alone. His mother, her face veiled as if with the charred embers of a backyard fire, stood motionless beside him. They might have been statues, the one carved off the other. I eventually realized that they faced the exact direction where the movie screen used to be. Perhaps Mrs. Vasilakis was describing invisible images to Theo, images that she knew he had loved. It was impossible to know from a distance, as I could neither hear her voice nor see her lips moving behind the veil. Or perhaps she was just as silent as her son, unable to alleviate his suffering with language. I couldn't forget what my mother had told me about Mrs. Vasilakis's difficult life – the final destruction of the theatre must have been just another hard example of the world's indifference to Theo's feelings.

For some reason, as I stared at them across the fifty yards of ruins and space, I saw another mother and son, a couple I had never actually seen before. It was as if I too was watching unreal but perfect images on a vanished screen, or rather one still distant shot from a silent film whose last nitrate copy was being eroded by the air right before my eyes. So when Mrs. Vasilakis took Theo by the hand, and they began to walk toward me, very slowly, like an image surfacing through chemicals in a darkroom, I had the sudden strange sensation that they were different people and that I had seen them before, in this exact spot. The feeling wasn't unpleasant, but it was unnerving, as if I stood inside one of the abandoned houses and awaited the embodiment of spirits approaching from the top of the staircase. For a few seconds, I even believed that Mrs. Vasilakis would lift her veil and I'd see another woman's face, and that Theo would look up into it with a love uncomplicated by the cruel dispensations of fate. In the last heat and light of a long summer day, I shivered with a knowledge that never fully reached me, until Keith's voice tore the gossamer between the worlds and the two figures descended into the tall grass shimmering like the sea around their sorrow-anchored house.

As still and silent as that evening had been, everything changed the next morning. The excitement of the massing Adams River run of sockeye filled the air, and a steady stream of pickup trucks, their beds heaped with tarp-covered nets, came and went from the government wharf. Hour after hour, the winch creaked and the boat engines roared, while the heavy metronome of the hammering of Edgar's new hull maintained a persistent rhythm.

But what should have been only excitement and industry was diluted by tension and anger. The canneries hadn't improved their offer, and so, with the membership's support, the union had called for strike action. When the river opened for fishing the following morning, most of the fishermen would form a picket blockade of boats just below the harbour, daring any scabs to cross it. Before then, however, in the early afternoon of the preceding day, confrontation was already inevitable on the government wharf.

Keith and I, drawn as boys always are to possible trouble, found ourselves lingering on the riverbank below the main net shed. The tide was low, so we pretended to ourselves that we were collecting empty beer and wine bottles out of the exposed muck. Every ten minutes, another three or four union fishermen appeared on the wharf, until a crowd of about forty had gathered, including my father, brother, uncle and cousins. But not, I noticed with mounting unease, Edgar or Keith's father.

A little farther along the bank, beyond a cluster of bulrushes resembling an armoury of old muskets, the clean white wood of Edgar's hull shone like a strip of moonlight on the dark river. On the dike above the hull, I saw Edgar standing with two older men whom I took to be his mysterious brothers. They were as dark but shorter than him, and dressed in the standard fishermen's garb of skullcaps, boots, cotton trousers and floater jackets. Yet there was something disturbing about them, about the way they slowly moved their arms and legs, as if trying desperately to untangle them from an invisible web. They seemed at once vulnerable and aggressive, as if the qualities of the fly and the spider had been mixed in each of their two bodies. I shuddered at the sight of them, for they threatened the sunlight that fell around them and their own flesh simultaneously. By comparison, Edgar never looked more comfortingly human. The trio, obviously deep in discussion, appeared oblivious to the growing tension on the wharf, and for a while I allowed myself to be distracted.

When I turned my attention back to the crowd of fishermen, I saw Keith scurrying up the nearby bank. His quick departure made no sense until I noticed a second group of fishermen – perhaps fifteen in total – loosely gathered so that they didn't even seem to acknowledge one another.

They stood on the dike, near the entrance to the wharf, and with a sinking feeling I saw that Keith's father was among them.

But I already knew, without even having to think about it, that the confrontation would be started by a different man, that it couldn't be anyone else who would attempt to walk through the union crowd to reach his boat moored on one of the floats below. In a begrudging way, I even admired his courage, for he took the shouts of "Scab!" and the shoves and the spits calmly, without any expression except perhaps the slightest tight smile, as he worked his way across the fifty feet of wharf until he stood freely at the top of the gangway, where he paused for a few seconds, and then, as if he couldn't help himself, turned and spat on the open planks behind him. As the shouts rose in volume, Kirkhoff allowed himself a broad smile, but only I could see it. And what I saw reminded me of my own capacity for hatred.

After all, I understood how much my own family had at stake in a strike. I understood, mainly from overheard conversations between my parents, about the importance of workers standing up for themselves, and together, as the only effective means of tempering the abuses of capitalism. But I also knew – in a much more visceral way, even if vaguely – that I hated Kirkhoff not just for his cruel kick at my dog and for his general air of unpleasantness, but mainly for his physical violation of Mrs. Hurry, his heavy, ugly, unquestioning sense of entitlement to the pleasures of her body, which was, in the most violent way, an attack on the sacred verities of my childhood.

By the time Kirkhoff had started up his boat, I had decided to ask Keith to deliver my anonymous note to Hurry. That way, my friend would know that I didn't hold him responsible for his father's disreputable behaviour, and Hurry would know that it wasn't my brother who'd been sleeping with his wife (even though I still had my doubts on that subject). Two birds with one stone, I thought with satisfaction, and turned to follow Keith onto the dike, where Edgar and his brothers – two stones and one bird – continued their intense and mysterious conversation.

XVIII

The deed was done. Now all I had to do was wait. Keith, delighted that I made no mention of his father, immediately offered to tell Hurry to his face whatever I wanted him to know. But I had come to cherish my secret, as if it was actually my own, and I was equally pleased by what I considered to be a more entertaining plan. Sending an anonymous note was just like lighting a long fuse to a stick of dynamite, except I couldn't be sure what kind of an explosion would follow. I didn't doubt that there would be one, so I made certain over the next few days to be at the bookshop or nearby as often as possible, which wasn't any kind of a hardship.

I was at the clock tower the next afternoon, listening to the shirtless Thomas Plum tell Nick all about his escape over the border into Canada.

"I've never been so lucky in my life," he started, leaning back against the door frame of the tower, hands clasped behind his head, his rib cage made more prominent by the position. "After I'd never been so unlucky. Anarchists! I still can't believe it. Canadian anarchists! A day and a half I crouched in those woods, smelling the pine sap and trying to work up the nerve to get my hair cut at the barber in Blaine. I kept kicking myself for being such an idiot. Why would a guy wait until he reaches the border before realizing he should probably not try to cross with hair down below his shoulders? And I figured the old bastard in the barbershop – he looked about ninety and was about as thin as a suspender strap – had turned his fair share of young scum like me in to the Feds. He probably had a direct phone line. I just couldn't bring myself to take the final plunge."

He reached down and grabbed his stubby brown beer bottle and took a long swallow. I tried to imagine him with hair down below his shoulders, but it was impossible to look past the shorter hair, long sideburns and full beard combination.

"What do you mean about being unlucky?" Nick asked from out of his usual cloud of pot smoke.

Thomas Plum grimaced. "Man, you Canadians just don't know how good you've got it. Probably haven't faced a draft since World War Two." He closed one grey eye against the sun, as if drawing a bead on an invisible target with an invisible weapon.

"I got a low number, man. One of the lowest. I'd be on the first fucking plane to the jungle, sure. Well, at least it made it easier to decide to get out of Dodge while the getting was good. It wasn't like I could wait around, hope for the war to end. But listen . . ."

He pointed the mouth of the bottle straight at us, sloshing a little beer on the pavement and almost losing his balance as he took a step forward.

"It's not like leaving your country is easy. It sure as hell ain't that. Like I keep saying, I'm a patriot. I love the good old U S of A. I love it enough to know that the government isn't the country, not even close. It's more of a feeling . . . like . . . like . . ."

Dreamily, but with a querulous tone, Nick asked, "What do you mean a low number?"

". . . like any other kind of love," Thomas Plum finished abruptly, gazing into the mouth of the beer bottle as if it was the end of a telescope. "Hey, man, did you notice?"

He stepped fully into the sunlight, and glowed as whitely as the hull of Edgar's new boat. With both eyes closed as he looked up, he said, "I got it working."

Like baby birds, Nick and I raised our heads in unison.

"Yeah?" Nick said. "It's not eight fifteen, morning or night."

"Come on, the hands are moving again. That's the main thing with a clock, man. What difference does the actual time make? It's the motion."

As I tried to puzzle out this curious idea, I heard raised voices from down the street.

"Uh oh." Nick dropped his roach to the sidewalk and pushed back his long hair with both hands. I couldn't imagine him trying to cross a border illegally either. "Sounds like Vicky's upset the old man again."

"Always been about the numbers," Thomas Plum muttered. "I should have seen it coming. A whole fucking childhood of clocks. Of course it would be a number that would get me. Ah well, it'll all come to the same sad end eventually. Five to one, baby, one in five, no one here gets out alive."

Hurry burst out of the pool hall and quickly looked up and down the street. From a distance, he appeared even smaller and older than he should have, but he still moved as swiftly as a crab scuttling out from under a lifted rock as he leapt forward into his beat-up pickup truck and slammed the door behind him, already reversing with a screech of tires. In seconds, he had raced toward the river and then turned toward the west, his truck rolling across the horizon like a billiard ball.

"Anyway," Thomas Plum said, "if you wait long enough, the time's going to be accurate eventually. Twice, in fact." He chuckled. "You just won't know when."

Nick looked at me, rolling his head to indicate that the American was well and truly sloshed. But Nick always loved to get Thomas Plum talking, so he asked him about the anarchists. I only half-listened, my eyes nervously on Hurry's truck until it disappeared. Why was he in such a rush to get to the western edge of town? There was nothing there but farm fields and Westham Island.

"Some big rally down from Vancouver. A whole shitload of freaks. So many that the cops showed up and all hell broke loose." Thomas Plum took a deep breath of immense satisfaction, as if memory was more of a scent than a thought. "The crowd did me a huge favour by crossing into the

States. The guards, of course, got all excited and left their booths. There was so much chanting and shouting of slogans going on, and music blasting out of transistors – I remember hearing Blood, Sweat and Tears. Yeah, I'm sure it was. I remember thinking it was like a welcome, you know, them being a Canadian band, I mean."

"Didn't they do that Jeremiah was a bulldog song?" Nick asked, winking at me.

"Nah, man, that wasn't them. And it isn't a bulldog either. It's a bull-*frog*."

Then the awareness hit me and, in truth, I felt sick. Kirkhoff lived on Westham Island. Easier access to poaching opportunities, my brother had once told me.

Thomas Plum pulled distractedly at his sideburns, as if they were caterpillars he couldn't quite remove. Then he burst out with a laugh.

"Three Dog Night. Ha! That's why you were thinking bulldog instead of bullfrog."

"So what did you do?" Nick asked, with a sudden legitimate interest.

"What would anybody do, man? I got right into the middle of all those beautiful Canadians and they carried me like a sweet tide right over the border. Then it was just a matter of avoiding the Mounties on the other side. But I'd been on the run for over a week by then, so I was pretty used to keeping a low profile."

He belched and the sound seemed to sober him up. He untied the red bandana from around his neck and mopped the sweat from his lean face. I half-expected the fabric to leave a bloody stain on his beard.

"It's a cold, cold city, Vancouver is. Unfriendly. There were times when I wanted to go home so badly that I almost began to think that fighting the Viet Cong would be better."

What if Hurry killed Kirkhoff? What if he shot him or stuck a knife in him? I hadn't really imagined anything as violent as murder, and all at once I realized just what a terrible thing I'd done.

"So why are you still here?" Nick said. "If Vancouver's so cold? The war's over, isn't it?"

THE MARVELS OF YOUTH

I couldn't tell if Thomas Plum had missed some sweat under his eyes or whether tears had dripped from his bottom eyelids. His Adam's apple was a stained burl of wood. "I can't do it, man. It's even harder in reverse. I even went back to the border crossing once. Had got myself a shave and a haircut and everything. Spruced myself right up. But there was one big problem."

"Yeah?" Nick said. "What was that?"

The American shrugged. "There weren't any anarchists around."

My brother's El Camino pulled up in front of the pool hall. A minute later, Mrs. Hurry came out and climbed into the passenger seat. Thomas Plum and Nick and the inaccurate clock above them dissolved to nothing. Standing in the full sun, I felt the heat close around me until I almost fainted. The hammer blows on Edgar's new hull kept raining down, just like the gunshots of the autumn hunters in the marsh. All at once, I could taste the violence I had initiated, the blood of it in the back of my throat as I swallowed, but I still didn't know what form it would take. Weakly, I climbed onto my bike and pedalled without enthusiasm to the bookshop.

"Here he is now," Mr. Edison announced, his broad face managing to be a blend of Buddha's serenity and Santa Claus's jollity. "We've been waiting for you."

Under the circumstances, his last sentence sounded more ominous than inviting, as if I'd been summoned to face a jury for my crime. Jay, standing at his usual place at the tall counter exactly opposite Mr. Edison, tried to play it cool, but the way he kept tapping the fingers of one hand on a thick envelope laid in front of him revealed his excitement.

"The Vengeance Squad is here," Mr. Edison said, reaching under the counter and placing a couple of bottles of pop on the surface. "This ought to be champagne, but I didn't think your parents would appreciate that." A little flustered, he took one of the bottles back and ducked out of sight. "I've got an opener down here somewhere."

"I haven't showed him yet," Jay said. "I only took a quick peek myself to make sure I got all the pages in the right order. You know, the numbers."

He kept shuffling his feet and drumming the manila envelope with his fingers.

Once Mr. Edison had opened both bottles and poured a little fluid from a silver flask into his coffee mug, he said, "To the first issue of *Cosmos*. And to many more!"

We all took a drink, and then Jay slid a stack of our very own comic out of the envelope. It was much smaller than a Marvel or DC comic – about a third of the size and with half the number of pages – and entirely in black and white, but when I held one in my hands and stared at the cover, and then looked inside at the title page and saw my own name there – as co-creator of Blackstar and creator and writer of the Vengeance Squad – I felt a thrill that put all thought of Hurry and Kirkhoff and my own guilt completely out of my mind.

"It looks terrific, boys. Congratulations!" Mr. Edison's powdery blue eyes trembled a little as he glanced up from the copy in his hands. Then, quietly to Jay, he said, "The collages came out great. You really did something there."

Jay shrugged. He hardly seemed to listen as he pored over each page, an intensity on his face more fierce than joyous. Later, he would tell me that he was disappointed with some of his compositions, that they looked too amateurish, the bodies not quite in proportion, but for now he finally allowed himself a half-smile of satisfaction.

Because it was such a hot day and the door was propped open, we didn't notice that someone had come into the shop until we heard a sniggering laugh and some muttered words. When I turned, the Grim Warper's purple-acned face hovered like the cratered full moon over the counter. His friend, who bought only war comics and had therefore been given the nickname of Sergeant Rockhead by Jay, was over six feet tall, pigeon-chested and wearing a Pink Floyd T-shirt. He pointed at our stack of comics and said, "Are those reserved or can anybody buy one?"

Jay pulled the stack toward him and started to open the envelope. "Not just anybody. You have to be able to breathe through your nose."

To my surprise, the Grim Warper didn't scowl or grind his teeth or make any comment about our comic at all. Instead, he took out his wallet, grinning at his friend the whole time. Then he pointed at the wall high above Mr. Edison's head.

"I'll take the *Fantastic Four* #1." He began to lay twenty-dollar bills on the counter, having shoved himself between Jay and me. "Eight, nine, ten. That's two hundred dollars."

Mr. Edison didn't move. His features had frozen, and for several excruciating seconds he didn't even look at Jay. I didn't have to, or want to, for I knew what I'd find there: an expression of shock and horror.

Plaintively, without even a pretense of self-protection, Jay finally said, "What do you want to go and do that for? You don't collect *FF*."

"How would you know?" The Grim Warper's smile was as wide and cruel as the Joker's. "You figure you know everything about everything. But you don't know dick."

"Language," Mr. Edison said, but with little conviction. He seemed to be thinking of something else, judging by the way he chewed on his lower lip and stared at the money on the counter.

"You can't sell it to him, Lari." Jay, his hand shaking, pulled out his own wallet.

Sergeant Rockhead elbowed his grinning partner. "Lari," he said in a low voice.

"I've got ten bucks here, and I'll be able to get twice that much by the end of the month. As soon as we get some more subscribers."

The Grim Warper gave a snorting laugh, but didn't say anything. He just pushed the stack of twenties a couple of inches forward on the counter.

For a terrible few seconds, I thought Mr. Edison's legs might buckle underneath him. His face had gone a dead-fish colour and beads of sweat glistened at the top of the red bubbles of his cheeks. Finally, he met Jay's imploring gaze and said dully, "I'm sorry. But I'm running a business here." Grim-faced, he picked up the twenties and counted them out slowly, as if each one had to be torn off his own skin. Then he turned his back and pushed a short wooden ladder of the type found in libraries directly under where the comic in question was displayed.

The Grim Warper took the opportunity to sneer at Jay. "Subscribers? Who's going to want to read your stupid little stories?"

"Lay off," I said, barely able to find the necessary breath. "Leave him alone."

The two older teenagers just laughed. As for Jay, he couldn't take his eyes off Mr. Edison as he descended again to the floor, valuable comic in hand. I'd never seen anyone move so heavily, as if his very breath had become leaden. Without looking at Jay, he slid the comic to the Grim Warper, took the bills and, stepping to the cash register, opened the till with a shuddering clang.

"What's the big deal anyway?" Sergeant Rockhead said, frowning at the cover of the *Fantastic Four* #1. "A mole creature? What sort of monster is that? Ooh, look, a giant mole in the ground."

"I think you ought to go," Mr. Edison said, still staring into the open till. "You have what you came for."

The Grim Warper held the comic out flat in both palms toward Jay, then slowly withdrew it. "Maybe I'll sell it to you. Let me know when you come up with some money. But you'll need more than two hundred. A man's got to make a profit, after all." Still grinning, he and his friend made no motion to leave.

Suddenly, the bell over the door tinkled and Nick Samaras sauntered in, bringing the usual cloud of pot smoke. Immediately sensing the tension, and not liking the Grim Warper any more than Jay did, Nick smiled drowsily and said, "Ah, the new copies of *Onan the Barbarian* must be in. Bet you boys can't wait to get your hands on an issue."

"Nick," Mr. Edison said.

"Just don't go getting any issue on your hands." Beaming, and clearly expecting a stronger response to his joke (which I didn't understand at all), Nick in his disappointment came up to within a foot of the Warper. "What is it with you and barbarians anyway? The family resemblance?"

"Nick." This time, Mr. Edison put more steel in his voice.

"Okay, okay."

It was obvious that Nick couldn't understand why his needling wasn't having the usual delighted reception. The grins of the Grim Warper and Sergeant Rockhead only widened until, chortling, almost giggling, they finally strolled past Nick and out of the shop.

When they had gone, an awkward silence settled over us. Finally, Mr. Edison banged the till shut. Looking at Jay, who didn't raise his head, he adopted – for one of the few times I'd ever known – a voice of adult authority, serious and practical, without modulation. "It isn't the only copy in the world. Another one will come along. As a business owner, I just can't afford to turn down such a big sale."

Just when I thought that Jay would never react, but instead would only stand there, motionless, his goofy white hat like the palm of some great Kirby celestial hand pressing down on his bare head to pin him in place, he nodded rapidly a few times and then reached for his bottle of pop. I could tell that he was afraid to speak, for fear that his voice would break with emotion. So I changed the subject by asking Mr. Edison about the shouting that had come from the pool hall.

"Oh, that?" He studied my face seriously for several seconds, as if trying to work out my relationship to his fractious neighbours. I was certain that he was still wondering about Mrs. Hurry's purchase of the *Amazing Spider-Man* #7 for me, but perhaps he thought it best not to mention the sale of any comics at that sensitive moment. "I haven't learned too much in my life about marriage, but I'm pretty sure that a forty-year age gap isn't that great for one."

Nick laughed, and was no doubt poised to make a lewd joke, when the phone rang. Mr. Edison, with a sigh of gratitude, turned to the receiver.

"You want to get a bag of chips?" I asked Jay, sensing that he really needed an excuse to leave the shop.

He nodded, and we stepped outside into the bright sunlight. I wanted to talk about Blackstar and the Vengeance Squad, about any subscriptions that had come through the mail from the advertising we'd done in other fanzines and in a few Vancouver comic collecting newsletters, but I realized it wasn't the appropriate time. So I just waited for my friend to bounce back from his shock and disappointment, trusting, in the same way that some people trust in God, that he couldn't subdue for long his true exuberant nature.

This time proved different, however, and the longer his wounded silence lasted, the more I began to question my faith, not only in my friend's ability to laugh down the world's assaults, but also in my own sheltered expectations of the nature of fate. As I watched our shadows on the sidewalk slightly to the side in front of us, they seemed darker than ever before, and it worried me that they weren't behind us, where summer shadows more properly belonged. Even worse, they stretched farther and farther ahead, spreading as if from objects much greater and more violent than what had yet been made visible to us.

XIX

Ordinary men like me don't get talked about much in the world, and for obvious reasons, I suppose. To be shy, quiet and entirely sane and harmless – an introvert with a love of books and dogs and a wariness of humans that has only increased with the decades – isn't very exciting, not the sort of profile that suits anyone's agenda. But as I approach the age of sixty, I'm comfortable with myself, even with my many regrets. Of course, I would have liked to have been in love, perhaps even to have had a family, and I wish I'd been more sensible with money. But taken all in all, I've done less damage than most men, an accomplishment for which I have little pride, for I did enough harm as a boy, and I saw enough harm done by others, that these subsequent years of reparation can only be considered justice.

I found my copy of *Cosmos* in the bottom of a cardboard box today. It is, at once, smaller than I remembered and even more impressive. That a twelve-year-old boy could draw so well isn't perhaps unusual, but how many, at that age, produce a fanzine that has subscribers in New York, Chicago, Pittsburgh, Toronto and – for some reason this place has always stuck in my memory – Willamette, Oregon? After all, in the 1970s, there was no easily accessible internet system capable of attaining tens of thousands of likes and followers. In late 1976, we had over fifty hard-earned subscribers, which was twenty more subscribers than I had for my paper route – and that was to receive the news of the actual world, not of the planet Lagamorra as dreamed up by a precocious fan of Jack Kirby's in a tiny fishing and farming town on the banks of an unheralded Canadian river.

But then, what is the real news? All that happened in my childhood in that time between the release of *Jaws* and the release of *Star Wars* has a greater power to move me than the latest statistics of coronavirus deaths or the ongoing and endless battle for one group or nation of people to stop hating another. Does this make me a heartless person, or merely human? I can't escape the repercussions of the right and wrong I learned in my formative years. Lari Edison is gone. Has been for a few years now. My memory has never been able to leaven the hard truth of death. I have tried all my life and failed, giving every springer spaniel I've ever owned – six so far, and counting – the same name in an effort to deny what can't be denied forever. That I have done such a thing isn't so strange, for didn't I also choose my career as a teaching aide for special needs children because of Theo Vasilakis, and my loneliness because of the old men and women moving slowly as spawners in the streets who couldn't die in the sun and the light with the waters of their birth streaming over their final vision?

XX

On the other side of our backyard, opposite the firepit, stood an ancient, gnarled Bartlett pear tree, its trunk plated like a stegosaurus and curved like a hunchback's spine. In the deep cool shadow of this tree, my father always repaired his nets, sitting on a wooden hanging bench and expertly manoeuvring hanging needles of twine as if he were playing the harp in a medieval court. No matter how hot the summer day, he always wore a white T-shirt covered in dried bloodstains and cotton work trousers. Normally, he'd be alone, with the buzz of wasps rising from the early windfall pears and his own low whistling of some '40s tune the only sound breaking the languorous silence.

But that morning, I found him there in conversation with my uncle. Blond, amiable and fond of wearing garish toques instead of a black skullcap, my father's younger brother by two years seemed like the last man who'd be living with terrifying memories. But like Jack Kirby, my uncle had been an infantryman after the D-Day invasion and he'd watched two close friends die in the cobbled streets of Holland, their brains splattered on the stone walls behind them. As a result, he had vowed to live his life to the fullest, with as much joy and curiosity as possible, since he believed he owed that much to his fallen comrades. But I knew from my mother, who knew from my aunt, how relentlessly the past could attack the subconscious, in sleep especially. That my uncle often woke in the middle of the night screaming and bathed in cold sweat was impossible to imagine whenever I looked into his cheerful face, but on this morning even he appeared subdued.

"It's just not worth it for me, Heck," he said, standing half in shadow above where my father sat mending away on his bench. "I can't be part of something if it's going to go as far as this." Without looking up, my father nodded. But his hand holding the hanging needle stopped moving. "Pouring acid on nets. I don't like that either, but I can accept it. Emotions run high, and I'm not going to judge anybody who crosses the line in that way. Jesus, I know how important standing up for your rights is. But there's a limit. I can even stomach a fistfight, or somebody waving a shotgun, stupid as that is, as long as they don't use it on anybody."

I had stopped twenty feet away. The conversation seemed as delicate as a spiderweb and I didn't want to break it. The aroma of ripe pear and the turned black soil in the nearby vegetable garden somehow made my uncle's words more disturbing, as if he had ushered evil into paradise.

At last, my father looked up. His cheeks were grizzled, his eyes bloodshot. I could see the dark smudge on one of his temples where he'd been rubbing it fiercely with his fingers for weeks.

"It doesn't change anything. You know that. We're not responsible for what others do."

My uncle stiffened. "His dogs, Heck."

"Yes, I know. It's terrible. But who's saying that a union member did it?"

"Who else?" My uncle waved away a wasp. "Given what's going on."

"A man like that. He's bound to make enemies, strike or no strike."

"You're not serious? A day before the river opens, and there's going to be a blockade, and the leader of the breakaway group has his dogs poisoned. And you're saying it isn't one of the membership who did it?"

My father picked up a ball of twine from the grass and began to fill an empty needle with it. He moved as slowly and meticulously as ever, until

I thought he wasn't going to speak again. Finally, he squinted up directly into my uncle's face.

"Kirkhoff is exactly the sort of man who'd poison his own dogs if he thought it would give him an advantage. Anyway, you know the members. Tell me, which one do you think is capable of such a thing?"

At the sound of Kirkhoff's name, I had begun to tremble. By the time my uncle responded, my whole body was shaking and I couldn't stop it.

"I can't believe that of anyone." My uncle raised his hand and plucked a red-tinged green pear from a branch. "I won't believe it. Not here. Not now."

"So I take it you're not coming tomorrow?" My father had resumed repairing his net, his head down.

"I'll sleep on it." My uncle bit into the pear with a crunch. Chewing, he said, "By the way, where's Scooter?"

"I don't know. Maybe Dan took him to the marsh for a run. Why?"

"I'd want to keep a close eye on my dog, considering. No telling what'll happen once things start heading in that direction."

In my shock, I must have shifted to stop myself from shaking, and the movement caught my uncle's notice. He smiled at me and asked if I'd been getting a lot of swimming in at Ashtons' pool. I managed to mumble something in response before I asked both men if they wanted a cup of tea. Knowing how I felt, it wouldn't be long before my stricken condition became apparent, so I needed an excuse to leave.

Back at the side steps to the house, I hesitated. My mother would sense right away that something had upset me, so I decided to carry on up the driveway and across to the vacant lots, just to have some time alone to recover. As I plunged into the waist-high grass, its earthy coolness for once not welcoming or refreshing, I thought I should go back and get on my bike and ride out to the marsh, just to warn my brother about the threat to our dog. For I was convinced that, if revenge was to happen, I had to be its victim – what other justice was possible? I had poisoned Kirkhoff's dogs every bit as much as Hurry had done, and I didn't even have a compelling motive. What Kirkhoff had done to me was indirect. But then I thought, what if I hadn't sent the note and Hurry had continued to suspect that Dan was the one fooling around with his young wife? Maybe Scooter would be dead, or . . . I couldn't comprehend the scope of Hurry's rage and violence. It was beyond my ability, far beyond what I could learn from comic books and movies or even the daily news. *This* act was immediate and intimate, and I wasn't a passive consumer, a watcher. No, I was a participant, and it didn't comfort me at all to think that my motive was sound. All I could imagine was the pain of the two dogs, their writhing spasms – and someone who loved them either witnessing their torment or finding their corpses. It didn't matter that that someone was a man I had come to hate. In fact, somehow, in a way I couldn't grasp but which was slowly advancing through my consciousness, my hatred made the situation worse, for I began to see how seductive and self-justifying hatred could be if given free rein.

When I reached the nearest abandoned house, its collapsing verandah and moss-grimed turrets as dark as ever even in the full summer sunshine, I sensed the ghosts watching me with an even greater concentration, as if I stood on the precipice of a truth that most of them had never realized, or realized too late, the erosiveness of the worst unchecked instincts, the grave-dirt colour of the ordinary heart burdened even with self-hatred, that spreads out and out in a wake that can disturb the surfaces of the farthest seas.

I stood listening to the whir of grasshoppers in the tall grass and the dull hammer blows falling at the waterfront, and I didn't move for a long time. There was, in fact, nowhere to go that wasn't guilt and fear and confusion. My mother, who was fond of using expressions that she'd learned from her own mother, would have said, "You've made your bed, and now you have to lie in it." And though I could hear her reassuring voice and the words as clearly as if she had whispered in my ear, I couldn't find the requisite wisdom there. Dull blow by blow, the summer was building a gallows for my crime.

XXI

I wasn't allowed to be on the boat for the next opening, because my father wasn't planning to set his net. He was going to participate in a blockade of the harbour organized by the union, an event that could turn violent.

But Keith and I knew we could watch everything unfold from a safe position on the dike, where we stood now, in the cool morning air, watching three dozen gillnetters, seiners and trollers being stampeded into place like wild horses. The racing of engines drowned out the chorus of insects and songbirds in the tall rushes along the bank, and the acrid stink of diesel and gasoline wafted up off the river as if the water had been replaced with burning motor fluids.

Keith and I didn't speak much. I knew he was afraid that his father might try to run the blockade, and also desperately hopeful that he wouldn't. For my part, I felt I had a responsibility now to be on the lookout for Kirkhoff at every opportunity. If he was in my sight, I thought innocently, then I could will nothing terrible to happen. If he was out of my sight, I could imagine only the graves he had had to dig in his yard and the vengeance he had planned to carry out as he threw the dirt over his dogs' bodies.

My brother drifted into position, but near our cousins and not our father. My uncle also took a place, but at one end, near the far bank, no doubt hoping to avoid any possible conflict. The river wouldn't open for nearly two hours, but the blockade had to be set up well in advance, in case any scabs tried to sneak out early. Often, fishermen would anchor on the drifts the night before a big opening, but the union, anticipating this move, had sent out night patrols.

"I don't see my dad," Keith said, and the hope in his voice almost made him breathless.

But my attention was focused on a single black gillnetter that drifted to within ten fathoms of the blockade, bow first, its slimy old car tires hanging from ropes off the gunwales, its mast without any kind of flag, its cabin windows and portholes more like knots in a tree trunk than glass for seeing through. Bullet was already in the bow, barking nonstop at the line of boats, and within a minute Edgar had darted out of the cabin and – to my astonishment – dropped into a seat that he'd positioned in the middle of the bow. And not just any seat, but the one he'd scavenged from the rubbish heap when the cinema had been razed. It looked exactly as if he'd decided to watch a movie, but one that he could stand up and join at any second.

"What's he doing? Is he going to try to get through?" Keith, every bit in the dark as I was about Edgar's possible behaviour during a strike, sounded relieved to have someone other than his father to focus on.

But I couldn't take my eyes off Bullet. Despite his usual feistiness, he seemed vulnerable to me, as if he'd drop dead before the next bark, destroyed from the inside. It was horrible to listen to him and watch him, expecting the worst. But then I realized, if Edgar didn't join the blockade, and since he hadn't been in the crowd at the union meeting, Kirkhoff couldn't possibly suspect him as the union member who'd killed his dogs.

The relief I felt didn't last, because the longer Edgar kept his boat pointed at the other boats, the more the morning tightened like a bow string, with Edgar the wildly unpredictable arrow. When the engines had all stopped racing, and many had been shut off, the voices of Edgar and the other fishermen could be heard clearly over the hammered-silver channel.

"You gonna scab now, Eddy? Can't pay off that fancy new boat if you don't, eh?"

"There's a few boats already gone," Edgar said gleefully. "You buggers gettin' blind as bats goddamn ya."

"Ah, so what? Where's anybody going to set that we can't see?"

"Got the whole river covered, do you? Looking down every slough?"

"Don't you worry about what we're doing. Worry about what you're doing, you silly bastard. What are you playing at now anyway? King of the goddamned river?"

Edgar straightened up in his seat, uncrossing his legs. I couldn't see his grin, but if it's possible to hear an expression or to read it through the movement of the rest of the body, then the grin was as apparent as a hand clap.

"I need a good seat to watch all the Adams go by that you're not going to catch."

"And you think you're going to, eh? Big brothers talked you into it, did they?"

I hadn't noticed before, but now, scanning the line, I realized that Edgar's brothers' large northern gillnetters weren't part of the blockade.

But Edgar's characteristic response – half witch's cackle, half hyena laugh – brought my eyes back to his boat. It was possible he'd remain there all day, just watching, and equally possible that he'd dart back into his cabin and suddenly gun his engine and ram straight into the other boats.

In the end, it was my father who broke the tension. He simply idled out of the line and drifted alongside Edgar's bow. I couldn't hear the words exchanged, but Edgar's posture loosened as my father stood on his main hatch cover, waving at one point back toward town. Edgar stood up then, and, wiping the back of his forearm across his eyes, gestured my father onto the bow with his other hand.

Then something strange yet very ordinary happened. My father removed his skullcap, bowed his head for several seconds and slowly lowered himself into the cinema seat. The whole time this scene played out – lasting several minutes – all the other fishermen remained silent. Even Bullet stopped barking. I could hear the trickle of the current fifteen feet below the dike, and Keith's even breathing right beside me.

The town hadn't stirred yet. It was as if the town no longer existed. My father, who I'd never known to go to a movie theatre, didn't look the way other people did sitting in such a seat. He seemed altogether too stiff, and the angle of his head would have carried his gaze far above any imaginary screen. At his side, Edgar also looked awkwardly formal, his arms like leaded ropes, his face pointed down.

I had an urge to turn and look up to where my father was looking, but I couldn't take my eyes off the two men, Edgar standing like a guardsman beside my father's regal stillness.

"What's going on?" Keith whispered. "What are they doing?"

I shook my head, feeling strangely calm despite my confusion. Something as great and mysterious as the river itself had pervaded the morning, something that could be sensed but not comprehended.

When, at last, my father rose, and put his arm around Edgar's shoulders, and both men retreated to their cabins and their boats began to move, my father's back into the line and Edgar's back to his float opposite the government wharf, I understood only that time had stopped. The pause didn't last more than a minute or so, but everyone and everything existed in it as if preserved in amber, but more vitally alive than ever, and permanently.

Nothing else of note happened that morning – nothing *could* have happened – before the gulls on the main net shed roof returned the hours to their raucous and ravenous appetite, and all the shops and houses in the town behind me began to open and close their doors like gills.

The tension mounted all week, made worse by the abundant catches that the Indigenous fishermen – who had their own separate food fishery – brought into harbour. Thousands of bone-white seagulls with crimson spots on their yellow beaks appeared, taking up positions on every piling head and net shed roof. For several days, their sharp reeling cries fell in weird synchronicity with the dull hammer blows on Edgar's new hull, and then the hammer blows stopped. The sizzling air deepened with the stench of rotted fish and brine, with the latter scent seeming to come into town strictly on the humped backs of the first million Adams sockeye as they tore open-eyed through the roiling silts.

Their desperation took up a reflected residence in the eyes of the striking fishermen, including my father, who smoked so much, and whistled so much when he wasn't smoking, that his lips moved constantly even though he almost never spoke, just worked meticulously on his net or sat gazing into the backyard fire. Other men hung around the waterfront, watching the natives unload their catches in the same way that they'd tongue a sore tooth.

Meanwhile, I kept a careful watch on Scooter and stared anxiously at any other dog I came upon. But Kirkhoff, whatever revenge he undoubtedly had in mind, didn't act, at least not with open violence. Hurry, however, suddenly embraced his nickname. He filed for divorce and kicked his young wife out. Much to my mother's dismay and my father's disgust, Mrs. Hurry moved into my brother's small apartment, confirming my disturbing suspicion that Kirkhoff's guilt was, at the very least, shared, though I made myself believe in the possibility of an innocent friendship between a man and a woman. Approaching twelve, I was old enough even to be jealous of my brother's libertine manhood, for Mrs. Hurry, despite the trouble she had caused me, still held out the mysterious promise of my own carnal future, which I couldn't separate then from the promise of love. The sultry August heat, the smothering musk of river and salmon, and the faintly erotic aroma of swimming pool chlorine whenever I swam at the Ashtons' and of ripening blackberries whenever I walked along the dike, added restlessness to my anxious guilt. For relief, I hid out as often as possible at the Haunted Bookshop.

Unfortunately, the good-natured creative atmosphere had dimmed with the shock sale of the copy of *Fantastic Four* #1. Nothing more was said about it, and the empty space on the wall had been covered up with an early issue of *Iron Man*, but Jay and Mr. Edison were no longer quite as easy with one another. Even more disturbing, Jay had become distracted and subdued, vague about his plans for the next issue of *Cosmos*. Whenever I asked about it, he simply shrugged and changed the subject. I knew, from the way he now fell silent whenever the Grim Warper or Sergeant Rockhead appeared in the shop, that something significant had changed for him, but what that something was I understood about as well as I'd ever understood anything about my unorthodox and brilliant friend. In any case, I was preoccupied with my own concerns.

One late afternoon, I biked home from the bookshop to find our driveway empty. In a panic, I threw my bike onto the crushed gravel and rushed into the house. My mother, at the kitchen table shuffling through several days of mail, looked up wearily, but tried to put some cheer into her tone.

"It's all right. I made sure to take all the comics out first. I stacked them on your desk."

Much to my astonishment, she seemed genuinely surprised that my expression continued to be distraught. I found it hard to speak, for, at my age, I didn't relish acting like a little boy, not even in front of my mother. But I couldn't keep the water from gathering in my eyes.

After several seconds, the penny clearly dropped for her. She sighed and fanned herself with one of the envelopes, looking like a tired, disillusioned geisha.

"This one's for the electricity. Others are for work done on the boat. With the strike being called, your dad thought the time had come. Roland Harris has been wanting an extra car for his farm."

I wanted to shout in response that she might as well have chucked the comics in the river, for they were worthless outside of the car. I wanted her to know that, as my mother, she should have understood this and fought my father over the sale, that she should have known what all my sanctuaries were and how essential they were to me. More than anything, I wanted not to have to explain, but to be respected enough to be included in such a big decision. Instead, I felt exactly five years old again, forced against my will to go to school. And it was the same shift – one incommodious world bullying a gentler and more comforting one right out of the way as if it didn't even exist. With so much to say, I ended up saying nothing, but just stood there, blinking, staring at the envelopes on the table as if each one contained an anonymous note that would further destroy what I had taken to be, if not indestructible, at least safe.

My mother adjusted her weight on the chair as if two invisible hands were pushing down on her shoulders. Dark hollows the size of fifty-cent coins hung under her huge green eyes, and her hands, flat on the table, were scoured pink from doing dishes. But even as I recognized her own worry and fatigue, they were almost nothing compared to my own, and wouldn't be for many years, a fact that, though in the ordinary nature of things between parents and their children, now fills me with shame and regret.

"Your dad's in the yard," she said. "He wants to have a talk with you."

But that was the last thing I wanted. My relationship with my father had always been easy, more of a grandson to grandfather relationship, or to use our nicknames for greater accuracy, more of a monk's to a ghost's, not exactly distant and impersonal, but somehow transcending the flesh and blood banalities and conflicts that existed between my brother and father. I had come late into his life, when perhaps he had not been expecting my arrival, and, as an extension of his middle age rather than his youth, I must have required a different mode of communication, one more suited to his growing need for solitude and silence.

I found him busy at his hanging bench in the pear tree shade, where he now spent so much time that he might have been making a new net from scratch rather than mending a torn one. But our family rarely trafficked in newness. Year after year, we fished the same nets until the lead line was so weak that a sneeze could snap it. I wasn't yet old enough to be embarrassed by want, but that time too was fast approaching, summoned by the seductive world of getting and spending and the deepening and even more seductive narcissism of adolescence.

The scent of ripe pear drifted only faintly through the fog of cigarette smoke. I kept my eyes on a wasp circling the rim of my father's mug, no doubt drawn there by the heaping spoonfuls of sugar in the tea.

"Take a seat," my father said, pointing his hanging needle at the wooden lawn chair six feet to one side of his bench. Thirty seconds passed heavily before he spoke again. "Your mother tried to stop me, you know. She even offered to take on extra shifts at the drugstore." He moved the hanging needle from one bronzed hand to the other. "But I told her, you'll be twelve in January. In a couple of years, you can be fishing your own boat in the summers."

At that moment, for the first time, I saw the yawning distance between my father and myself; it wasn't a result of temperament or values, but of expectations borne out of our very different personal and cultural backgrounds. He had known a degree of poverty and violence particular to his generation, whereas I had been more broadly and gently shaped by privilege and the fantasies of the American entertainment industry. Undoubtedly, for my father, my brother's refusal to pursue mysterious scholastic and athletic achievements had only confirmed for him the necessity that I should inherit his world without any such trivial dalliances getting in the way. But for me – as much as I loved the river and the boat – the idea of becoming a fisherman was as foreign as the idea of becoming prime minister. In any case, I wasn't even prepared, as I stood there trembling, to take the first step toward adulthood. But how could I articulate any of these inchoate feelings to my father?

"It wasn't being driven," he said, and deftly moved the hanging needle among the meshes. "And that's what a car is for, after all."

I didn't have it in me to argue, but neither did I want to show myself unworthy of his acknowledgement that I was growing older. So, after a minute, I found voice and nerve enough to change the subject. It was as if the smoke-thick air had parted, and I was able to step into another stage of my life, simply by using thought and language. Upset as I was, I did experience a strange and fresh confidence.

"What happened between you and Edgar at the blockade? Why did you go and sit in that theatre seat?"

My father froze. The muscles tightened in his neck and jaw. He didn't turn to me for several seconds, and when he did, I was shocked to see the beginning of a mist in his pale eyes. All at once, as he began to speak, the strength drained out of his body. His shoulders slumped. His arms hung limp. The grizzle on his cheeks might have been lead filings, for it appeared a challenge for him to keep his head lifted.

"Your grandmother was a very caring person. Too caring for this place."

Something in the tone of his voice made me aware that he wasn't just talking about our town. He seemed to have drifted away from it himself, the shade beneath and around the hanging bench suddenly bottomless and much colder.

"She used to take Edgar to the movies. When he was a little boy. Every weekend. During the week, too, when she could find the money. It was the best she could do for him. Oh I have no doubt she'd have adopted him if she could, just to get him away from that house. But . . . it's strange . . . I don't think he'd have gone. There's something about family, even when it's wrong, a kind of hold that's not just from the outside."

My father's face had drained of colour but he had fought back any tears. His eyes, however, were a paler blue than I'd ever seen, almost without blue at all.

"She cleaned up his cuts and bruises at least, so he could go to school and not make the teachers too curious. Their interest wouldn't have done any good. If Edgar could choose his father over *her*, what chance would anybody else have had to help? She'd try to feed him, too, leave meals for him in some of the places she knew he liked to go, a shack in the marsh mostly. It puzzled us at the time. Bothered us, too, to be honest. Everyone thought the Winterbournes – except for the mother, and she'd been dead for years, died when Edgar wasn't more than a few years old – weren't worth anybody's time or effort. But she'd say, 'Charity begins at home,' or 'There but for the grace of God,' or else just clamp her mouth shut, her way of telling us that we were invading her privacy. Later, I figured out that she needed Edgar as much as he needed her. Maybe even more. We were all grown, you see, and once your grandfather was gone, she must have just found herself at a loss. She had always done for others. It was her nature . . ."

My father's voice broke and he lowered his gaze to his hands motionless in the meshes. When he spoke again, he didn't look up; he didn't even seem to be speaking to me, but to himself, haltingly, putting words for the first time to an emotion that mostly reduces all language to trivial noise.

"When she died – after terrible, terrible suffering – it was . . . the thing was . . . I had never really understood what death meant. The war wasn't like that. Losing people. Even if you didn't admit it, even to yourself, there was always gratitude that you had survived. And losing my father . . . that was harder, but, of course, she was still there, and she had always made it her job to ease everything for us, even that, even when she must have been in great pain herself.

But when it came, she couldn't do anything to make her loss easier. Once she was gone, and I knew that I would never hear her voice or look into her face again, it changed things. I would think, this pain . . . I can take it to her, she will know how to cope with it. Then I would remember, and it was like I was swimming and I just kept swallowing wave after wave of brine. Almost ten years ago, and it's just the same. I think, when I've had a good opening on the river, wait until she hears about this. Or, I've had a bad day, and I can taste the exact flavour of the tea she'd make, as if I was still drinking it."

He licked his lips but the effort must have been futile, for he kept speaking in the same unworldly, heavy way.

"Maybe it's true what they say, that time heals some wounds. But not the biggest ones. Easier to put the guts back into a sockeye and get it to swim away. Edgar, you see, more than even my own brothers, understood. When the theatre shut down a few years back, that was . . . well, it wasn't final. He could still go by there, and stand there, and remember, and call her back somehow. Maybe it was like he could see a movie of her in his head, I don't know. But when they knocked it down, I suppose he needed something that he could keep with him that was more than what he remembered. If he could sit in one of those seats, out on the river, and look at the sky, maybe he could feel her there beside him, maybe the whole painful world could just be some sort of movie. And when it's over, you know the big curtain will draw back again, and you'll have your bag of popcorn and a couple of hours away from everything . . ."

THE MARVELS OF YOUTH

Scooter, with that curious instinct that dogs have for human emotion, had risen from his spot near the trunk of the pear tree and limped over to lick one of my father's dangling hands. But my father didn't react. As if he had struggled to climb to the top of a long ladder plunged in blood and space, he finally looked at me and came back to himself, or, rather, to the self that he had to inhabit in order to exist in the responsible world.

"People will always be telling you that you can recover from everything. But it's a lie. You don't recover from the worst. You go on, but it isn't the same. You'll know. You'll know when your own mother dies."

He seemed poised to say more, perhaps about what a man could expect from the woman he chose to live with, but that must have been too complex a subject, or too intimate, for him to broach to me.

"I'm sorry we had to sell the car. But it was necessary."

He turned and let his hand scratch Scooter's muzzle. I saw that sweat stains had spread like large bruises under the armpits of his T-shirt. He had aged twenty years right before my eyes, and I didn't know how to respond. Even if I had possessed the maturity to try to comfort him, it was obvious that he wasn't seeking comfort, that he had moved far beyond it and into a stoic acceptance, cold and unrelenting. Besides, I was a child, and callow as children often are. Faced with my father's transformation from one kind of being to another, I waited until my confusion naturally returned to disappointment and selfishness. Because his pain could only exclude and bewilder me, I had no option but to inhabit the body and consciousness of the years that were my own. The car's gone, I thought, and already I missed the comforting smell of the old vinyl seats and the feel of the cracks in their surfaces and the sound of the rain on the roof and hood. I missed, too, the solidity of the car's presence in my life, how its small contained interior redolent of damp and that antique must of weathered comics offered itself to me as a refuge whenever I needed it. Now a small resentment began to grow, for I realized that I didn't even have the opportunity that Edgar had had outside of the condemned theatre, to stand and contemplate the cherished past that had existed – no, *still* existed there – nor would I ever be able to wrest a material reminder from the wreckage and install it in my present as a way to face the darkening future. It seemed, then, that my father's grief and pain were selfish, that they made no account for me at all, and so I didn't regard his confidences with either gratitude or sympathy. I simply rose from the chair and walked weightlessly across the cold, deep shadow past my father's numbed self, and eventually saw again the great blank space in the driveway, which made a much larger hole in my life than the demolition of the theatre had made, and carried on into my bedroom until I finally stood over my desk, above the stack of worthless comics, breathing in the must that was now entirely without comfort or magic, but mockingly dead, the wake of a past that I could never recover. Petulantly, self-righteously, I picked up the top comic and ripped it in half. Then I threw myself down on my bed and wept the last of my childhood tears.

XXII

How long does it take for nostalgia to be a salve against approaching death? For that is clearly what it is, despite all our cultural attempts not to be serious, to brush everything off as just innocent, harmless pleasure. If a middle-aged man wants to surround himself with the artefacts of a simpler time in his life, what of it? He could spend his days and his money in much worse ways, of course.

I make no judgments on that score, for what are memories but artefacts that no market can value, no shelf can hold?

My apartment was small, contained and suddenly pungent with the must of old comics, but it wasn't a haven in the same way that my father's undriven Ford had been a haven in my childhood or that the local cinema had been a haven in Edgar's. That pandemic summer afternoon, opening yet another cardboard box, I had the overwhelming urge to rip the top comic in half and to keep on going until I had destroyed the material collectible value of all of them. For I knew, all at once, what I had really known for years – that I was my father's son, and that, in the most important sense, I too had moved beyond comfort. And that distance had nothing to do with the apocalyptic zeitgeist, but only with the barnacle accretion of sunsets and the chilling awareness that nostalgia wouldn't work its protective and restorative powers on me. My memories, as worthless to the world as any stack of torn *Archie* comics, possessed a value that was as unrelenting as the truth my father had to carry alone in the abyss of the absence of his mother's capacious love. That is, a value unredeemable in the marketplace, bought and sold only by the heart and the conscience in the middle of the most sleepless nights.

I began to sweat, though I held no hanging needles and I spoke to no son. The *Jaws* doormat mocked me from the near wall. Such items in relation to the vibrant, creative and tragic world I had lost were paltry and pathetic, just as my plans of selling the artefacts of that world were mean and disloyal to the only sense of self that means anything, the sense of self that my father and Edgar lived with, and so many others. Perhaps, in the end, those war victims of my childhood cast a shadow of death too vast to be outdistanced. Perhaps all I could do was accept the responsibility of inheriting a human sadness that, despite the best efforts of my parents and those of the trivial and denying world, was as inevitable as breathing.

I made no final decision. Putting the old comics back in their box, I faced once more the forgiveless fantasy of the real.

XXIII

I saw Kirkhoff once in the last days of the strike. He had pulled his truck up to the gas pumps at Brownlows' garage just as I was riding past on my bike. In anticipation of a big salmon run, fishermen often carried extra jerry cans of gas on board, just in case the federal government extended the opening by another twelve or twenty-four hours. To leave the fishing grounds and return to harbour for fuel was an unpleasant task when the catches were at their peak.

Kirkhoff didn't look altered in any way, which surprised me given what had happened to him, but my attention was drawn to the emptiness and silence of the bed of his truck. Two excited black Labs should have been circling around in it, and putting their paws up on the sides, tongues hanging out, tails wagging furiously. Perhaps I had just become too accustomed to absence, but there suddenly seemed to be a hole in everything when you really looked, and if there's one thing you learn growing up on the flood plain of an estuary, all holes eventually get filled in before they empty out again. Since the tension of the strike still permeated the town, I wasn't sanguine about what would rush in to fill the absence. Mostly, I couldn't accept that a man like Kirkhoff wouldn't seek vengeance for the murder of his dogs, especially when I took careful note of his appearance.

The permanent scowl on his leathery face was like a slightly bleeding gash. Even his haircut – trimmed to not quite a stubble – seemed like an act of ongoing violence. I thought I could see the blood throbbing in his hard skull, as if he held some other life captive there. But everything else – the black gumboots, the plain trousers, the olive-green T-shirt covered by an open flannel shirt even in the full heat of the day – said only that he was a responsible and determined fisherman preparing for work.

But he wasn't like most of the other fishermen, a fact made obvious when old Mr. Brownlow himself – tall, gaunt, bespectacled and wearing a grubby mechanic's monkey suit – walked out of the dark and greasy garage entrance and, in a cold voice, announced, "Your custom isn't wanted here," and stepped forward to take the spout of the gas pump from out of Kirkhoff's hand.

Kirkhoff didn't even argue. He just took out his wallet and dropped a five-dollar bill on the oil-splattered concrete. "For what's already in the can," he said, and hoisted both red containers into the bed of his truck where the barking and circling dogs should have been.

"Keep it. Since you appear to love it so much. Just keep it." Mr. Brownlow turned and walked away, and I was disappointed that he hadn't shown at least a little kindness, given what Kirkhoff had suffered. But the fisherman had already climbed into his truck, slammed the door and started the engine before the garage darkness had swallowed Mr. Brownlow's figure again.

I waited a few minutes, my eyes fixed on the money, asking myself in a kind of frenzy if Kirkhoff's five-dollar bill was, in fact, good to me. It seemed a simple question with an obvious answer, yet I found myself unable to act.

The seagulls circled and cried high in the azure depths above, and the sun hammered its heavy yellow blows on the heat-rippled pavement. Slowly, I coasted into the heavy chloroform of the gasoline fumes, convinced that Mr. Brownlow would return for his money, but knowing as well that he'd no sooner do that than beat himself to death with a lug wrench. There was a steeliness in most of the men and women of the older generations in our town, and though I didn't fully understand its source, I could always recognize its presence. Even so, five dollars wasn't an insignificant amount of money.

Cautiously, I picked it up and pocketed it, telling myself as I biked away that I didn't have to spend it, that I could reserve my decision on the rightness of using such a windfall. But already I felt as if I had received at last the second half of autumn's bribe, that somehow Kirkhoff had acknowledged to me his complicity in that carnal deception. But as I had already betrayed him, or at least not accepted his efforts to silence me, I didn't know what this money meant, except that it connected me to him all over again, a connection I told myself I didn't want. Yet I had taken the money, despite being the agent of the atrocity he'd recently suffered. I didn't realize it then, but I was beginning to face the complexity of a moral world within an indifferent universe. Some instinct of that approaching and deepening confusion must have registered, for I had never parked my bike and entered the Haunted Bookshop with such a palpable feeling of escape.

The five-dollar bill already felt heavy in my pocket, and the conversation I came upon only increased the weight.

Mr. Edison, looking even more like a Santa Claus down on his luck – his white T-shirt more of a used-dishrag grey, the image of Thor on the front so faded that the Norse god was more of a ghost, the words "Journey into Mystery" only visible as "Joy stry"; his long greying hair uncombed; his overall demeanour simply exhausted – was speaking with exasperation to a red-faced and fidgeting Jay.

"Of course it isn't fair. It isn't just. The people with money are almost always the worst people. That's the way of the world. You can fight – you *should* fight – but you have to pick your battles. You can't go around being superior to people and think that they're just going to take it. Why should they? You wouldn't."

Jay started to interject, but Mr. Edison put his large working man's hand up like something dramatic and final sketched by Jack Kirby.

"Anyway, justice is more complicated than you think. You have to be honest with yourself. Sure, he bought the comic that you wanted, and sure, he probably did it only to spite you. You say that's unfair. But is it? From his point of view, he had justice on his side. He thought he was just evening the score. Ah, but me no buts, Jay. I've tried to get you to stop riding him, haven't I? You ought to consider yourself lucky. He's older than you, bigger, meaner. So he bought the *FF*? I'm just glad that he didn't decide to beat you to a pulp instead."

Jay looked two years older than the last time I'd seen him. His face was leaner, and he'd let his hair grow almost to his collarbone. Most remarkably, I couldn't see his goofy white Gilligan hat anywhere. He made a dismissive gesture with one hand.

"That dork can barely roll a spine without running out of breath."

Mr. Edison opened his mouth, and then, after a slight pause, closed it and shrugged his broad, rounded shoulders.

"I guess you'll just learn these things on your own. The hard way. No one can help you if you won't even listen."

He turned to me, which was a surprise since I didn't think that either of them was aware of my presence.

"You could learn a lesson from Sean here. He's a very good listener. Too good, maybe. At the next swap meet, you two ought to swap a bit of your characters. Trade some arrogance and energy for some humility and stillness."

As soon as he'd made the comment, he appeared to realize that he'd gone too far, made too intimate a revelation about us, revealed an awkward level of caring. Abruptly, he reached under the counter.

"*Eternals* #2 is here," he said, and placed a mint copy on the counter. "I have to admit, Kirby's always good at building suspense. You'd be a pretty dull character if the phrase 'The gods are coming' didn't make you sit up a little."

He smiled until the creases under his powdery eyes deepened, but the effort seemed forced. Jay, with his characteristic silent ravenousness, began to flip through the pages, no doubt concentrating on the compositions, the draughtsmanship. I was relieved to see that he hadn't lost his idolatry for King Kirby, but the talk of money and justice weighed on me. As I stood there, breathing in the must off the yellowing pages of the old paperbacks, watching Mr. Edison sip at his tea mug, listening to Jay flipping pages, I understood that I needed to give the five-dollar bill to my mother. I needed to do something else, too, but I'd have to wait for a time when Jay wasn't around. Given his bitterness at losing out on the *Fantastic Four* #1, he wouldn't have understood – and I didn't want to have to explain – why I'd choose to sell my copy of *Amazing Spider-Man* #7 back to Mr. Edison. Jay's parents were professionals in the city, so he had no idea of the realities of a strike in the salmon fishery. But I knew how much the extra money would mean to my mother, if I could get her to accept it.

After a few minutes, Jay slid the comic over to me, the usual brightness in his eyes.

"It's great. Magic. There's this character called Ajax and . . ."

I walked out an hour later into the taut, sensitive silence of a fishing town on the edge of violence – either between men, or between men and nature. The gasoline fumes wafting over from Brownlows' garage smelled like blood because the two fluids ran from the same tap of commerce. Now that the theatre was gone, the large patchwork quilt of vacant lots; a few occupied lots; six-foot-wide ditches; ancient pear, plum, cherry and apple trees; blackberry bushes; and derelict Edwardian houses appeared much larger than usual, and even emptier as a result, like the surface of some newly reached planet. Sunlight and shadows spread rich comic book inks and colours over the scene until it resembled a full splash page with a background and foreground but no figures.

Up the street, the time on the town clock, though still wrong, was closer to accuracy. But Thomas Plum must have been asleep or passed out – or even gone – for I couldn't hear the Doors playing on his beat-up portable record player.

As I climbed onto my bike to deliver my papers, I glanced at the pool hall. It was strange to realize that Mrs. Hurry – soon to be ex–Mrs. Hurry – would never sit behind that till again, never jingle the charm bracelets on her wrists as she flirted with the patrons. And strange, too, for a few fleeting seconds, to feel pity for Hurry, a pity that shocked me, for I knew the atrocity he'd committed. But worse than my knowledge was the fact that, once again, I hadn't acted on it, out of fear and shame for the despicable part I had played.

Without pleasure, I shifted the full canvas paper sack in my wire carrier and pedalled slowly toward what I dimly apprehended to be an inevitable and unforgiving fate.

XXIV

Under normal circumstances, summer days and nights were the longest, richest and most delicious of the year. Because school was out, I had no curfew, unless I was going fishing in the morning, which meant that I was free to roam the fields, streets and riverbanks at almost any hour. And Keith, who had no curfew at any time and who often didn't even bother attending school, sometimes slept the summer nights away in the bottom of a skiff or in one of our forts constructed of cardboard boxes and drift lumber in the blackberry bushes. Even with the tension surrounding the strike, my parents were too preoccupied with their own concerns to worry about the possibility of violence in those intriguing electric hours between the fall of dark and the emptying out of the hotel pub and the Legion at some point after midnight.

That day, at dusk, Keith and I were sitting on a great beached log on the riverbank, watching the harbour for signs of activity that might lead to something interesting. The stillness was like the inside of a church bell, promising more than resonance. Occasionally, a figure appeared on the wharf, or a gillnetter drifted from one side of the harbour to the other. The union wanted to maintain a presence to keep the scabs away, but I knew as well that fishermen, when idle, mostly preferred to be idle beside or on the river. With the smell of salmon, brine and mud so heavy on the August air, the idea of staying home was especially torturous. So every ten or fifteen minutes, a different fisherman emerged through the greying threads of dusk. We could hear their pickup trucks coming and going on the road behind us.

"You want to look for bottles?" Keith asked. "Tide's low enough now."

I shook my head. "There's not enough time. It'll be dark soon."

Keith bent and picked up a rock from the marsh grass and hurled it into the channel. The tiny concussion was like the snuffing out of one candle. "Ah, there's plenty of time. Come on. We can stay around here, in case anything happens."

Since the killing of Kirkhoff's dogs, I hadn't said anything to Keith about Hurry's guilt, because that would have been an admission of my own. For his part, Keith either didn't make the connection or chose to mind his own business. I suspected that, because his father was non-union, just like Kirkhoff, my friend preferred not to mention the latter, which suited me fine.

Just as I was about to agree to Keith's suggestion and get up from the log, a blue heron croaked somewhere in the pewter air beyond the spire-like poplars on the opposite bank. Seconds later, it appeared – like a broken umbrella or upside-down Victorian bicycle – seeming to fly straight out of the poplar branches. Then it cried its hollow, echoing call again. Or else the next heron did, for a second had followed almost immediately behind the first. Within a minute, all up and down the harbour, other blue herons – hunched like old men – joined the sudden angular flight toward town.

Keith and I didn't speak. As five birds became twenty, and twenty became fifty, we could only glance at each other before giving our full attention to this strange exodus. It was as if the herons were fleeing, as if the imminent mass arrival of the salmon had terrified them. Their deep, broken cries sounded no different than usual, but to hear so many at once somehow made me want to fling myself down on the muddy bank and cover my head with my arms. It didn't help that the breeze had grown stronger since the herons' rising, as if their great slow-bellowing wings had summoned the change.

It took twenty minutes for the dusk to resume its empty greyness and for even the echoes of the herons to dissolve into silence. Keith and I had turned to watch the birds disappear south over the town, and once they were gone, we couldn't think of anything to do except to follow their example and move on.

By darkness, when the streetlamps had fully blossomed and everything outside their shimmering reach had withdrawn into mystery, we found ourselves by the clock tower. Thomas Plum was nowhere to be seen or heard, and we figured he was likely in the hotel bar, drinking with the usual assortment of locals and bar hoppers from surrounding towns. Often, Keith and I hung around the hotel after dark, because sometimes a drunken patron, fumbling for his keys, might drop some money on the street. More likely, he'd leave his empty bottle on the curb. Some nights, we'd collect a couple of cases of empties that way.

We hadn't been there long – the clock hands hadn't moved very much but that could have meant anything – before, almost simultaneously, the door to the hotel bar swung open and police sirens broke over the silent streets. Several bodies that seemed joined into one whirled onto the sidewalk, pursued by shouts and screams and the breaking of glass. Within a minute, a crowd had spilled out from the bar, throbbing music behind them, but the crowd was entirely separate from and focused on one figure. At first, in the faint light from the corner streetlamp, I couldn't identify the man, except to see that he reeled wildly from side to side, and then, as if concentrating his energy, entered a half-crouch before springing forward at the assembled onlookers, who rushed back like a rapidly departing tide line. Another figure, who'd just been wrestling with the crouched man, limped away, holding its jaw, dripping blood and shouting curses.

The sirens screamed louder, so that even the shouted curses couldn't be heard over them. All at once, the crouching man emitted a long and horrible laugh that rose above the sound of the sirens, just for an instant, before breaking off as if chopped by an axe. Then the figure sprang forward again and seemed to rush straight into the back of a pickup truck parked at the curb. As soon as I heard the weird laughter, brief as it was, I knew that the lone figure was Edgar. I also knew that it wasn't any version of Edgar I had ever witnessed before.

He suddenly lifted the back end of the truck a couple of feet in the air, and the crowd seemed to move forward and backward at the same time. The truck held its new position for several seconds, and then crashed with a dull sound to the pavement as the sirens and flashing police lights descended on the scene. Now everything became a criss-cross of red-and-white light beams and shadows and a sudden diminishment of time that was like an inverse explosion. Two officers hurried up to the crowd – which consisted of perhaps thirty or forty men and women – and ordered them back while two others, more methodically, approached Edgar, who stood, heaving great breaths and dripping blood from his face. As they came close to him, without – I saw with relief – their guns drawn, he raised his head, black hair swinging across his eyes, gave out an unearthly howl, then jerked his body away from the police and turned in the direction of the river. Even I could tell that he was homing in, that left to his own devices he would carry his rage away and let it burn down in private by the water.

But the police advanced against his turned back. When one of them grabbed his shoulder, Edgar reared and, in a flurry of quick, savage movements, lifted the officer by the armpits, flung him like a dead salmon through the air and then broke into a careening, staggering run and was soon swallowed by the night. By the time the other officer had helped his fallen colleague to his feet, the other two had ordered the crowd back into the bar. All that remained of Edgar's presence was the unmistakable wake of sweat, blood and, now, alcohol that seemed to be a part of the brine and the fish slime smell washing over the town from the west, drowning the softer confections of ripening fruit and pool chlorine, a part of the wake of the intensifying summer itself.

Keith, who at eleven already traded in muskrat pelts and who seemed drawn to the violence inflicted upon nature, wanted to follow Edgar as if tracking a wounded beast. But I was frightened by what had happened, and

THE MARVELS OF YOUTH

I didn't think that the resumption of silence and the eventual withdrawal of the police cars signalled a return to normal. When Keith took out his flashlight and trained it on the pavement, finding a trail of blood spatters and running from one to another as if on a gruesome treasure hunt, I watched him vanish too into the darkness, another part of Edgar's wake, a shadow of the same isolation and wildness. Despite my sympathies, despite what I knew of Edgar's past, I just didn't have the courage to follow. I wanted only to get home and to tell my father what had happened.

As almost always that summer, I found him in the backyard, this time crouched close to the firepit, for the fire had burned down to its orange-red embers and he was seeking the last of the heat. When I told him what I'd seen, I expected him to be upset, even to rise up and hurry to the waterfront, just to check on Edgar, but he only nodded and said, "I thought that was more sirens than usual," before returning to poking at the embers with a branch he'd cut from our cherry tree for the purpose. I wanted to say, *Aren't you going to help him?*, but somehow, in light of my father's posture, the question sounded pointless. All questions did, including why Edgar had exploded in this way. If my father knew, he wasn't planning to tell me, that much was obvious. An air of deep and final resignation inhabited his whole being – and that frightened me as much as Edgar's display of violence. I didn't think that the past, like a living thing, could suddenly rouse itself for a final reckoning with the present and future, and not thinking it, I lacked even a cold philosophy to temper my fear. As for my father, he retained enough of a worldly sense of responsibility to say wearily, "I think it's time you got yourself to bed."

The next afternoon, telling the story of Edgar's fight and escape to Jay and Mr. Edison at the bookshop, I began to feel ashamed by their interest, which bordered on amusement.

"Sounds like an issue of *The Incredible Hulk*," Mr. Edison said. "Lifting up a vehicle and everything."

Jay looked at me. "And you really didn't follow him? Why not?"

"He was only going to go home and sleep it off." I didn't mention that Keith had followed him, and partly, I realized, I was protecting not only him and Edgar, but also the whole fishing and river culture.

Jay wanted to go out and find the bloodstains, and I went without enthusiasm. The street looked transformed in the brilliant sunshine, as vibrant as a comic book panel. But the bloodstains were there, and real enough.

"Let's get some chips," I said, eager to diffuse Jay's interest.

As we neared the clock tower, which remained silent and still, I remembered something that gave me a chance to change the subject.

"Hey, did you ever find out what Civil War battle it was that happened in Vermont?"

"What?"

"You know, the American said he couldn't remember."

"Oh, that." Jay, who loved *Captain America* and was always reading American history, never seemed to neglect an opportunity to pick up bits of information. "It wasn't much of a battle. More of a raid. I forget what it's called."

We walked on in silence through the watery heat haze on the pavement. I didn't know it then, but I was also beginning to walk out of one world while another was rapidly receding from me. No matter how hard I tried to follow the latter, the smell, the taste, the bloodstains – all of it would be dissolved, scoured away by the sun and the moon. But I could follow, and alone, because it seemed unjust and disloyal – it still seems unjust and disloyal – not to do so.

XXV

The news was all over the river within a few days. I heard it first from Keith, of course, who had overheard it being discussed by some fishermen on the wharf. But soon after, my mother brought the subject up, as it touched her natural sympathies and therefore, briefly, reduced her usual reticence about spreading gossip.

"His own brothers," she said. "I just can't get over it. How could they do something like that?"

"How much money?" I asked.

My mother put the dishcloth down on the counter beside the sink. The sum seemed too much to speak of in a normal tone, so she lowered her voice.

"More than forty thousand dollars. Everything. All his savings."

"But how does everyone know that the guy ripped him off? Maybe he'll come back and finish the boat. Maybe he's just taking a break."

"They say that the builder's gone to Mexico. Allard says that the fellow was even talking about leaving a few days before. Poor Edgar."

"But won't his brothers do something? Didn't they hire the builder?"

My mother sighed. "Apparently, they told Edgar he was a fool for paying all that money up front. That he had it coming to him if he was stupid enough to trust anyone that much. Even though they were the ones pressuring him into getting a new boat."

Because I couldn't accept the naked injustice of what had happened, I pressed on, my voice growing more and more desperate.

"But can't he take the guy to court? Can't he sue? Can't the police do anything?"

My mother picked up the soiled rag as if it was a wounded songbird. "Can you imagine Edgar hiring a lawyer? Or going to court? Even if he had the money and somebody was willing to help him?"

Of course, it was absolutely the last thing I could imagine. For many in the fishing world, justice was rough, if it took place at all. And not only in the fishing world. Hadn't Hurry taken matters into his own hands? But then, as far as I knew, sleeping with another man's wife wasn't a crime, at least not of the type that you could go to jail for. If Edgar was going to receive any justice, it would have to be personal, and that would require patience. Forty thousand dollars would probably last a good while in Mexico; that builder wasn't returning any time soon.

In a final desperate sally, I asked if Edgar might do something to his brothers, perhaps frighten them into helping him out financially. The clinking of dishes signalled that my mother had exhausted all her opinions on the matter. She said only that Edgar wouldn't dream of harming his brothers, no matter how much harm they'd inflicted upon him.

"But I can only imagine," she concluded, "how betrayed he must feel. And the fact that he's being laughed at by some of the men at the waterfront – even if it's just their way of trying to keep things light and ordinary – won't help."

Not surprisingly, my father refused to talk about what had happened, and Edgar himself disappeared for a while. Keith and I kept a daily watch on his boat and net shed, but it seemed obvious that he'd chosen to stay out of sight. As for the half-finished new hull, it shone white as the moon on the muddy riverbank, at least until the restless seagulls started roosting on it and leaving their droppings behind. By the fourth or fifth day, rumours of a settlement to the strike replaced the interest in Edgar's situation, and the town shifted its focus back to the great massing schools of sockeye out in the Gulf of Georgia.

As abruptly as it had begun, the strike ended. The canneries increased their offer, but only marginally and for a set quota of fish, but the union members didn't feel that they could risk missing out on the biggest run of the four-year salmon cycle any longer. The general feeling was, we'd made our point, the companies shifted a little and now we can get down to work.

Once again, the growling chorus of boat and truck engines swamped the neighbourhood, and the air thickened like champagne infused with blood. Now every tide rose and fell like adrenaline and the flight of birds and the crooked wanderings of tomcats and stray dogs took on a greater urgency. The heat increased, as if the sun had moved closer to witness the violence, and everywhere you walked in the streets closest to the government wharf smelled heavily of cigarette smoke, for the fishermen in their growing tension lit another stick while the butt of the old one hit the cracked pavement.

But even as the river opened, even as all the expected boats slotted into their usual places on the drifts, Edgar still hadn't appeared. His gillnetter, however, had vanished from its moorage spot – exactly when, no one could say – which suggested that, at the very least, he wasn't planning to miss out on the anticipated bounty. If anyone needed a big month of catches, of course, it was Edgar.

The nets rolled off the drums at exactly 8:00 a.m. all up and down the river, and the next four hours passed like minutes. My father, normally so meticulous and patient, had no choice but to wrap some fish on the drum, an abhorrent necessity that bruised and reddened the valuable flesh and put a deep frown-line on Vic's forehead. But in such circumstances, when the fish were so plentiful that they "sunk" nets (meaning there was so much weight in the meshes that the corks were pulled below the surface), not even the fastidious packer could object to the less-than-pristine harvest.

By mid-afternoon, with the sun blazing and the tide finally approaching slack, my father and I had time to move the hundreds of salmon from our latest set into our main hatch (we had already filled both side lockers). Even as we did so, the hand claps and frothing spumes of more fish striking at the cork line continued to violate the stillness. Scales flecked my father's grizzle and slime and blood smeared his bright yellow nylon apron. I kept wiping sweat from my eyes as every step that I took sloshed another dead and gaping salmon off to the side of my gumboots, as if I walked on a river of flesh.

In truth, I felt sick looking at the dead fish and breathing in the heavy fumes of gasoline and slime that coated the air in invisible layers of varnish. Even my father worked grimly, deriving no pleasure from the task, continuing to smoke so rapidly that I suspected the endless clouds off his cigarettes had become a mask that covered both sight and smell for him.

We didn't speak much, or even look at each other. At some level, we understood that we were the stewards of slaughter, and perhaps my father, himself caught in meshes that he hadn't seen coming thirty years earlier, already realized that his own time – and mine as well – in such a visceral and merciless culture was doomed.

As the tide turned again, and again, the deep turquoise sky and pounding heat dissolved to dusk and the temperature of a lukewarm bath. After so many successful sets, it was daunting to know that the approaching dark set could be overwhelming, that we might have to face a thousand dead and struggling salmon as darkness settled over the river and the current hurled us faster and faster toward the sea.

But all of a sudden, a hundred fathoms above us on the drift, a familiar black shape drifted out of a slough mouth. In the thickening motes, it seemed that the boat itself was made of dusk that had already hardened to midnight.

"It's Edgar," I said, as much to myself as to my father, who stood in the stern, a fresh cigarette between his lips, his right hand as usual resting on the taut cork line. Below us and around us, our engine throbbed like a pulse, and the light bulb of our pickup light brightened by the second. In fifteen minutes, it would be pitch dark.

Like a block of black ice, Edgar's gillnetter glided across the channel to the far bank and almost vanished in the gloom. Then, in the traditional looping fashion, it regained definition as Edgar slowly laid his net on the drift, ensuring that the meshes would hang loosely below the cork line. I should have been relieved to see him there, in his familiar place at the towhead, making a set as he'd done so many thousands of times before, but the suddenness of his reappearance was unsettling. I looked at my father, and could tell by his fixed gaze and posture that he too found Edgar's resumption of normal activity as disturbing as comforting.

A minute later, Edgar finished setting his net and his gillnetter settled within a few fathoms of the near island bank, still a hundred fathoms north of us. I could just make out his figure in the stern, bending and rising as he doubtless arranged his gaff hook and knife in readiness for when he picked up his net. The sky was a plum-black above and around him, and a clutch of low stars could just be seen in the thickening billows of dark over Vancouver. On the near bank, five fathoms from our boat, the island treeline of poplars, maples and cottonwoods was dissolving, sliding under the night's hurrying tide. The faint forms of late-feeding bats darted over the shoreline as the oily musk of the river rose like steam.

My father coughed. When I looked at him, he stood out as sharply in the vivid pickup light as if drenched in the glow of a full moon. But the night was moonless, and the current as black, cold and unending as any stretch of space above us. I turned away, a little afraid, as always, of the river's gathering fierceness.

Suddenly, more like a shadow than a body, Edgar flung himself from the stern toward his cabin. Over the thrum of our engine came a loud splash, as if he'd thrown a big chunk of driftwood overboard. I opened my mouth to say something to my father. At the exact same instant, Edgar's boat exploded in a whirling ball of red and orange. It was as if my eyeballs had burst. The whirling inrush of air might have happened inside me and also somewhere between the planets hurtling toward the Earth from their terrible shivering distances. Seconds later, Edgar's boat was engulfed in crackling flames and black smoke. Yet it was far enough away from us to appear small, blazing like a child's birthday cake.

My father yelled something, but I couldn't make out the words. All at once, he put his drum in gear, released the remaining fathom of net and let the whole thing go. As he plunged the boat forward toward the flames, I saw the tiny head of Bullet, no larger than a muskrat's, revolving on the rushing current as the terrified dog pawed the waters in a futile effort to get back to his master. I shouted at my father, but he had already swung broadside into Bullet's path and somehow, as if it was the easiest motion in the world, like lifting an apple out of a full barrel, brought the barking, desperate animal on board. Almost simultaneously, we broke into a wall of intense heat, and my father, moving as if the darkness was weighted, managed to reverse the boat just before the temperature overwhelmed us. My father yelled Edgar's name several times, or at least I thought I heard him do so over Bullet's frantic barking and yelping. The air reeked of oil and gasoline, smoke and burnt rubber. Drifting broadside to the flames as the current continued to pull both boats south toward the sea, we could do nothing but study the surrounding light-flickered waters in the hope that Edgar had jumped free in time.

Meanwhile, another boat had arrived from above the drift, throwing its powerful searchlight wildly in all directions. The crackling and snapping of the fire, and the rolling surf of black smoke, visible for seconds before merging into the darkness, prevented us from getting any closer. Bullet, however, dove into the weirdly glowing current and managed a fathom of progress before the river threw him back toward us. This time, when my father got hold of him, he shut the frantically barking dog in our cabin.

Minutes later, with no sign of a body in the water, and with nothing to be done, my father left the supervision of the burning scene to the three other gillnetters that had now arrived, and raced downriver to rescue our net before it wrapped around the headland of the island.

In an intense display of dexterity learned from decades of fishing, he picked up his net, removing the thrashing hook-snouted sockeye and the occasional slab of spring salmon as though he was a steel worker torquing ingots of lead out of a sizzling forge, except he carried out his task on a river erupting seaward like black lava down a volcano's side. Above the sound of the engine and the drum and the thumping of dying fish, Bullet kept whining and scratching at the cabin door, and I didn't know what was worse: my father's manic skill or the dog's uncontainable grief. The current quickly whirled us past the headland and down a narrow slough, until we could no longer see the flaming ruin of Edgar's boat drifting at the same rapid pace behind us. Only a dull glow low in the sky suggested an event out of the ordinary.

Eventually, with our net and several hundred salmon on board, my father, dripping sweat, his face and apron scale-flecked and blood-spattered, raced us back up the slough. Before we reached the headland, Edgar's burning gillnetter emerged like a raised palm of fire, as if in a warning to keep us away. Not surprisingly, his net had wrapped the far point of another island, so that his boat would inevitably catch and hold like an anchor at the end of a long chain. There was nothing to do except to wait for the heat and flames to die down enough for the watching fishermen, their boats drifting a safe distance alongside, to turn their hoses on the flickering wreck and to haul in Edgar's bunched and torn refugee of corks, meshes and, as it turned out, several hundred strangled salmon.

We joined the drifting procession as the boats increased in number and the grim faces in the diminishing fire glow trembled like scorched blossoms overhanging a trench of whirling ash. Under the ceaseless noise of Edgar's stricken dog, the death-throes of the equally desperate sockeye under my father's drum sent their intermittent and mocking applause into the constellations now fixed like torches against the fathomless depths above us.

The remainder of that night and the next morning have grown indistinct over the decades, blurring and compressing, so that I can't be certain whether we continued fishing until the tide changed again or stopped for several hours while we plied the waters south of the drift, hoping that

Edgar had somehow survived, or whether in fact my father, already accepting the worst, only joined the search for Edgar's body once the river had closed. But I do remember that, at some point in the teacup-fragile dawn, with the planks of the government wharf still slick and dark, Bullet, finally released from the cabin, scrambled up the gangway and burst along the dike to the west, presumably intuiting that his master lay in that direction.

The rumours began almost immediately, generated by three main factors: no body was ever found; Edgar's boat engine appeared to have been tampered with (this was never concretely proven or disproven, but the police showed little interest in the possibility); and Edgar himself had obviously been in a chaotic state of mind on account of the theft of his life savings and the lack of support from his brothers. With regard to the last point, most people, including my father, dismissed the idea of planned suicide (why take Bullet along or set his net?), but couldn't wave off the possibility that Edgar might have been drinking himself toward destruction ever since his disappearance. Setting his net one last time on familiar waters, then, would have been a final symbolic act carried out in an almost comatose drunken state.

If nothing but gossip and mystery surrounded the fate of Edgar Winterbourne, the opposite was true of my last real childhood summer in almost every other regard. First of all, the Adams run of sockeye turned out to be one of the largest on record, resulting in a glut on the market that saw prices slashed week by week, despite the union's best efforts, until, by the time school resumed in early September, the whole town reeked of dead and rotting unsaleable salmon. Many had just been dumped overboard and left to wash up on the banks at low tide. But my father spent most of that month pushing wheelbarrows full of sloshing, silver-auburn corpses home to be buried in his garden for compost.

But before that, in the last week of August, I was walking home from the Ashtons' pool, the last beads of water evaporating from my shoulders, legs and arms, when I saw Mrs. Vasilakis, still veiled, still in black, standing with Theo and Stevie beside a large panel truck in their driveway.

I hadn't seen much of her that summer, and I was shocked by how thin she had become. The black dress hung loosely from her, and her hands and forearms were not much thicker than twigs. Theo, too, with his hair now almost to his shoulders, looked like another person, years older overnight, suddenly a teenager who'd smoke pot and listen to Pink Floyd, except he still wore a little boy's short trousers, high socks and a kind of peasant blouse. But Stevie, to my relief, was the same lean-muscled, sharp-jawed, large-eyed figure as always, looking every bit the clean-living greaser in his jeans and white T-shirt and with his hair smoothly gelled. His expression, though, was uncharacteristically grim. He shrugged as I approached.

"I had no say in it. And it wouldn't have mattered anyway. My dad says we had no choice."

Wrapping the towel as respectfully as possible around my bared skin, I followed Stevie's look to the large red block letters on the side of the truck, which revealed that it was, in fact, a moving van. For a moment, I couldn't take the reality in. Somehow the emptiness of all the other abandoned houses in the neighbourhood had made the Vasilakises' presence more solid and stable in my mind. Not only that, but I couldn't remember a time when they weren't there. In fact, one of my earliest memories involved being invited into Mrs. Vasilakis's kitchen to eat some of her freshly baked and icing-sugared Greek cookies. I could almost taste again the delicate flaky pastry beneath the sweetness and – painfully – see the healthy, smiling, red-cheeked face of a younger woman through the veil.

"Where are you going to?" I asked in a kind of half-sob that made Mrs. Vasilakis turn and step toward me. She spoke something in Greek, the first words I'd heard her say in months, which is no doubt why they lodged in my memory: *Elpízo na boró na páo spíti tóra.*

"Ma," Stevie said, his own voice breaking, "please don't."

Mrs. Vasilakis bent slightly toward me and slowly lifted her veil. It was all I could do not to gasp and step back. Her eyes seemed roughly chipped out of her pallid skin, but they possessed an unearthly brightness.

As if to reassure me, she took both of my hands in hers. The touch was at once icy and clammy. "You're a nice boy," she said, her voice barely a whisper. "Always so good to my Theo. And you will be a good man. I know this to be true. A very good man. A good father."

I tried to meet her eyes, and to smile. But it was as if she'd become a black wax candle that had burned out centuries ago below an icon in some far-off church. Already, she and Theo seemed to have left the neighbourhood, as if they were ether, as if they'd never been there at all.

And suddenly, they were gone, as silently and easily as the droplets off my skin. With tears in his eyes, Stevie said that he needed to help with the packing. When I asked him what he had meant about having no choice, he explained that the town was planning to redevelop all the vacant lots.

"They're going to knock everything down and fill in the ditches, cover everything with sand. Build some sort of complex after that. I don't know the details, just what I could get out of my dad. But it's sure going to be a lot different around here."

I nodded, afraid to ask the most important questions – where were they moving to, and what had his mother said to me in Greek? Somehow I intuited that the two questions were related, and related as well not only to my vanishing childhood but also to the rest of my life. Answering those questions would have approached an answer that doesn't exist, a paradox that has only come to haunt me more with each passing year. On that late August afternoon in 1976, however, I felt only the shiver of the ineffable, as if the wake of an orbiting planet briefly crossed over the surface of the earth and breathed its glacial emptiness on my naked skin.

When Stevie too had gone, I stood on the cracked, oil-smeared grey concrete driveway, as grasshoppers from the crowding edges of the waist-high grassed vacant lots spurted briefly into view. Far away and near, simultaneously, the seagulls cried without cease. The air smelled of ripe blackberries and rotted salmon, and when I squinted up at the sun, it seemed hostile, intent on destroying everything that its heat had generated. Already, behind me, my footsteps all the way down the sidewalk from the swimming pool had disappeared.

THE MARVELS OF YOUTH

*

Because it was a weekday morning, I didn't expect to find Mr. Edison or any of the comic book collectors at the shop. He worked at his city window-cleaning job until three every weekday, and so Jay and I and Nick and Dagwood Bumstead, even the Grim Warper and Sergeant Rockhead, only showed up in the late afternoon hours or on Saturdays.

But I was restless, and upset by the apparent death of Edgar Winterbourne and the Vasilakises' move away from our threatened neighbourhood. The Haunted Bookshop's musty stillness, even without Mr. Edison's calm and good-humoured presence, offered a welcome distraction. I didn't want to think too deeply about my role in the events leading up to the explosion, for I couldn't entirely rule out the possibility that Kirkhoff, in an act of misguided revenge, had tampered with Edgar's boat engine. The tragedy wasn't considered suspicious by the authorities, and there was still no discovery of a body, but I nonetheless felt culpable in some way. So retreating to the one part of the neighbourhood completely separate from the river and the fishery was more than necessary; it was, given my interests, temperament and the direction of my own future, inevitable.

As soon as I reached the front of the shop, I knew something was wrong. Nick Samaras stood on the sidewalk, staring into the window, and for once he didn't reek of marijuana; there wasn't even a whiff of it on him.

He seemed surprised to see me, even a little uncomfortable, but he composed himself quickly.

"I was just thinking," he said in a voice so clear and strong that for a few seconds I thought that somebody else was speaking, "that I really ought to read that book."

I looked at the tattered copy of Christopher Morley's novel in its worn red-cloth binding, and couldn't for the life of me figure out why a fan of *The Fabulous Furry Freak Brothers*, *Fat Freddy's Cat* and Robert Crumb would want to read an old book that almost certainly had no drug-taking in it. Before I could ask, a car pulled up behind us and Dagwood Bumstead, dressed in a suit, climbed out.

"I came straight from the office," he said. "But I feel like I should have stopped and bought a wreath for the door."

Nick flashed him a furtive scowl.

"What? Doesn't he know?"

"Shh. For Chrissakes."

Dagwood laughed. "Well, how long do you think it'll be before he notices that the paperbacks are gone?"

With a sickening feeling, I followed them inside the shop, only to find Mr. Edison and his wife removing paperbacks from the tall shelves and packing them in cardboard boxes.

Straightening up from folding over the four sections of a box top, Mr. Edison caught sight of me and immediately turned red. "Ah," he mumbled, rubbing the dust from his hands. "Ah, well, yes."

In what seemed a strange act of courtesy, as if I was the most important guest checking into a five-star hotel, he hurried behind the counter to take up his usual position by the cash register. His aging cherub's face was hollow-pouched under the eyes, and his moustache, usually under control if not exactly neatly trimmed, seemed several inches longer and an inch thicker.

"I wanted to make it until after Christmas," he explained heavily. "I really did try. There's just something about a comic shop at Christmastime."

Because his powdery eyes were damp, I controlled my own tears, in yet another strange act of courtesy. Though, perhaps, not so strange at all, for the relationships and the interactions at the Haunted Bookshop had been, for the most part, more decorous than those in the outer world, for here existed the tacit acceptance that creativity and imagination were not childish things to be put away, but rather the very foundation of a sustainable and healthy life in a violent negating world destined to come to the same cold end for everyone.

"Does Jay know?" I finally managed to ask.

It was as if I'd struck Mr. Edison in the face, for his eyes widened, he grimaced and he put both hands on the counter as if to steady himself.

"I'm still going to be a dealer," he said, and it seemed now he was giving a rehearsed list of comforts to Jay even though he wasn't present, "out of my garage. In Richmond. And I'll still have a table at swap meets and conventions. Maybe I'll even open up another shop one of these years."

He saw me look beyond him to where the most valuable comics were still displayed on the wall.

"I'm not taking the comics out until the end of next week. After you've gone back to school."

I recognized this decision as yet another act of courtesy, giving us the whole summer, right up until that first harrowing bell of servitude.

"It's just one bus ride to Richmond. Fifteen minutes. Oh, and I'm just a couple of blocks from the McDonald's. You can get a burger and a shake and then walk right over."

I nodded, but wasn't taking everything in. Behind me, Nick and Dagwood were speaking to Mrs. Edison, and I could hear box lids being folded into place. Obviously, they had come to help with the move.

Mr. Edison spoke my name, and waited until I met his moist blue gaze.

"Let me tell him, okay? As soon as he comes in. I want him to hear it from me first."

"Okay," I agreed so quietly that even I wasn't sure I had spoken.

"Here. I have something for you." He reached under the counter and pulled out a bright fine-condition copy of the *Amazing Spider-Man* #28. The villain Molten Man blazed against the solid black background. I was grateful, of course, but the image made me think of Edgar in flames, and how was Mr. Edison really supposed to comprehend how I felt about that? Fortunately, he took my silence for the more appropriate emotion. "I know *Kamandi*'s your favourite. But these early *Spider-Man*s are a better investment."

He spoke in full confidence that I wouldn't sell my comics for a long time, if ever, and that confidence, more than anything else, made my own eyes water.

After what seemed an eternity, I thanked Mr. Edison and said a solemn goodbye to the others, only realizing when I was outside again that I should have offered to help. But I knew that going back inside was impossible, at least on that day, so I crossed the street and passed the empty row of shops and dropped off the curb into the tall bluejoint grass whirring and crackling with grasshoppers, feeling exactly like Kamandi, alone in a destroyed civilization. Turning back once, I saw my shadow, as black as the background of the comic in my hands, sink like a weighted net into the blades.

Then I realized that I wasn't alone. It wasn't the same prickling sensation that I felt when wandering through empty buildings, but how could it have been? That feeling came from an awareness of the dead, and the person who had been following me, who now, seeing me turn back, raised her hand slightly in greeting, was perhaps more alive than anyone I've ever met. When she dropped her hand, I swear that the music flowing off her charm-braceleted wrist was like a shivering between the spheres in some cosmic comic book I was years away from being mature enough to read.

"You're not an easy guy to keep up with," she said with all the laughter in the world in her voice, as well as just the faintest breathlessness. But the latter was enough for me to avert my gaze quickly from the bare skin below her collarbone. "Are you always in such a hurry?"

Slowly turning my gaze back on her, I shook my head and forced out a weak smile. I knew that my awkwardness had a great deal to do with her physical attractiveness, but I also knew that a kind of reckoning must be coming, for we had been silent partners in all that had gone so horribly wrong in the past year.

Mrs. Hurry – and again I couldn't bring myself to call her by her first name, for the intimacy was too much – smiled, revealing the beguiling gap in her front teeth, and held up what looked to be a small pamphlet. Curious though I was, once more I looked quickly away, for she was wearing short cut-off jeans and the white fraying at the edges played against her bronzed thighs like the fringe of an exotic surf. I grew increasingly aware of my swallowing.

Perhaps recognizing my embarrassment, she didn't close the distance between us, but merely stood, waiting for me to look back at her, which I forced myself to do. With her free hand on her hip and the buttery sunlight in her violet eyes, she seemed to be posing for all the photographers in the world and completely oblivious of them at the same time.

"I just wanted to ask you to sign this for me," she said at last.

It took me several seconds before I realized that she was holding out a copy of *Cosmos*. Then I became even more confused and embarrassed.

All of a sudden, she seemed to spot an advantage. Stepping a few feet closer, she held both arms out, framing her body. The laughter in her eyes and smile was like a massing storm.

"It's really good. But the drawings of the women . . . if we were really built that way, we wouldn't be able to stay upright."

"Oh?" I said, the blush spreading over my skin as swiftly and obviously as the shadows spreading over the tall grass. "Oh, yeah, I guess."

She let her arms fall back to her sides. "You must be as smart as your brother, to make something like this."

I shrugged, waiting. For somehow I understood that the copy of *Cosmos* was only an excuse, something she felt she needed to break the dark ice between us.

With a startling directness that reminded me at once of my brother's opinion of her, Mrs. Hurry said, "Your dad doesn't like me, does he?"

Taken aback, I didn't know how to respond.

But she pushed beyond my surprise. "He probably thinks I'm not good enough for Danny. Not smart enough."

Falling back on my mother's courtesy, I shook my head and opened my mouth to protest. But Mrs. Hurry had opened the floodgates now.

"Maybe not school smart, sure. I didn't exactly get the chance to be any good at that sort of thing. I've always had to make my own chances, you know? And some of them . . . well, I'll admit that they weren't always the best idea. But it's easier for men, isn't it?"

With this comment, I realized that, by "it," she meant everything was easier. And by the chances, I knew she meant Hurry, Kirkhoff and probably even my brother, though I could tell that she thought the idea of my brother was a much better idea than the previous two.

My blush deepened as I had these thoughts. It wasn't possible now to avoid the real issue, and so she pressed on.

"What you saw on the boat that night, it was wrong. It was a mistake. But I didn't think I had any choice then. I needed to do something to..." She sighed deeply and ran her free hand over her black hair, all the way from her forehead to the back of her neck. "Oh it doesn't matter. What's done is done. But you tell your father, okay, that I'm plenty good enough for Danny. That we love each other. That I'm not the sort of woman he thinks I am."

I couldn't fully take in what she was saying, partly because I wasn't old enough to work out the complex relationship between sex and love, and partly because, over her final words, a dog began to bark somewhere up on the dike, and the sound immediately brought all the guilt and shame I'd been feeling to the surface. It was all I could do to keep the tears from my eyes.

Apparently sensing my emotions, Mrs. Hurry softened her tone. "It's not your fault. None of it's your fault. It was just bad luck, you being there. But if it'll make you feel any better, you being there helped me to change my life. Because it was you, I took it as a sign, you know? A sign that it was Danny I wanted to be with." She smiled and jingled the charm bracelet on her wrist. "As you can see, I put a lot of faith in signs."

When the dog finally stopped barking, I became aware of the even-more-distant crying of gulls out over the river; it was unpleasantly similar to some of the sounds I had heard that rainy night on the wharf, and I couldn't meet her eyes.

"You don't have a pen, do you?"

I shook my head.

"Ah, stupid me. I didn't think to bring one. Here." She held the copy of *Cosmos* out and I had to force myself to step forward to take it.

"You can sign it and then give it to your brother to give to me. Okay, Sean?"

She was close enough now that I could smell the mixture of sweat, suntan lotion and cigarette smoke flowing off her skin, could feel the sound of my own name on her lips. The sides of the universe closed in as the grass blazed into flame. Watching her walk away, I didn't notice that I had almost crumpled the comic in my hand.

XXVI

Three months have passed. Now it's late October, already well below freezing, a skiff of snow on the lawns and rooftops. Like the rest of the country, Edmonton is preparing for the first pandemic winter. Infections are increasing at an alarming rate, but the government refuses to impose greater restrictions on social interactions for fear of damaging the economy. The money-first values of our society are proving even deadlier than usual. And the months ahead are expected to be grim, isolated, long and cold, regardless now of whatever health measures are taken.

But last week, after putting off the journey for so long, I finally overcame my indecisiveness and, frankly, my low-level depression, and walked six blocks south to a comic book shop punningly called We Have Issues. By this time, online research had revealed to me certain fundamental truths about modern comic-book collecting culture, so I wasn't likely to be shocked.

In the first place, I knew all about raw versus graded comics, which reminded me of nothing other than the terms "in the round" and "dressed" as applied to salmon. Graded comics are comics that have been "slabbed" (or encased in hard plastic) by a third-party company that assesses the condition of your copy on a scale of 0 to 10 and puts that grade on a label also inside the plastic. Now your 9.8 *Eternals* #1 (books that get a 9.9 or a 10 are so rare that they're called unicorns) could be worth over a thousand dollars, but no one will be able to read it or look at the artwork inside (you need a raw copy for that). In other words, comics are now fully fetishized as commodities on a speculative investing market. Long gone are the days of casual browsing and carefree trading, of buying comics at the drugstore when you're shopping for a new toothbrush or of reading worthless copies of uncollected titles on the floor of a bookshop or in the backseat of an old Ford. The world is a more controlled and serious place, even in its fantasies, and comic books are well and truly a part of that world. Even Jack Kirby had to go to court in the 1980s to force Marvel to return some of his valuable original artwork to him. Since his death in 2002, his heirs have tried, mostly without success, to claim some share of the massive profits the Disney Corporation makes annually from turning Kirby's creations into cinematic blockbusters. Without exaggeration, as many comic book critics and fans point out, Jack Kirby's influence on American culture is greater than any other individual's, yet hardly anyone knows who he is.

The artist, who spent his whole working life inside a factory-production system and therefore could never relax about money, created characters and worlds from his one teeming brain that now generate billions of dollars. But that artist, that streetwise Brooklyn kid and World War Two infantry soldier, understood in his core that the battle for justice, for good to triumph over evil, was a permanent battle, in an individual's life as well as in a planetary and cosmic context. And what defined a person was his willingness to take up the fight, again and again, while believing in the cause: the wonder and grandeur of the ordinary searching imagination.

I kept my mask in my pocket and walked out into the bright, clear day. High overhead, the same sun of my childhood hung low in the deep blue sky, the sun that dried the water on my shoulders and hair when I walked home barefoot from the Ashtons' pool, the sun that set over the estuary of the Fraser River in a gush of salmon-blood red. But the world this northern autumn sun looks down on has changed considerably. Perhaps there's nothing really new under it, for planets and species have died before, but in 1975 the sun wasn't a killer (we wore suntan lotion but not sunscreen) and the zeitgeist, despite many early warning signs and calls for action from a tiny minority of scientists, wasn't so remorselessly apocalyptic. As children, we had no sense that our future would be any different than it had been for all the generations before. There would be trouble, yes – wars, economic slumps, disease, a whole range of social ills and injustices – but a widespread belief that we had entered the beginning of the end simply didn't exist. Walking south along the sidewalk of a busy arterial road, the car exhaust much thicker than my remembered scents of ripe blackberries, swimming pool chlorine and salmon musk, I felt, more than ever before, like Kamandi, the last boy on Earth. Except, of course, I wasn't a boy.

About a half-block before I reached my destination, the past abruptly and shockingly pushed itself with greater resolve into my consciousness. A group of about a dozen men paced in a loose rectangle outside of a business called Cessco, which turned out to be a steel fabricating plant. I slowed down as I approached, stunned to see a picket line of blue-collar workers. After all, nothing says the '70s and '80s more than labour action and workers' rights. That world, too, like the world of a friendly sun, has largely gone, especially in a place like Alberta, which generally caters to corporations, especially when they're foreign-owned. But I remember five hundred thousand people in Vancouver's streets in the early '80s marching for solidarity with the average working person, and I remembered, on that sub-zero Edmonton day, the fishermen standing on a wharf in the shimmering moonlight, prepared to make a collective sacrifice for their livelihoods. So deeply affected was I by the presence of these lonely looking picketers wearing aprons that read "Locked out in the Cold" that I overcame my usual reticence and, from the required six feet of social distance, asked one of the men – who, at over six feet tall and with a grizzled beard, reminded me of an aged Rosie from the fishing grounds – about the situation.

In short, the company, seeking to eliminate virtually all the rights the union had won over decades, had left the bargaining table in July, hired scab workers and locked their former employees – some of whom had been with the company forty years – out. And, as my interviewee soberly put it, there was no indication of any willingness on the company's part to return to bargaining, and no support from the government for the workers either.

"They're fighting with the doctors and nurses, for Chrissakes. Not going to get any fuckin' help from them."

I said a few sympathetic words, wished him well in the struggle and carried on from cold reality toward fantasy, which I reached in less than two minutes.

Donning my mask, I pulled open the heavy door in the side of a nondescript warehouse building and crossed over once more into the parallel universe.

Lari Edison is dead, well embarked on his own journey into mystery, and the Haunted Bookshop building was demolished decades ago, and yet here the shadows flicker again to life. I walk into a small vestibule, not much larger than my childhood bedroom, and am greeted by a cheerful man behind a counter. Despite his Batman-design pandemic mask, I can tell, by his hair, the crow's feet around his eyes and his old-fashioned manners, that he is not many years my junior.

Within fifteen or twenty minutes, during which no one else enters the building, I learn a number of things about Paul and his comic-dealing business: that he's from Saskatchewan and remembers bugging his mom to drive him around on the weekends to all the used bookshops/comic shops in Regina; that he's been buying whole collections, even whole store inventories, since the 1990s; that no matter how affordably he prices back issues of popular comics, he can't attract children to collecting (too many competing entertainments); that he has a signed-by-Jack-Kirby copy of *Journey into Mystery* #83 (slabbed, of course) on offer for $15,000 (O where is the Grim Warper now with his disposable income?); that, yes, he'd be interested in purchasing my comics; and that the high prices of comics from the 1970s are entirely unpredictable, linked directly to rumours about whatever new character or plotline might appear in the MCU.

THE MARVELS OF YOUTH

"The beauty of comics," he says, explaining in particular his fondness for those titles from the Golden, Silver and Bronze Ages (roughly the late 1930s to early 1980s), "is that they're a real time capsule. Everything that was going on in the world is reflected in the comics of the day."

As he speaks, I notice that there's no foolscap paper covering the counter, no valuable comics hanging on the wall (they're locked in a nearby safe) and no sound of a jukebox's bass pounding through the walls. I doubt too that any elderly Scotswomen have wandered in recently looking for Agatha Christie novels. However, through a narrow doorway into an adjoining room walks another masked man, also near my age, his black T-shirt dusty with wood chips (it turns out he's been building shelves). I don't catch his name, but he joins comfortably in the conversation, speaking too of the joys of comic collecting in the 1970s, when you could still buy new issues in the corner store and when the whole superhero culture was anything but mainstream. He's happy, of course, that there's so much interest now in the medium he loves, and he does mostly enjoy the blockbuster films and Netflix series, but it's obvious that, for the three of us, the past has a special lure, nostalgia, in this community (the word that comic fans attach to the whole culture), not something to be ashamed of or denigrated.

As the minutes tick away, I realize that this nameless man probably spends entire Saturdays in the shop, just hanging out with the owner, chatting, looking at comics and hoping that someone like me might walk in with a few rare comics to sell.

Then Paul says, "I guess you'll want to look at the comics." And he leads me through the doorway into a warehouse-sized space exploding with comic book wonder: posters of superheroes all over the walls, shelves of toys, glassed cases displaying slabbed copies of valuable hot "key" issues and dozens upon dozens of waist-high bins – hundreds of feet of them – containing Mylar-sleeved and back-boarded back issues of every comic book title imaginable. The ceiling is so high that I keep looking up to see if the Silver Surfer might be passing over.

"We're still getting set up," Paul explains, gesturing toward the distant reaches of the space. "There're thousands of others I haven't unpacked yet."

Whole collections I haven't even looked through or priced."

That accounts for the wood chips and power tools, the intermittent drilling and hammering, I think, as he returns to the front counter and I am left alone, like the journalist-narrator at the end of *Citizen Kane*, overwhelmed by the acquired riches of a lifetime, cast adrift on the vague meaning of material possessions in a world of elusive spirit. Yet I didn't possess millions of dollars' worth of great art and junk – no classical statues or cast-iron stoves; just a few cardboard boxes of old comics – and there'd be no slow pan of my accumulated treasures, no dramatic close-up of a beloved childhood object being tossed into the flames. There'd be only the transient image of a man vanishing into fire and smoke and the sound of eerie laughter across water, where phantom boats slide like searching hands past the scattered jigsaw pieces of the little silt islands.

At the end of *Citizen Kane*, a reporter asks the narrator, "Whaddya been doing all this time?" It's a haunting question that every human life must confront if not fully answer. But it feels as if I have reached the end of a journey without really knowing that I had embarked on one. The warehouse, as huge as a salmon cannery, is still and silent and smells faintly of wood. No music plays from a portable radio, no must rises off the yellow pages of the plastic-covered comics to seep into the air and no one says my name with pleasure and affection. I think of glassy-eyed Nick Samaras in his faded denim and permanent cloud of marijuana smoke, and for a moment consider searching for issues of *Fat Freddy's Cat*, as a kind of long-overdue homage.

But it isn't necessary. And besides, as I stand there, the walls and ceiling drift farther and farther away, until I'm no longer even aware of them. Minutes pass, or an hour. Like the Silver Surfer or one of Jack Kirby's other cosmic-travelling characters, I'm moving so rapidly through dark space that time and worlds no longer exist, at least not until I decide to descend into the vibrant colours and black inks of my chosen story, which, like all stories, all lives, has also chosen me. And my story doesn't have its origins in words or pictures, but outside the panels, in the seasons and the creatures of the one vanished world, vital and glorious in the senses,

THE MARVELS OF YOUTH

shadowed by suffering, loneliness and war, my parents' world, Jack Kirby's world and, strangely, most potently – it rushes back to me now in the organizing winds and water and sky filling the chaos around my one beating heart and restless seeking memory – the world of Edgar Winterbourne.

XXVII

The tide is slack, the surface of the river a thick impasto of black and grey-green in which the brown, yellow and red autumn-leaf fall has been smeared. It is a late November morning, just past daybreak, in what the fishermen call "dog season" – "dog" being the slang term for the chum species of salmon on account of its large cur-like teeth and fierce strength when fighting to escape the nets. My parents, as they sometimes do, have allowed me to miss school so that I can be out on the river for some of these shorter fall openings, usually lasting from dawn to dusk.

A thin fog thickens around our boat, and soon we can't see more than the first thirty fathoms of cork line stretched out from our stern. Moisture drips off the rollers and glistens in a web that a daring spider has built near the gearworks of the drum. My vapoury breath and my father's cigarette smoke slip into the fog again and again. There are other gillnetters on the drift, but we can't see them. Occasionally, though, the sound of an anchor-chain scraping or a bucket being lowered into the current tells us that we aren't alone.

Somewhere below us, my brother is shivering in his dew-drenched poncho in the stern of his fragile skiff, listening to his transistor radio, and

THE MARVELS OF YOUTH

perhaps thinking of the change in his life. He and our father still aren't on speaking terms, and it seems that Dan and Mrs. Hurry are now a definite couple. Over the next decade, in fact, they will live together out of wedlock (shacked up, as my father puts it), and have a daughter, but the relationship will falter a few years before my brother, drunk at the wheel, drives off the river road into a black tide and a premature death.

But I'm thinking of my own life now, as I hold a mug of sugary Red Rose tea in my hands for warmth and watch my father's familiar grizzled profile, cigarette dangling from his mouth, black skullcap pulled down to his eyebrows. His bare left hand, as always, rests on the cork line, feeling for the tug of the giant spring salmon. He is still a kind of god to me – permanent, all-knowing, even a little remote – and I rely on his steady presence to cope with my losses.

The Haunted Bookshop didn't hold out more than a week after the packing up of the paperbacks. And though Jay and I did take the bus into Richmond to visit Mr. Edison's new "shop" in his cement-floored garage, it just wasn't the same, and we knew it. We also knew, without discussion or any kind of acknowledgement, that our friendship was ending too. At almost fourteen, Jay was spending more time with Nick, talking about art and ideas and eventually smoking pot and drinking. A year before, I hadn't been too young, but now I must have seemed like a little kid to him. It was a sad change amidst all the sad changes, and I didn't yet know how to live with it.

The river is as black as creosote and as thick as sludge whenever I look down. It's hard to imagine that the salmon and other species in that water can swim at all, that they aren't already dead, preserved in a frozen gallery, as still and distant as the stars only just disappearing in the wan sunrise. Around me, the fog is as thin and cold as my breath. From up on the main river, or out toward the sandheads, the deep bellow of a foghorn rolls over the coagulant fathoms.

Then an old silence settles on the slack water. My father drags on his cigarette and exhales. The spider is pupil-still in its web. The fog shifts, slowly breaks. All at once, no more than thirty fathoms from our stern, a great bulk explodes from the dark river and hangs in the air. Two seconds pass . . . almost three. I see the armour and prehistoric shape, the sandpapery grey-green body beneath the reptilian head, gills like flanges on the dredged-up first motor of the world. Then the image plunges back down, a concussive slap encircles the river, the islands, the ocean, the spiderweb fragility of the dew-stippled still-sleeping town of war veterans and war widows, and echoes long after the black water and the white air resolve again into the neat selvedge of the elements.

For some reason, I turn and look over my shoulder, to the west, convinced of some human sound or motion, but there is only the fringe of the island treeline showing through the wispy fog like a blurred X-ray of a far-off spring, and, beyond, those murkier fathoms of space and water as inexplicable as the blood circulating through a single life of time.

When I look back again, all that's left of my parents and their world is the river.

ACKNOWLEDGEMENTS

I wish to thank the Canada Council for the Arts, the Alberta Foundation for the Arts and the Edmonton Artists' Trust Fund for their support. My gratitude to the jury members who supported my writing in these competitions.

To Paul Vermeersch, Noelle Allen, Ashley Hisson, Jen Hale, Jennifer Rawlinson and everyone at Wolsak and Wynn and Buckrider Books, I extend my appreciation for their hard work on my behalf.

A special thank you to Penny Doukas for her insights into the Greek Canadian experience, and to Peter Cocking for his exceptional design skills and long-standing friendship.

And much gratitude to the following writers, whose conversation, either in person or via email, continues to remind me that the passion for literature is always local and intimate: Theresa Shea, Jay Peterson, Curtis Gillespie, Marco Melfi, Jacqueline Baker, Russell Thornton, Chris Wiesenthal, Don

McKay, Colby Stolson, Peter Christie, Jean-Marcel Morlat and William Heyen.

Finally, I wish to thank my family, in Alberta and on the West Coast. Your willingness to understand that fiction is indeed fiction is greatly appreciated.

Tim Bowling is the author of twenty-two works of fiction, nonfiction and poetry. He is the recipient of numerous honours, including two Edmonton Artists' Trust Fund Awards, five Alberta Book Awards, a Queen Elizabeth II Platinum Jubilee Medal, two Writers' Trust of Canada nominations, two Governor General's Award nominations, two Canadian Authors Association Awards and a Guggenheim Fellowship in recognition of his entire body of work.